AF241198

OMG! Not Another Gay Erotica Anthology?
Copyright©2013 Barry Lowe
ISBN 978-1-909934-06-1
Cover art and design by Dawné Dominique

First published by loveyoudivine Alterotica

Published by
Lydian Press 2013
Find us on the World Wide Web at
www.lydianpress.com

OMG!
NOT ANOTHER GAY EROTICA ANTHOLOGY?

Barry Lowe

Lydian Press

CONTENTS

All the above titles were originally published as individual eBooks by loveyoudivine Alterotica.

OMG! MY DAD'S
A STRIPPER!

*Once the zipper comes down,
everything is out in the open.*

The man himself was making his way toward me. Well, toward the table at which I was seated with mates, Dazza, Franco, and Tick. I was so excited I almost shit myself. As always, he had me wriggling like a worm on the end of a hook. This special man. The man I'd had the most enormous crush on since I hit puberty.

Gage.

Just the sound of his name made my cock so hard you could hammer nails with it.

His body was incredible. He was obviously past his twink years – that was a plus for me as I like older men – but he kept his body honed to perfection. Not steroid perfect, but gym toned; the sort of body that takes dedication, still a turn-on for a muscle worshipping freak like me. As it came toward me, okay us, the body was part-hidden by an intricate crisscross of leather straps and metals rings that highlighted its pecs and its biceps.

A man could die happy cradled in those powerful arms. This man certainly could.

Tick nudged me. "You're drooling, mate. Put your tongue away."

As to whether my dream man was handsome as fuck or ugly as a fundamentalist's personality, I couldn't care tuppence. Just as well, the currency changed decades ago. It was the body I craved. I had horny schoolboy scrapbooks filled with publicity photos and flyers of Gage and his dance buddies. In every single public picture, however, he was wearing his signature leather hood, only his mouth and his eyes visible. It just made him that much more sexy.

The paparazzi left him alone because his fame was so minor and so specialized. As a result conspiracy theories were rife about his true identity, ranging for the bizarre to the ridiculous. He was either a Phantom of the Opera-style figure whose face was so hideously deformed as a result of a childhood accident or because of a jealous lover's acid attack revenge, or a moonlighting politician/actor/sportsman whose fetish for flashing his dick would cripple his career if it were to become known. I didn't subscribe to any of these romantic flights of fancy, preferring to think of Gage as just a regular Joe who wanted to keep his identity private so he could have precisely that: a private life.

None of us was even sure he was gay. Sure, he threw himself into his performances with the sort of relish you'd expect from a guy who wants everyone to admire his body and his…um…rather large tackle, but there were plenty of examples of gay-for-pay performers in the nightclub tonight. I tended to avoid them as far as possible; they offended my nascent gay political sensibilities. There were plenty of gay guys, however, who liked nothing better than the fantasy of converting a straight man or being on the receiving end of his straight cock.

Our GLTQBI support group at college had often debated whether sticking your dick in another dude's ass made you gay. We'd come to the unsurprising conclusion that it wasn't the gender of the person on the receiving end of your cock that defined you, but the gender of the people you fell in love with. Affectional preference was the key.

"Anyway, should we really be into all this defining shit?" Dazza said one evening to close down yet another boring argument that had bogged down in semantics. "Labels are so passé."

Not necessarily. I had enough labels to describe Gage that they'd cover his entire magnificent torso. There's one label: magnificent. There was also hot, hung, huge, horny, huggy…well, you get the picture. And don't get me started on the other letters of the alphabet to describe his rounded ass. I could bury my face in there and never come up for air.

"How are you gentlemen today? Enjoying yourselves?"

I couldn't speak. The deep masculine tone was just perfect. Not too educated, not too working class, and not so deep as would be the envy of James Earl Jones. That was too deep; I never found it arousing.

"You're doing it again," Franco hissed.

He, my he, was standing so close I could have reached out and run my fingers across his lightly haired chest, the oil glinting under the subdued lighting of the club, his nipples perfectly erect and just begging to be tweaked and chewed on. His biceps had that divine vein running the length of his arm. I wanted to lick it, to feel the pulse of blood beneath.

Oh, those abs; his washboard stomach, again with a slight mat of hair that trailed down, down, down until disappearing under his leather pouch. Oh, dear God, did it ever get any better than this?

He put his big oily hand on my shoulder. "Okay, son, I think you should try to breathe now."

I was frozen in admiration. I gasped, oxygen flooding my lungs causing me to cough and splutter.

Way to impress, Dion.

He patted me on the back, the print of his powerful hand indelibly etched on my brain.

"I have that effect on people sometimes," he whispered conspiratorially. "But not usually on young dudes who are cute as apple pie and twice as mouthwatering."

I knew he was flirting as part of his job but that did not make it any less appealing.

"You gentlemen must be people of some importance," Gage said, his hand on my shoulder. "They only give me the VIP tables and it's usually a group of rich older men who believe it's their right to prod and squeeze me as if I'm a product on a supermarket shelf."

That's what I wanted to do.

He must have read the embarrassed look on my face, for he added quickly, "Not that it wouldn't be an honor to be poked and prodded by handsome young gentlemen such as yourselves." His emphasis on 'poked' and 'prodded' was almost enough to make me shoot in my jeans and, I'm afraid, I groaned. Yep, I groaned out loud so that everyone at the table heard me.

Let me die now.

"Don't mind us," Dazza laughed. "He's the one you need to take care of. We're in a relationship." He pointed to the three of them.

Gage chuckled. "Polyamorists."

"Yeah," Franco said in surprise, although it came across as patronizing.

"We're not all bozos," Gage said, without rancor. Before anyone could feel embarrassed about patronizing him, he went on, "So why isn't this cute young thing part of your circle?"

"His heart belongs to someone else," Franco admitted.

"Ah, he's here tonight to try to forget that someone?" Gage asked.

"No, you are that someone," Tick said.

Franco slapped him on the shoulder. "Don't scare him off."

Gage squeezed my shoulder. "Son, you look like a nice level-headed young fella. The last thing you want is to be involved with someone in this profession. We're all miserable sons of bitches who earn our living flashing our cocks and selling our souls to the next rich bastard who comes along. But if it's a quick shag in the dressing room after my spot before I have to get ready for the private show…" He did that irritating thing of using his fingers to do quote marks in the air. "…then come along. Bring your mates if they're so inclined."

"Seriously?" Dazza said with just a little too much interest.

Gage began to walk away because the PA system was announcing the show would commence in fifteen minutes. "Seriously. And guys, you don't need to impress by shoving cash in my jock strap. Keep it in your wallet. You need it more than I do. Get yourself an education. Don't end up like me. I might have the body and I might have the looks, but it's the guys with money who control everything."

With that he was gone.

"Cynical bastard," Tick muttered.

I watched Gage's back as he pushed his way through the crowds.

Franco prodded me in the chest. "He likes you, Dion."

"He's a bit of a downer though," Tick added.

"I wonder what this…" Dazza imitated Gage's air quotes, "…private show is?"

"A cousin of mine," Franco whispered, "used to date one of those straight strippers and she said what goes on at private parties was unbelievable. She said there are no holes barred."

I was confused. "No holes...?" Then I twigged. "Oh."

Franco sought to reassure me. "Of course, that was straight guys and pussy."

Dazza was sarcastic. "Your cousin still dating him?"

"Hell, yeah. She loves what he does. She's his manager now."

We ordered another round of drinks and some nibbles so that we didn't get too drunk and raucous. As the lights dimmed and the music began quietly, a hot guy dressed in black stretch tights that did nothing to hide his excitement strode out on to the stage. He was naked from the waist up, his torso gleaming with oil. His costume was topped off by a bow tie which wiggled when he spoke. As he welcomed us to the club, I noticed Franco, Dazza and Tick move their chairs closer together and their hands disappear under the table.

Maybe if I were more adventurous... No use going there, I was here for Gage.

The MC enlightened us about each of the dancers, revealing the sorts of biographical details that humanize the men although none of it was convincing enough to sound even remotely possible, especially when he announced Gage was a former classical pianist who'd had his fingers crushed in a car accident and could no longer play...the piano.

"Doesn't mean he can't play with other…um… things." Winking for emphasis, he added, "If you know what I mean."

The room full of gay men erupted. It was gonna be one of those nights.

The strippers must update their biographies on a regular basis because my scrapbook was full of Gage's life before he became ecdysiastically inclined: he'd been a marine, jet pilot, cop, international banker, fireman, cowboy, house painter (are house painters really fantasy figures?), and now a classical pianist.

I shrugged. It was all fantasy. Except my fantasy was all muscle, and he'd invited me to his dressing room after his performance.

I was impatient because the guys who entertained us first seemed imperfect, awkward, uncoordinated somehow. In my eyes they just didn't measure up, although I was definitely in the minority because the audience exploded every time one of the strippers got bare and bashful. Sure, they were all buff and beautiful but they appeared plastic alongside the man mountain that was Gage. Everyone else was enjoying the floor show, including my mates whose hands seemed to be pumping frantically below the table and whose groans and panting were coming, if you'll excuse the use of that word, with increasing frequency.

The dancers mingled with the audience allowing a quick grope of their crotch or a squeeze of their ass; to the extent I thought they must go home black and blue with bruises after each show. Some audience members brazenly attempted to cop a feel under the jockstraps of bulging crotches or snake their finger between naked bubble butts to find the entrance to heaven.

We were warned not to go 'too far' as there may be police spies in the audience who were keen to shut down this sort of entertainment. Too far seemed to have a flexible definition as I noticed a number of the dancers stopped overenthusiastic groping, while others actively encouraged more intimate touching. I just hoped none of the crowd tried any of that shit on Gage or I'd break their fuckin' fingers.

After what seemed like an interminable wait that, to be fair, no one else seemed to mind, we were at the pinnacle of the evening. A prop grand piano was pushed on stage, the lights went out, and the PA system screeched to life and the announcer, sounding as if he could barely suppress his excitement, screamed the simple, "Gentlemen, the moment you've all been waiting for. Gage."

The audience rose from their seats applauding, whistling, stamping their feet, the noise just short of pandemonium. I joined in. Even my three mates stood up, adjusting their crotches as they did so. We screamed along with the best of them. I just hoped it didn't mean they'd be accompanying me back to Gage's dressing room.

Suddenly, I had a sinking feeling in my belly that maybe he'd invited a lot more people back stage for afters than just me. Damn, it never occurred to me that he might be an insatiable bottom and just be looking for a tag team to round out the night.

Shit! My mind always does that; goes for the negative, the worst case scenario. I needed to relax.

A spotlight found the side of the stage and a few seconds later Gage emerged – in a tuxedo! – as if blithely unaware of the audience. He strode to the baby grand to the PA soundtrack of Grieg's Piano Concerto. He adjusted the stool, cracked his fingers, sat, adjusted the stool some more; he sure knew how to tease an audience. Flexing his fingers once again, he dismissed the piped music with a sweep of his arm. It stopped on his command. He gave a little nod to the audience and then began to play. Chopsticks!

Laughter rolled around the audience like a Mexican wave. We sat back down again to watch the performance. He sped up his version of the hoary old waltz as it took on a harder, disco beat. It obviously wasn't Gage playing any more. His body shook to the new tempo as if in a frenzy of sexual frustration. He ripped off his collar as he gyrated his hips, his groin tantalizingly inviting. Then he jumped on the piano stool and from there, on to the reinforced piano lid. What began as a soft shoe shuffle to a slower tempo Chopsticks morphed into a bump and grind.

He tore the tuxedo off until his upper body was on open display. He'd discarded the leather harness of earlier, so his torso now rippled muscle glistened with sweat and oil. If I were an old-fashioned sort of guy, I would have swooned. But I didn't want to miss a second of his performance. He held the waist of his trousers and yanked; they came away in a single smooth movement. Clad now only in construction worker boots and his leather jock, he dropped to his hands and knees, his perfect bubble butt facing the audience as he ground his crotch against the piano, making hot passionate love. He rotated his body as he simulated fucking until he was facing us again. I can't imagine there was any man in the house that didn't wish he were the baby grand that night.

He was up and off the stage so quickly I thought he'd fallen. Gyrating his way through the audience as hands pawed his body and his ass, he made his way to me. Once I was within range, he swept me to my feet to plant a kiss on my open mouth, his tongue pushing against my own. All I could do was welcome him in. He squeezed my butt cheek, running his finger down the crease where my ass crack trembled beneath my jeans.

"Mmm, tight butt, I like that," he mumbled through the kiss.

His hand moved around to my cock which he squeezed; that was almost too much and I had to concentrate not to blow my load. Picking me up, he threw me over his shoulder in a fireman's grip and then carried me through the crowd of waving and clutching hands, until we hit the stage.

I felt the heat leaching from his body as he positioned me face down on the piano lid. He leaned closer to whisper in my ear. "Just relax, play along with me. This is all in fun. The serious shit will come later in the dressing room. If you want."

Oh, I wanted all right.

He positioned his body over mine and began grinding, ordering me to place my hands above my head and leave them there. He rubbed himself along my clothed body until he wedged his crotch against my butt. Even through my jeans and his leather pouch I could feel how stiff his cock was. He began to dry hump me, pushing against me so hard it was causing my own cock to rub against the piano lid.

Suddenly he flipped me over to an almighty roar from the audience. He was playing to them, looking out over the sea of excited gay men who probably wished they were me if only for fifteen minutes. His hard crotch slammed against mine so that we both felt the throbs of desire in the other. I'm sure he must have thought I was a tramp the way I was succumbing to his performance. His face was right next to mine. "Happy birthday, cutie," he whispered, licking my ear and then tracing his tongue to my lips.

WTF? It wasn't my birthday. Dazza or one of the others must have organized this special treatment by lying about my birth date. Had Gage been feeding me a line all night? Maybe Franco had come up with some extra cash to buy me some time with my idol. Did I care?

There was no way this god was going to settle down in the suburbs with yours truly and raise daffodils and dachshunds. There was no way I'd allow him to continue in his chosen profession if he did and, if his playing of Chopsticks was anything to go by, he could kiss his career as a classical pianist goodbye – crushed fingers or no crushed fingers. So there was no way any sort of permanent relationship would evolve from this meeting. I'd have to settle for what I could get.

Even though he continued to rub his body against mine, his cock still as hard as ever, he watched me with some puzzlement. At least that's the emotion I read on what little of his face was revealed. I guess I had a glazed look on my face because I was seconds away from dropping my bundle. He asked, "What's your name, kid?"

That was the moment my balls chose to spew their guts up. I was so horny, the cum shot out the end of my prick with the force of bullets. I groaned, "Dion" as my spunk puddled in my boxers. It was obvious even to the patrons seated at the back tables that I was in the throes of orgasm. My body juddered. Through the slits in his mask I saw Gage's eyes glaze with horror like he'd just met his worst nightmare.

For fuck's sake, what did he expect rubbing his glorious prick against mine? I'm only human.

He sprang off me like I'd committed a huge faux pas against common decency, took a perfunctory bow to number of catcalls and exited the stage. I'd been responsible somehow for his truncated act. He hadn't even showed us his prick. Thankfully, the curtains closed on my public mortification. I stumbled off the piano wondering if I could make the toilet in time to stop a revealing wet patch from appearing in the front of my jeans.

A stage manager pointed me in the right direction and with the help of a lot of toilet paper and cold water from the ancient wash basin, I got myself tidied up and respectable. My boxers were a dead loss and I crammed them in the bin.

I would have to seek out Gage and apologize for my behavior although I couldn't believe it had never happened to him before. He was sex incarnate; I doubt anyone could have held back when he did what he did to me. If nothing else, he'd got me off. I smiled at small mercies. We may not have a future, but we'd always have the Zipper Club.

I sighed as I gave my face a last look over before making my way outside and along the corridors toward what I hoped were the dressing rooms. Other people were crowding around, a couple of them clapping me on the back in congratulations for my performance, telling me they'd pay to watch me strip some time.

Yeah, right.

Fortunately, the dressing rooms had names crudely written in black marker pen on white cards taped to the doors. Right at the end was Gage's. He wasn't sharing with anyone and he alone had what looked like a leftover

Christmas tree star tacked to the door. If I knocked and waited it would give Gage a chance to reject me outright. I didn't want that; I needed to explain, so I knocked and entered.

I heard the shower running in the bathroom of his dressing room. The door was open although it was so full of hot water mist I couldn't see anything. I knocked on the open door.

"Is that you, kid?" he called.

"Yeah, look—"

I didn't get a chance to apologize.

"Hey, kid," he called. "I can't hear you in the shower. I'll be out in a second. But if you're here for what I think you're here for, then do me a favor."

"Anything," I shouted.

"Good boy. Strip out of those clothes of yours. You'll find some Vaseline on the make-up table. Grease your ass up nice and loose."

Holy crap, he's going to fuck me. Okay, it's a bit impersonal but...he's going to fuck me. Where's the downside in that?

"Bend over one of the seats and look at the floor. Okay."

I snapped to attention. As did my cock. "Yes, sir."

I heard a snicker from the shower.

Determined to make it up to him, I was out of my jeans and casual shirt faster than if they were on fire. I found a jar of half-used grease, a momentary twinge of jealousy stabbing my heart before I thoroughly coated my hole until I could insert three fingers. I knew how thick his cock was and three fingers were only part-way there.

I noticed a line of coke that he'd obviously prepared for when he got out of the shower. I went back to the bathroom door.

"Ah…you got nose candy…"

"You want some, mate?"

"Yeah, if there's any going."

"You like it rough?"

"Sex, you mean?" I had visions of Gage dominating me and fucking me through the floor. My cock oozed its approval. "Love it hard."

"Help yourself."

It had been a while since me and my mates had the cash to afford life's little luxuries. In fact, we'd saved for months for a ticket to Gage's show. If it was the difference between food or the show, Gage always won. I would have sold my ass to pay for a ticket, I'm not proud. Otherwise why was I here in Gage's dressing room, kneeling in a tub chair, my ass exposed, already greased to save time and foreplay, rubbing the residual coke on my gums? I was a sad human being. God was I hot for it, though.

"Keep your head down, boy," his voice said as he came out of the bathroom. I was disappointed he didn't sound as sexy now that his hood was off. It must have been the Adrenaline the crowd was pumping that gave his voice that edge. But, I wasn't here to fuck his voice and, anyway, it still made my balls tingle.

I heard Gage snort a line. My head was already buzzing as I felt a sharp slap on my ass cheek. Then another. He kept it up until my ass was warm as a spring day.

"It sure looks pretty, all red like that," he said. "Only thing better would be to see my name tattooed right there." He prodded my left cheek and I made a mental note to look into getting inked.

He fingered my ass slowly, pushing two fingers inside my warm ass cavern until I clenched my muscles.

"Fuck, dude, that's hot. Let me get greased up, 'cause this is gonna hurt, no matter how experienced you are." I heard the lid on the jar and the squelch of grease being liberally applied.

None of the strippers were exactly small, obviously chosen by the inch rather than their choreographic skills, but Gage came up trumps in both departments.

I felt his knob circling the entrance waiting for the right moment. Naturally, I tensed. He leaned forward and rolled one of my nipples between his fingers before clamping it between his finger nails, shooting pain through my body. At that precise moment he rammed his cock straight through my sphincter so that I had two sources of pain. My brain was so coke soaked it didn't know which to concentrate on, until he wrapped his hand around my dick and began to milk me slowly, the residual grease making for a smooth action.

There was no holding back and he began pounding mercilessly, my ass on fire, his length feeling like it was being pushed up into my stomach. Fuck, he was so big and thick, and oh-so-worth-it.

Once I'd got used to having him impale my ass, I began to clench when he entered and also when he pulled out.

"Looks so fuckin' hot, babe."

"Feels so fuckin' hot."

Then he began the name calling. Slut, faggot, whore, cum dump. Much as I considered myself a modern politicized homosexual, the nasty words had a frisson that went straight to my ass, making me push back against his cock invasion, insisting he be rougher. He was eager to oblige, squeezing my balls, pinching my nipples, choking me until I thought I'd pass out, all the while ramming his cock through the battered sphincter gate of my ass.

He'd pull all the way out so that when he forced his way back in, the head of his cock spread my ass wider than if he'd left it inside. The pain was amazingly good. I begged him to treat me like the cock whore I was. I am. I was in another dimension, so that when he grabbed my hair and pulled my head up to confront the enormity of our coupling in the dressing-room mirror I cared little that it wasn't Gage tapping my ass.

I must have gasped because he snarled, "Not who you thought it was, babe? Too late now. I ain't gonna give up your sweet ass for no one. You were born to be fucked, mate."

The guy behind me was the dancer known as Gigantor. He was huge and, if the feel of his cock in my ass was anything to go by, he was the equal of Gage in every department. It was time to just relax and enjoy the experience.

Gigantor lifted me bodily from the tub chair, kicking it out of the way in order to twist me around, laying my back on the make-up table in front of the mirror. He had a sneer which made him appear evil and debauched and he spat saliva on my face and body every time he croaked out his dirty talk.

"Let me taste your cock, dude," I whimpered.

He was eager to please. Uncoupling from my ass, he wiped his greasy cock with a tissue so I wouldn't get a mouthful of lubricant. As it was, I could scarcely get my mouth around the thick weapon but he cared little for my comfort, pushing in slowly until I had most of it wedged in my throat. I'd never sucked a cock this big before but the ritual is the same no matter the size. Breath control is everything and I'd mastered it as best I could. Gigantor seemed pleased at my ability to take him so deep, praising me in his twisted humiliating way, allowing me to breathe at regular intervals so there was a minimum of gagging.

Eventually, though, I wanted him back in my ass. He was happy to oblige because that snug hole didn't require breath breaks so he could plough it to his dick's content. I was beginning to like Gigantor and if I hadn't been in pursuit of Gage I could have quite happily settled for this hunk of spunk.

My ass felt like it had been split open no matter how lubricated it was and I was pleased when he announced in words as crude as my desire, "I'm gonna breed your slag ass, boy. Fill it so full of spunk it'll foam out your nostrils. I fucked your ass so good I've spoiled it for any other man." He gripped my throat as his face contorted and he shot his spooge deep in my anal canal. I grabbed my dick to bring myself off while he was still pulsing inside me. A string of expletives turned the air blue as my load shot all over my chest and stomach. I flopped back exhausted. Gigantor kissed me briefly, the only time he'd shown any sort of tenderness. Not that I asked for any.

He pulled out, my ass gaping, sorry for the loss, and he slumped in the chair.

"Some ass you got there, mate. Dunno why Gage ran out on you like that."

"Is it because I blew my load in my jeans while he was writhing on top of me in front of the audience?"

"Nah, most guys do that. Can't help themselves when they have a stud like Gage on top of them grinding away at their boners."

I swallowed the jealousy because I needed answers.

"Did he say where he was going?"

"Special show." Those fucking air quotes again. What was it with these guys?

"What's a special show?"

"It's no secret but I shouldn't be telling you this. Dancers don't make a lot of money just from stripping. It only becomes lucrative when you start getting the big tips. And for the tips that make the difference between eating and starving you gotta work at it. Gage works at it like crazy. Like a man possessed."

"Has anyone seen his face?"

"Nah, he always wears his mask to work. At least that Gage does."

"What do you mean 'that' Gage?"

"There's a whole load of Gage's out there, dude. Sure, the one you saw tonight is the original and the best, but he's a franchise. The company figured if they make so much off one Gage, think how much they could make off two, or ten, or twenty."

Shit! How was I ever gonna track him down.

"You know where he's playing next?"

"Nah, we don't usually swap destinations. Gage and me aren't that close."

"You were in his dressing room."

He shrugged. "He asked me to tell you, 'sorry.' Said he wasn't the right guy for a kid like you."

"So, you delivered the message and fucked me into the bargain."

"What can I say?"

"Thanks."

"Okay, thanks. It was only a fuck. A very good fuck. Hey, maybe we can repeat it some time."

It didn't hurt to keep him hanging. "That would be good." I paused as if I was thinking something over. "You think I'd make a good stripper?"

"Can you move?"

I ad libbed a few dance movements, miming stripping off my clothes because I was still naked.

"You're a shoo-in, mate. The punters like good-looking twinks. You'll be very popular at the specials, especially since you bottom. Most of the twinks don't take anything up their ass."

"About the specials."

"As I said, don't expect to make loads of money except by the tips and the specials. Those are the private parties the company organizes for you. Strictly cash in hand. But the guys who do the hiring are demanding bastards. They like it up close and personal. Very close and very personal."

I nodded. I thought I understood.

"You can make a couple of grand on a good night at a special. And Gage usually does. But he's prepared to put himself out there."

"Meaning?"

"Kinks. Double acts, that sort of shit. Most guys won't go that far, so they don't make the bucks."

"How do I join up?"

Naturally enough, Tick, Franco and Dazza tried to talk me out of my wild scheme. They didn't understand.

I'm not sure I did either. Gage had become a life-altering obsession. I don't know what I expected once I tracked him down; for starters, he might not remember me. There was no reason he should. There was just something unfulfilled about our initial meeting. It wasn't just the perfunctory way he left the stage, although I did want an answer to his behavior if only for my own self-esteem. There was more to it; I felt a connection.

I know everyone says that.

I tracked down the promotions company that franchised the strippers but they were tight lipped and no amount of subterfuge could crowbar any information out of them. Certainly not Gage's real name, address and contact number. I even tried convincing some snotty-nosed company apparatchik named Jaeson (what a wanker) that I was the president of the Gage Appreciation Society – to no avail. Nor could anyone tell me where the 'real' gage would next be appearing.

The next step was a no-brainer, in every sense of the hyphenated word. I had to do it but it was perhaps the most foolish thing I'd ever done. (If there was a keystroke for shrugs I'd insert it here). It was my life, it was my future I was throwing away; or perhaps not. But everyone I knew believed I had no brains after I sent in my CV, my very revealing photographs and video suggesting a future in stripping was something I'd always hungered for. Those pics and video got me an interview and an 'audition.'

Expecting the worst of the audition, I popped a Viagra a few hours before my appointment, but it was not necessary for the initial contact. I was fully prepared and had choreographed an entire number and prepared the necessary costume. It was crude but effective. Because I had limited finances I went as a Big Game Hunter who stripped off to become a jungle boy.

"Very impressive," said the dreaded Jaeson of telephone rudeness fame. In the flesh, Jaeson was very appealing with or without the pretentious extra 'e' in his name. I was treated very differently on this occasion although no one was to know it was me who'd hassled them mere weeks ago about Gage. In the flesh and auditioning as a dancer, I was taken seriously, especially when the Viagra worked its magic a little too well.

He squeezed my crotch as my briefs did little to hide the enormity of my embarrassment. "J.G. will be mightily impressed," he added. "Especially if the rear stacks up as well as the front." So saying, he pinched my butt.

Normally that sort of behavior would get you slapped, but I had to remember what sort of job I was applying for; taking liberties with my private parts was a given.

"Who's J.G.?" I asked.

"The Boss. Capital B. No one gets employed without his say so."

"Will I have to…?" I mimed giving a blow job.

Jaeson laughed. "J.G. is so straight surveyors use him to mark out property boundaries."

"When will I meet him?"

"I'm taking you to see him now."

J.G.'s office was as large as the man himself. A florid gentleman whose rosy cheeks matched the nasty burst capillaries in his nose. He was pudgy and breathless. It wasn't difficult to see the reason for his lack of vigor. He had an ash tray overflowing with butts and ash, and a decanter of what looked like scotch to one side with a glass half-filled with the amber pacifier.

"Dion, come in, be seated. I hope I may call you Dion?"

"You can call me anything you like."

He made no effort to stand or to shake my hand. I noticed a tank of oxygen and a rubber-ringed plastic face mask discreetly just to one side of his desk.

"You must realize, Dion, that you would not have made it this far if Jaeson had not approved. If you don't make the grade you are dismissed with a polite, 'We'll be in touch.' I don't have an eye for male flesh, I leave that to professionals. It's why I employ them. Jaeson is one of the best. Should you choose to accept the job, he will be your tutor. You will do everything he tells you. Understood?"

"Definitely."

"Good. You will undergo six weeks of training during which time you will be given a name and a persona. We'll try you out in some of the less, shall we say, discerning cities until you find your feet. Then we'll let you loose on the world. It's up to you to seduce them with your dancing. Welcome to the firm, Dion."

This time he did stand and clasped my hand in a remarkably strong grip considering his fingers had the shape and consistency of frankfurters.

"Dion," he added as Jaeson ushered me toward the door. "Gigantor speaks highly of your ability in other departments. Says you would be perfect for our special parties."

He did not do air quotes around the words.

I already knew what they were, of course, but thought it politic to feign ignorance.

"Special parties?"

"We'll speak of that later. Once you are broken in."

With that, he dismissed me by picking up a paper from his desk to read.

Jaeson beamed once we were back outside J.G.'s palatial office. "That went well."

"About the special parties?"

"If Gigantor recommended you then you must know that his name is no lie. And you must have had it up that pretty little butt of yours. That's a very high level of achievement indeed. Speaks volumes for your talent," Jaeson said. "If your cock is as accommodating as your ass, then you will fit into the very exclusive elite tier of talent."

I grabbed a handful of Jaeson's very pert and very muscular ass cheeks. "Why don't we adjourn to your office and test it out?"

I would have been perfectly capable of spreading Jaeson over his desk and buggering the ass off him without the help of the Viagra, but the medicinal help certainly meant I could fuck him into the floor as he kept demanding even after he'd swallowed my first load of the day. In fact, I could have gone on all afternoon but he called a halt to our sexual activity.

"Fuckin' hell, Dion. Do you fuck like that all the time?"

"Only if they look like you."

He turned serious. "I know Gigantor must have told you a little about the specials."

"A little," I admitted.

You know they won't all be as good looking as me, don't you?"

"Of course."

"And some of the clients who ask for specials can be very demanding. And not at all pleasant on the eye."

"I guessed as much."

"You don't say a lot, except when you're fucking the ass off a guy."

"I know when to keep my mouth shut, and when to open up."

"Admirable qualities if you want to get on."

"And I do."

"Loose lips don't sink ships in this business, they sink reputations. Where are you staying?"

"I thought I'd doss at the YMCA tonight. I have to head back home tomorrow to pack everything up and transplant it here."

"You're welcome to spend the night at my place," he said, with a mischievous glint in his eye.

"Do you have a guest room or is the invitation to share your bed?"

"Either."

"Then I choose your bed."

He moaned facetiously. "You're gonna wear me out."

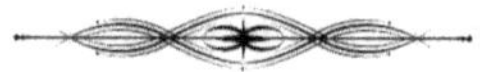

My mates and my lecturers attempted to talk sense into me but I asked for, and received, a year's grace. I could begin all over in a little under twelve months' time. I hoped I would have achieved what I'd set out to do well within that time frame. I didn't realize then how optimistic that calculation was.

I donated most of my belongings to charity shops around the city, trashing items that were long past even their second-hand use-by date. My buddies threw me a spectacular farewell party with copious amounts of booze so that I crawled onto the plane the next day and slept the entire journey. I had to be roused by a cabin attendant when everyone else had disembarked.

Jaeson was waiting at the airport for me, greeting me like a long lost comrade.

"I know just the thing," he said after he'd looked at my blood-shot eyes and smelled my hundred-proof breath.

He bundled me into his car and then stowed my luggage in the boot. I was hoping he'd take me straight to his house where I was staying until I found suitable accommodation so I was pissed when we pulled up outside a spa — until I walked inside. The place was all luxury. After a disgustingly healthy breakfast of juice from some sort of Tibetan weed mixed with the teardrops of a rose fairy or some other shit, we ate dry toast made with seventeen grains found only in the highest peaks of the Andes and the Himalayas containing enough fiber that it bypassed your stomach and you shit it straight out thus ensuring only minimum weight gain.

I jest, of course, although the food and drink did taste like something witches would brew in a cauldron.

It was the sauna and the massage which got my head screwed back on the right way. By the time we got to Jaeson's and I'd set up in the spare room, although we both knew I'd be spending most of my time in Jaeson's bed, I was ready for action. We christened my bed before we got down to business. Jaeson had drawn up a punishing schedule but that was okay by me because the sooner I got to Gage, the happier I'd be.

Those weeks of choreography, gym training, costumiers, skin care experts, and all the other professionals a hot tanned booty boy needed to look his best, certainly paid off. Even I barely recognized the man who stared back at me from the dressing room mirror. Fuck, I was hot. I made my own cock hard. I'd do me.

Jaeson was fussing over me. He'd completed his stint as Professor Higgins and now his Eliza Doolittle was about to be catapulted onto the world stage. This was the ultimate test. J.G. would have the best table in the house and he'd be surrounded by a rowdy bunch of gay bar patrons who'd responded to an advert in the gay press for free tickets to a strip show.

Fortunately, I was not on my own. A couple of the guys who'd been in the business for more years than my cock had inches were in support. If there was any inkling that I was not their equal or better, there'd be hell to pay. I was not the main attraction which took some of the stress off me. Unfortunately, Gage was not on the bill, either the original or one of the franchisees.

I guess I was too nervous to enjoy myself. I was also uncomfortable that they dressed me as an airline pilot. That was about as sexy to me as a lawyer or an accountant. The audience, however, seemed to like me if their pinches and gropes were anything to go by. The other dancers proved to be adept at helping me whenever anything threatened to get out of hand. I was grateful. I was also exhausted at the end of the night. Once the Adrenaline wore off, I was pooped.

It was all worth it though when J.G. called me to his table to introduce me to Mrs. J.G. and a number of married men and women. The men were stand-offish as I would have expected straight men to be, but their wives and girlfriends were instant fans. As were a small number of gay men who hovered until I was free so they could ask for my autograph and/or my phone number. I was free with one but not the other. J.G. watched as I handled my new fame.

When I returned to his table he was alone. He pumped my hand. "You've done us proud. Congratulations. I made a few notes." He tapped his forehead. "There'll be a debrief tomorrow. You, me and Jaeson. But I'm pretty pleased with your progress. We'll look at getting you on the road soon. And, Dion." He nodded to the crowds clamoring around the other dancers. "Never give away for free what you can charge for."

As J.G. made his way to the entrance where his wife was waiting for him, Jaeson couldn't contain his delight any further. "You were wonderful," he screamed, planting his lips against mine. When he'd calmed down, he asked, "What did J.G. say?"

I repeated the line about 'pretty pleased.' That sent Jaeson off into paroxysms of delight. "That's high praise from J.G. Enthusiasm is not one of his strong suits. You want to go out and celebrate."

Truth was I was totally buggered. Jaeson could read it in my body language. I appreciated it when he said, "I know. Let's just go home and cuddle. That would be a nice way to end the evening."

I hugged him in thanks. I was asleep before my head even hit the pillow.

The next day at the debrief, J.G. was generous in his praise while wily enough to suggest a number of fine-tunings that would improve the act. I shouldn't have been surprised by his perspicacity as he'd been in the business a long time, and had the success to show for it. I tried complaining about the persona that had been chosen for me but it did no good. On that point I'd bide my time.

By week's end we'd incorporated J.G.'s suggestions and the improvement was marked. I'd also received my schedule as I was being sent out on the road. Jaeson would accompany me for the first month to ensure everything ran smoothly. It was just as well because up until now I'd had the comfort of a full dressing room virtually to myself including my coming out performance. I'd been coddled for so long that the first time I had to negotiate a dressing room cluttered with other dancers and their costumes and make-up I was floundering. Jaeson steered me through the first few performances. It didn't help that we never traveled as a troupe, we were individuals sent our separate ways after one or two nights at a venue.

Sure some members of the audience had their favorites but the scattershot programming meant stalking was kept to a minimum which would explain why the company was so adamant it would not release any details about Gage when I'd rung all those months before. I occasionally ran into men from previous engagements but there was no time to form friendships or attachments. I'd grown quite fond of Jaeson and I could tell he thought he'd found a soul mate in me. If I hadn't been so set on my path, I may have considered his unspoken offer.

He invited me to stay with him any time I was in the vicinity and I promised I would. We made slow, passionate love on his last night as my chaperone, and we parted with genuine reluctance. But while I enjoyed his company I was also glad to be free for the first time in ages. Not because I wanted to screw around but because I needed a clear head and a selfish attitude to plan. Having to take another man's feelings into consideration could become wearying.

In those weeks he was with me I'd asked Jaeson about other dancers and who I should emulate. Gage's name came up on more than one occasion but I played it cool, explaining I'd seen Gage in performance and was wondering if anyone knew why he wore the hood. If Jaeson knew anything, he was not willing to tell. I learned nothing that was of any use to me in my pursuit.

For three months I toured the country getting no closer to Gage than before I'd joined the organization. I was beginning to wonder if my mates hadn't been right after all. My popularity up to that point had been building steadily but I was still only mid-range. I knew I had to do something to draw attention to myself, and it was while reading a manga that I came up with the solution.

In a few weeks I was scheduled to perform in the city that housed our corporate headquarters. What better time to try something different? It would either make or break me. I couldn't stand this stasis in which I found myself. I practiced in secret, spending some of my hard-earned cash on a new costume. At the last moment I sent out invitations to gay newspapers and magazines and gossip columnists. I had a new set of photographs taken and jpgs ready for publicity. I sent the press release out the morning of the unveiling of my new stage persona. That was in time for the gay papers published at the end of the week by which time my new career would be made or broken.

Jaeson, of course, plus J.G. and his entourage were to attend to ensure the standard of my act – the old one – had not declined. I paid the MC a bribe to change my introduction. I was bathed in nervous perspiration when my time came.

"Gentlemen," he shouted over the din, "We have a surprise for you this evening. For the first time on any stage…"

I glanced through the peephole at the side of the stage and saw J.G. and Jaeson in angry conversation. Too late now.

The MC went on, "We are proud to bring to you for the first time on any stage, that man of mystery, that man with the mighty muscle, the man himself, Young Gage."

He shouted my name over the general excitement in the crowd. Once my new name was announced there was uproar. Gage had a following and I was about to expand the franchise.

My hood was not a replica as it only came down over my face to the bridge of my nose and then covered my cheeks. I'd found I couldn't breathe properly if it covered my entire face; even with breath holes, I'd felt like I was suffocating.

In a satiric exploitation of Gage's tuxedo, I'd dressed as a hip young businessman except that under my suit I wore another outfit to double the tease. In stripping, I went from a Friday office worker to a weekend surfer. I even carried a surfboard with my briefcase. I'd arranged the stage so that it stood upright on its stubby nose and I could use it as if it were the closed door to a dressing cubicle, ducking behind it to prick tease.

The audience went berserk, clamoring for more though once you've shown your tackle to a crowd there doesn't seem much more you can do apart from peel off your skin and that is so anti-erotic not to mention painful and life threatening, I had no intention of going there.

I briefly glanced at J.G.'s table, the occupants of which had the appearance of thunder. That did not auger well. As I took my seventh curtain call, I watched the company brass exit, underlining the shit I was in by loudly demanding people 'get out of our fucking way!'

Bert, the stage manager on our show, shook his head when he came to the dressing room. "Tomorrow. Nine o'clock. Office." The message was as short as J.G.'s temper. Bert sighed but made no comment once he'd delivered the coup de gras. Oh well, I could always try going freelance but as the company pretty well had a monopoly on male strippers, I'd be blackballed and out of work.

I didn't care to be put through the grinder by Jaeson, plus I didn't want to involve him in my problems, so I stayed away from home that night which drove him frantic. After about the dozenth call or text message asking me to call him, I switched off the cell phone. I was still seated at the mirror in the dressing room considering my options when Bert stuck his head in to check all the lights were off before he went home. He came and sat astride the chair next to me.

"Kid." Bert called everyone kid because there was such a huge turnover of dancers and actors through the theatre he didn't have time to learn everyone's name. "Kid, that was one of the gutsiest displays I've ever seen. You ran rings around the rest of them tonight. Just thought you'd like to know that. Something to hang on to tomorrow when he reams you a new asshole."

He clapped me on the shoulder. "Come on, you can sleep at my place tonight."

I knew it wasn't a come-on as Bert had been happily married to the same woman for over thirty years. How did I know? I made it my business to talk to the stage manager and tech crew everywhere I performed. Those guys can make or break your career. I've seen them do it to guys who acted like assholes.

I packed up without a word, clearing everything away as I had a sneaking suspicion I wouldn't be back the next night, and then silently followed Bert out to his dilapidated old bomb parked in the alleyway behind the club.

"She doesn't look much," he said as he wrenched open the door for me, "but she'll get you where you wanna go as long as you ain't in a hurry."

He was right. We weren't in a hurry and she did get us there in her own time. I was exhausted and as soon as Bert made up the sofa bed I was grateful to be left alone. It was late and he wanted the warmth and comfort of the woman he loved while I just wanted the sweet oblivion of sleep.

Things did seem a bit brighter in the morning and I could greet Bert's wife with a modicum of cheerfulness as the sounds and smells of breakfast wafted from the kitchen. I dressed and wandered in to meet Merle, Bert's wife. There were no embarrassed introductions. With her back still to me as she prepared something on the bench top she said, "Oh, there you are. I hope I didn't wake you. Plonk yourself down at the table, honey." She placed a steaming mug of coffee in front of me. "Get that down; you'll need it from what Bert tells me. You want eggs with your waffles?"

"Sure."

"How you like 'em?"

"Scrambled will do just fine."

She went back to the stove and left me to my regrets. It wasn't until she slid the plate in front of me that I remembered I wasn't alone.

"No use brooding over it, honey. What's done is done. No use unpicking the sweater once it's been knitted."

I laughed at the homily.

Merle was the same age as Bert; mid to late fifties at a guess. She had an easy manner that made you feel welcome right from the start without any of that messy introductions and shit. In fact, we were having a right old chin wag by the time Bert put in an appearance.

I excused myself to shower and prepare for the carpeting I was about to receive. When I approached Head Office I was as calm as any man before his execution, although in my case it was merely the end of a career. I'd enjoyed myself, made a few friends including…

"Where the hell have you been?" Jaeson's face was in mine. "I was worried sick."

"I stayed at Bert's place. I needed to think."

"No, you needed to be home with me so we could work on a strategy together."

"You don't have to involve yourself in my shit."

He shook his head impatiently. "Of course I do."

Just then we were called to the big man's office. Jaeson entered first and I followed with as much bravado as I could muster. J.G. paced as if I'd single-handedly brought down the Western Alliance. But I was not about to sit back and take my medicine.

"Was it all your own idea?" J.G. demanded.

Jaeson surprised me when he began to take responsibility.

"Wait a second," I yelled. "Jaeson, it's very noble of you to want to protect me but I don't need that sort of help. I'm an adult; I can accept responsibility for my own actions." I turned to J.G. "It was all my own doing. Jaeson had nothing at all to do with it. Knew nothing about my intentions."

"Why?"

"I told you on a number of occasions I was uncomfortable with the moniker you saddled me with and I was equally pissed off with the character you chose for me. So, I created my own, something that I did feel suited me better."

"Yes, it does. Much as I hate to admit it. However, that is not the point here. I don't pay you to think. I pay you to obey commands."

I decided to stand up for myself for the first time. "If you don't allow me to continue in the role I did last night, then you won't be paying me at all."

"I don't think you understand the rules here, Dion. You don't dictate the terms to me, I dictate the non-negotiable terms to you. Get it?"

"No, not really."

I saw Jaeson wince at my provocation. He interceded before I went too far. "J.G. I think you should look at something before this goes any further."

"That will give this hot head time to reconsider his position," J.G. snapped.

"That's your final word on the matter?"

"Yes." He turned his back on me and went to join Jaeson at the computer.

I shrugged. "Okay. I quit."

I turned on my heels and strode toward the door.

There was mumbled conversation between the two company men before J.G. shouted, "Hold it."

I stopped in my tracks and waited.

"Just for my curiosity, Dion. What will you do now?"

As I spun around to confront him, I removed my wallet from the back pocket of my jeans. I went to his desk and poured the contents of the pouch on to his desk.

"What's all this?" J.G. asked, totally unimpressed.

"Just the business cards of your most important customers. They asked if I could give them a private show. One of the specials. Asked if I'm available for parties, bar mitzvahs, marriages, you name it. I always turned them down." J.G. ran his index finger through the cards obviously noting the names. I scooped them up, returning them to my wallet.

"I have enough offers of work here to tide me over for months, if not years. And what's great about it, I don't have to share with a middle man. Enjoy your day."

I got to the door this time and was turning the handle when J.G. called. "Dion, baby. No need to get all twisted up about some little disagreement. I'm a reasonable man. We can talk this through."

Obviously, Jaeson had shown him something on the computer that led to this change of heart.

"You know if you're unhappy, all you have to do is come to old J.G. here and we can work something out. All amicable like." His belligerent tone belied his words. He must have realized because he smiled which merely gave his face the appearance of someone scarcely able to control his temper.

Jaeson had mainly remained silent through most of my dressing down. "I think what J.G. means is that we're all one big happy family and there's no need to resort to anything underhand." His eyes pleaded with me to take a few steps toward a compromise.

"I suppose I might have been a bit precipitous in going ahead with my plan without asking," I admitted, while including enough weasel words to totally negate the meaning.

J.G. beamed. "Apology accepted."

Jaeson frowned a warning that I interpreted as 'Let it go if you want to keep your job.' Either that or he was feeling particularly constipated that morning.

The boss beckoned me over to the computer. "Come and have a look at this, Dion."

I wasn't predisposed to think kindly of him but it was better to let it go in order to concentrate on what I wanted most. A meeting with Gage. Perhaps I could turn this around yet.

I couldn't believe my eyes. Jaeson and J.G. were watching a clip on YouTube. It was of my performance from the previous night. OMG, I was so hot I felt myself getting hard. I sneaked a look at Jaeson's crotch and it was obvious he had a boner.

My secret life was safe as I was wearing a hood. "Where did they get this footage?"

"Someone must have taken it last night," Jaeson said, turning the palest shade of red as I looked at him. "That was the first time you did that act, right?"

"Yep," I said.

Jaeson tapped the screen. "It's gone viral. In less than twenty-four hours you've received almost half a million hits."

"And you're all over the Twitter sphere. Who is that masked man seems to be trending. There are a couple of others, but you get the drift."

I did indeed. Someone had gone to work on my behalf and had saved my ass. I winked at Jaeson.

J.G. buzzed his secretary. "Get me Publicity, get me Human Resources, and get me Bookings. Have them assembled in my office at…" He consulted his watch, "One o'clock on the dot. Ring that deli on the corner and have them cater. Oh, remember Sid is vegetarian and Valerie is Halal." He finished his conversation and turned to us.

"Right, gentlemen. I want you back here as well. On the dot. Dion, I want you pumped and ready for a photo shoot in your new look. Jaeson, work with him on refining his moves, and see if you can get someone who's good with costumes to do a quick job on his threads. That's it, gents." We were dismissed but now was not the time to hand in my list of demands. J.G. was buzzing and if I were to interrupt, I'd get stung. "Oh, Jaeson, tell Lynne to send someone from the Art Department. ASAP."

Suddenly Head Office was a flurry of activity and I was glad to escape to the comparative calm of Jaeson's studio. Fortunately, I had my costume and my music with me. Jaeson fingered the flimsy material and awkward stitching. "You do this yourself?"

"Uh huh," I said proudly.

"And you call yourself gay? Look at this needlework. A five-year-old child could do better." He yanked at a seam, tearing it apart. He grabbed his cell phone. "Marta, hi, it's Jaeson. I'm in the studio. Could you duck up here, please? And, Marta, bring your sewing machine."

He slid my music disc into the portable machine he used for rehearsals. Before he could press play, I wound my arms around him and planted the sweetest kiss on his lips. He shook me off, but with the widest of grins. "There's time for that later."

I wasn't going to rile him; after all he'd bailed out my ass. Big time.

I went through the motions, he didn't expect a real performance, he was merely watching in order to finesse my routine. He stopped me and suggested I try something a little different. Most times it was a drastic improvement, sometimes it didn't work and we jettisoned it. I loved working with Jaeson like this. It's what I'd missed on the road; once I realized having my own space meant he wasn't around.

Marta, a middle-aged woman who looked like a potato, wheeled her sewing machine in on a trolley. She also had a selection of fabrics with which to reinforce my flimsy home-made costume.

"Dion, show Marta your bump and grind."

I knew Marta of old so I was unembarrassed to gyrate and thrust my hips at her. Every now and then she yelled 'stop' and I froze in position so she could examine the stress and pull on the costume. I took the trouble to go through the entire production number so she had the best possible chance of picking up where the outfit needed strengthening. Then she sat quietly at her sewing machine and proceeded to transform my amateur effort into something totally amazing while Jaeson refined my choreography.

I was proud of what I'd achieved but not too proud that I couldn't accept help from experts. This was no profession for temperamental divas.

By meeting time the costume was complete and my new moves had been incorporated and I felt much more relaxed. Jaeson and I were the last to arrive at J.G.'s office and we could hear the chatter of excitement down the hall. When we entered there was a spontaneous outbreak of applause. I accepted it as my due without letting my ego get the better of me. While I withstood the backslapping and congratulations of the departments who were there to promote me, Jaeson piled a plate with the sandwiches and savories I particularly like. I had to go easy because there's nothing worse than dancing on a full stomach. I nibbled to take the edge off my appetite as the Art Department showed the adverts for Young Gage that would appear in local gay papers close to where I was to perform. Publicity detailed their saturation social media bombardment which would help make me a gay household name, and Bookings revealed a tentative schedule that meant I would cover all the major cities in the next three months.

It was in the middle of my new choreography that a very nervous secretary knocked on the door and poked her head in.

"What is it, Lynne?"

"Phone call—"

"Didn't I say—?"

"I think you'll want to take this one, J.G. It's Gage."

I had continued my performance through the conversation because J.G. had his eyes on me while talking to Lynne. The mere mention of that name threw me off balance. I would have fallen to the floor and perhaps injured myself if Jaeson hadn't caught me in his strong arms.

"Put the call through," J.G. instructed. "Gents, this call is an omen. A good luck omen." He picked up the phone. "Good to hear from you, mate. Hold on, I'll put you on speakerphone so the other guys in the office can hear you."

Gage's slightly distorted voice echoed in the quiet room. "…young twink pretending to be the young me. I saw the clip on YouTube. Very talented. Very hot. What's he look like under the hood, J.G.? Would I fuck him?"

"Oh, yes," J.G. said.

"In that case, send him on over so I can teach him a few of my tricks."

Yes, please.

"I know the sort of thing you want to teach him, Gage."

"I never mix pleasure with business, J.G. You know that."

Damn.

"Listen, while I've got you on the line, mate," J.G. said, "Got a few minutes so I can throw a few ideas at you?"

"Sure."

"Nothing definite yet, but we thought we'd send the kid out on the road, generate a bit of buzz, leading up to a major pairing of you two on the same bill right here in our own theatre. Maximize the profits, create interest, then give it to them full throttle. Maybe Jaeson could come up with a routine that included both of you."

"You know I don't duet," Gage said.

"No, what I meant is, with your approval, of course."

"If he's as good as the word on the street and it's not all hype, then I'll consider it." He must have remembered I could hear every word he said. "Sorry, kid, nothing personal. I got a reputation to uphold."

"I understand perfectly," I said.

"Sexy voice."

"Um, thanks."

J.G. interrupted our love fest. "I'll call you in a day or two and update you on what we decide."

"Good." Gage hesitated. "Ah, J.G. can I talk frankly."

"Sure. Go ahead."

"That young guy you sent over to do specials. He's not gonna hack it. Too flighty, too fussy, too particular. Great little dancer but he's not cut out for the back-room stuff."

I saw J.G.'s eyes light up. "Hey, how's this for an idea. You and the kid here as a tag team. How does that sound?"

"He done any specials yet?"

"No, but…"

"Don't screw this up, J.G. I got a really big paying gig coming up."

The boss turned to Jaeson. "Is the kid ready for specials?"

Jaeson looked as if he'd rather tear his tongue out than answer the question. "Yeah, he's ready. We just need to test him out."

"We can do that once he goes out on the road. I have the utmost faith in Jaeson's judgment."

"Even if I tell you, the special's for Mischa Roberts?"

"Ouch!" Jaeson said.

"Jaeson?" J.G. waited on confirmation.

He groaned. "He'll be ready, Gage. In fact, I think he'll surprise you."

"I hope you're right."

After a few more pleasantries between the boss and Gage, he hung up.

"You never mentioned you thought I was ready for specials," I hissed at Jaeson.

"It was going to be a surprise."

"Well, gents, you all know what you have to do, so let's get to it." The meeting broke up as everyone went back to their departments. "Kid, Jaeson. Tomorrow at eleven. I want to go over a few things."

We both mumbled agreement, my indiscretion seemingly long forgiven if not forgotten.

Back in the security of Jaeson's studio, I locked the door and swept him into my arms.

"Okay, what did you do?"

He shrugged out of my grip. "If you'd had the decency to take my calls, you could have helped me. I merely began tweeting about the masked stripper. I have enough accounts to start a trend. I also took the precaution of having a friend in the audience. He had an uninterrupted view of your act, plus the latest digital camera so he could capture it all in perfect focus."

"How could you know…?"

"Dion. You think you're so clever, but I can read you. You're transparent. When you insisted we all be at your performance, especially J.G. it was easy to guess you were going to spring a surprise."

"You're always one step ahead of me?"

"Babe, you don't know just how far ahead of you I am."

"I'm beginning to learn."

"Your new act is very good. Hell, it's better than really good, it's fucking amazing. I'm so proud of you."

"Really?"

"Which part are you querying? That your new act is amazing? Or that I'm proud of you?"

I hit him playfully on the arm. "I know you're proud of me."

"I don't think you need me to stroke your ego anymore."

"Why didn't you tell me that you think I'm ready for specials?"

"Because I hoped you'd never ask."

"Is that why you looked so sad when you told J.G. I was?"

"Partly."

"Is it because I'll be fucking other men and they'll be fucking me?"

He nodded. "Partly that, too. I tried not to let it get to me because I know it's part of the job. Especially for an ambitious young man like you. I've never met anyone as focused, as single-minded as you, Dion."

"We have something special, Jaeson. I'll always be fond of you."

"Fond?"

"What more can you expect of a…a stripper?"

"What more do you expect, Dion?"

"What do you mean?"

"You must think I'm a fuckwit. From day one you've had your eye on only one prize and I've seen you ruthlessly pursue it. You'll use any means at your disposal to get it. What chance is there for me?"

"What prize?"

Jaeson's eyes were glistening. "Oh, come on, Dion. You think I didn't notice. The way you always manage to steer the conversation around to Gage. The way your eyes sparkle when you hear his name. The way everything you do is to wangle your way closer to him."

"But you helped me. In fact, you more than helped, you pushed me. Why the fuck would you do that?"

"Because I love you, and I can't bear to see you unhappy."

It was painful for both of us, but Jaeson accompanied me for the first few performances I gave under my new moniker. He also organized the specials for me, ensuring that I got less demanding clients at first until my confidence was such that I felt I could take on anyone. My next special put paid to that when the customer roped and gagged me and whipped me painfully with his belt. He left welts across my body and I was 'retired ill' for a few days until the marks disappeared. J.G. did not like to see his dancers out of pocket particularly when it was no fault of their own so he managed to persuade the sadistic bastard who'd marked me to cough up two weeks wages (with tips) by sending around two rather large gentlemen with knuckle dusters and a large dollop of aggressive intimidation.

"It doesn't pay to get too cocky," Jaeson said as he changed the dressing on a rather nasty wound.

"Tell me about this Mischa character."

"Nasty piece of work but he works within boundaries. It's just his parameters are so far out of an ordinary person's concept of decency as to blow the whole concept of morality totally away."

"Sounds like a total charmer."

"That he is. What you need to know is that he and his buddies will tag team you while Gage taps the ass of the bottoms. You'll be fucked until you can't stand up. But that will be after the floor show."

"Let me guess, Gage and I are the floor show."

"You don't have to look so pleased that your fantasy is about to come true."

The night Jaeson confessed his love for me was one of the longest of my life. I genuinely liked him, but while I had Gage in my head and, I guess, a little in my heart, there was little room for anyone else. I didn't want to lead him on, give him unrealistic expectations. I was honest with him, up to a point, although he had deduced most of it. A little too perceptive is Jaeson. Not sure I could love a man who knows what I'm thinking before I've thunk it.

To his credit, at no time did he attempt to talk me out of my path, in fact he encouraged me to go for it. There was no begging, no whining; he was all understanding to the extent he got on my wick. I would have relished an all-out screaming match.

Then like a mother hen sending her chicks out into the big wide world, Jaeson was gone. I had no opportunity to miss him, I was so hyped up on my prospective dance date with Gage. It had taken ten months but I had achieved – almost achieved – what I set out to do when I gave up university. Whether I would return would depend on a lot of things.

My cell phone buzzed. I didn't recognize the caller's number.

"Hey, kid."

I couldn't speak.

"You there? Speak to me."

"Hi, um, Gage. I just wasn't expecting it to be you."

He laughed. "You got one huge man crush on me, mate? I'm your hero? You've loved me ever since you hit puberty? I've heard it all before. Why should you be any different?"

That was not the way I wanted our first conversation to go.

I tried to play it cool but my voice gave me away by squeaking when I wanted it to sound deep and masterful. "What can I do for you?"

"Look, kid. Let me lay it on the line. You can hero worship me as much as you want, but it's all strictly business with me. I do sex, I don't do love, so get those thoughts out of your head right now. And I don't do sex with fellow dancers except in the confines of a specials. Got it?"

"Got it."

"Then we'll get along just fine. You got your hood and your costume to hand?"

"Yeah."

"Where are you staying?"

I gave him the address of the motel I was holed up in on my trajectory toward our famous dual stripping routine. It was fairly simple routine but we'd not had a chance to rehearse it together.

Gage surprised me. "Get yourself in costume. I'll be outside your door in about…let me see…fifteen."

He disconnected before I could reply. Arrogant prick. What if I'd had other things to do? Nah, he knew what it was like on tour. He knew there were no other things to do.

He was right on time. I opened the door as nonchalantly as I could manage. The huge hunk of muscle that stood in the doorway was even hotter than I remembered from our previous encounter of almost a year before. This was the real Gage. He looked me up and down, whistling appreciatively. "J.G. was right. You are exactly my type. No, don't go getting any ideas. There are plenty of others out there who are not in the industry and who are also exactly my type. I don't shit in my own backyard."

I locked the door behind me. "Where are we going?"

"I thought you and me should hang out together before the big night."

"Dressed like this. We'll be arrested."

"I was thinking more along the lines of the club. No one's using it now and we could go through our steps."

"I was warned you're a thorough professional."

"And also, let me think, cold, unfeeling, a taskmaster, a perfectionist, and, oh, a fuckin' pain in the ass."

"From what you seem to be packing in those trousers of yours, that's a given."

He laughed.

"So you're not always the serious son-of-a-bitch you're painted. You can actually have fun."

"I take my work seriously. Everything else is up for grabs."

"What about your love life?"

"Listen, kid, and listen good. I allow one mistake and one only. You want me to pull the car over and toss you out on that pretty bubble butt of yours, just mention the words 'love' and 'life' again. That should do it."

"Point taken."

"I can't keep calling you 'kid.' If you told me your name I musta missed it."

"I like it when you call me kid."

We sat in silence until we pulled into the gravel parking lot of the club which had seen better days. In fact, it was hard to imagine that it had seen any worse. It was misleading because inside the joint was warm and inviting in that way only Trailer Trash Modern can be. Subdued lighting, leatherette booth seating around laminated tables. Well-worn carpet the color of vomit and stale beer, a forlorn mirror ball that looked as if it had taken one look at its surroundings and refused to glitter.

Gage must have seen my look. "It scrubs up okay at night. It's amazing what sort of flaws an audience can cover over."

I was tense and awkward as I guess anyone would be in the presence of a legend. We stop/started our rehearsal so many times because I lost the plot, I thought Gage was going to lose patience.

"You need to relax, kid," he said. "You're too tense. I've got the perfect cure for that." So saying he unzipped his costume and flopped out his dick. It was semi-tumescent. I must have stared because he nudged me and said, "Go on, you can touch it if you want."

He stood with his hands on his hips, his legs spread apart as I pumped his cock. I heard the sharp intake of breath and felt his dick thicken under my touch. "Too much of a good thing." He removed my fist. "I gotta save that for tonight." He carefully tucked himself away. "Well?"

"Well what?"

"Fair's fair. Your turn."

I felt somewhat ridiculous hauling out my cock for examination especially since it wasn't a patch on the size, shape or beauty of his.

"You've got nothing to be ashamed of in that department," he said as he gave my rock hard dick – it had been that way since he arrived at the motel door – a quick jerk or two. He must have anticipated his effect on me because he removed his hand a few seconds before I would have shot my load.

"Now, let's try those dance steps gain."

He was right. It all ran smoothly from that point on. During numerous breaks in rehearsals he asked me about my life and why I'd given up university, recommending I scoot back there asap.

"This is no life for a kid," he said. "Pay's lousy, conditions are worse, and the shit you gotta do to earn enough to live on I wouldn't wish on my worst enemy. Nah, uni is where you belong."

He was free with the advice but no so free in revealing anything of himself.

Even though the perspiration was pooling in our leather hoods neither of us removed it. Eventually as bar staff and other club workers began arriving for the night's show. Gage slapped me on the butt and said, "Okay, let's do it. Dry run in tonight's show. How's that sound?"

I stuttered. "Fantastic."

He dragged me down the dark corridor, the fluoro tubes flickering, in desperate need of replacement. He opened a few doors, closing them quickly until he found what he was after. "Here you go. Make yourself comfortable. Try and get yourself some sleep before the show. It's what I do. There's a shower. I'll bring you over a towel. My dressing room's the one with the star." He said it in such a matter-of-fact way there was no chance to laugh at his ego. "We'll go on in the second half. I'll tee it up with the sound and lighting guys. You okay with that."

I was pumped. "Hell, yeah."

"I'll come and get you about thirty minutes before our set."

"Sounds good."

I lay down on the tatty old lounge and the next thing I knew was the roar of a crowd on the other side of the door and down the corridor. There was a clean towel on the back of the divan and a small lamp was illuminating the far side of the room. I stumbled over to read the time on my cell phone. It was late. Shit, I had to get ready.

I'd showered and freshened up by the time Gage came to collect me. He looked me over, then declared, "You need some oil."

He took me back to his dressing room where he rubbed oil all over my body until I thought my cock would explode. When he began rubbing my ass cheeks he accidentally on purpose brushed his thumb across my throbbing hole. I gasped.

"You'll be so popular with the gangbang crowd, kid."

I examined myself in the mirror. The oil made me look hotter than ever.

Then before I knew it our act was being announced and we were on. I didn't have time to worry, the screams, the testosterone, the hands like the tentacles on a thousand octopuses that I could never quite dislodge, the act climaxing when Gage and Gage Junior look at each other through a mirror and get so turned on that we jerk off until our spunk spatters against the other's body. I was so fuckin' turned on; I wanted to do it all over again.

Gage was complimentary on my performance. "You did good, kid. Go take a shower and I'll drive you back to the motel."

"You wanna go out for a drink?"

"Afraid I can't. I got a special every night I'm in this shithole," he said, but he didn't seem too bitter about it.

Back in the dressing room, I was careful not to dislodge Gage's cum from my body. I went into the bathroom and stood in the shower stall without turning on the spray. I scraped Gage's drying spunk from my body and sucked it off my fingers while the other hand jerked my cock until I sprayed the tiles with my second load. By the time Gage came to drive me back, I had just about calmed down.

We repeated it for the next three nights, never once seeing each other's face, and me unloading a second time in the shower to the fantasy of Gage spooning me while ramming his deadly weapon in my tight hole.

Word got around about our double act and how we honed it to perfection out of town. Some very professional footage appeared on YouTube, courtesy of Head Office although J.G. denied any knowledge of its origin. That created even more demand for tickets.

Our official opening night was complete with a number of A-list pop stars and television actors who were far enough out of the closet that they could afford to be seen at a gay strip show, plus a sprinkling of top-dollar as well as up-and-comers in the porn industry. I was awestruck that those who weren't there to be seen were there to see me. It was enough to give a boy a complex.

I was confident in my own ability, mainly from the positive reinforcement from Jaeson while he was training me and now Gage as we worked in tandem. All this adulation could go to a boy's head. It already had in the case of my smaller head.

The biggest surprise to me was that Gage seemed not at all envious when my popularity began to rival his, or that the overwhelming majority of publicity for our big night was about me. It wasn't of my doing but that didn't prevent a certain amount of guilt.

Gage and I had our own dressing rooms; I guess so we could take our masks off and relax without fear of exposure. Quite funny when you think about it. I had a steady procession of visitors, including J.G. who was more nervous than me, a handful of celebrities who had their photos taken with me (hooded, of course) in case I turned out to be anyone important.

The man I was most pleased to see was Jaeson who knocked shyly just before the half hour call. I'd chosen not to stay with him this time and J.G. put me up in a moderately pricey hotel. I hugged Jaeson warmly. "Well, this is it, Dion. The culmination of all you've worked for. In every respect." I won't see you after the show because they whizz you off to the special. I hear Mischa paid a fortune to secure your services. I only hope some of it filters back to you. I hope Gage is everything you hoped he'd be."

He was eager to go, although I wanted to keep him with me a little longer.

"This is for you," he said, thrusting a small box at me.

By the time I finished saying, "You shouldn't have," he was gone.

I opened the gift to discover a doll that was an amazingly lifelike representation of me – in my stripper's outfit. I'm not a total idiot and I can recognize a work of love when it's shoved under my nose. I ran to the door of the dressing room but the hallway was empty. I propped Little Me against the mirror so that every time my eyes strayed over to it, my face lit up. I sighed. If only everything wasn't so complicated.

I didn't have time to stew over the maybes of life. A knock on the door for the half-hour call and soon enough I found myself on stage for my solo number in the first half. It went exceptionally well, but the audience was so buzzed I think they would have applauded a caterpillar crawling across the stage. The commotion at the intermission was all about Gage and Young Gage's dual strip, emanating to a large extent from the table at which Mischa was holding court with his entourage. When people learned that we were going to perform at Mischa's private party, men clamored for an invitation.

We'd rehearsed our duet so thoroughly it was a bit of an anti-climax to perform it again although the audience, new to the double act, almost took the roof off with their screams of encouragement. In the euphoria of the adulation it's easy to get carried away and at one point I was about to drop to my knees and engulf Gage's cock in my hungry mouth but he warned me off with an imperceptible shake of his head. If there were cops in that night, we'd be arrested and the club closed down.

We took our bows to a cacophony of cheers, foot stomping, and applause. The audience was informed another evening performance had been added to the schedule, making it eight in all. It would probably be sold out before we left the venue.

Gage shepherded me to his dressing room where, behind closed doors, he hugged me to his oily chest and planted the wettest, hungriest kiss on my mouth. I melted into his arms. I felt his heart thumping against his chest, hoping it was me making it pump so wildly.

He held me at arm's length. "Look, I know you don't like taking orders but, believe me, it's essential that you listen to me tonight. I've got a second sense for these things so if I tell you to do something, don't argue, just do it. It's for your own safety."

"Okay. I promise."

"Now, bend over the chair."

Wow, I was going to get my wish. I spread my ass and felt him probing my hole. I felt something greasy slip inside me, something much too small for his cock. I turned my head, "What was that?"

"Just a little something to help ease the...um... discomfort. Just how many guys have fucked you in one night before?"

"One," I said proudly. "But he did it three times."

"Wait until I get my hands on Jaeson. He said you were ready."

I took umbrage. "And he was right."

I was about to march out the door when I was grabbed by the scruff of the neck and another kiss planted in my mouth. The difference this time was there was something unfamiliar on Gage's tongue. He pulled out and held my lips closed. "Swallow."

I did as told, then looked at him questioningly.

"Viagra. It will help keep you excited."

"I won't need it," I boasted.

"I'm not going to argue. There will be a car waiting for us at the back of the club in half an hour. They get a bit pissy if we're late."

I was at the designated spot with five minutes to spare. Gage was already there chatting to the driver. Calling the vehicle a car was a total misnomer. It was a limo. I scrambled into the back and lay along the plush leather seat wishing I could travel like this every time. Gage got in and sat opposite me. God, I loved that guy but I wished just for once he'd take off his hood.

"When we get to the house, Mischa will tell me what scenario he wants played out this evening." Gage snapped, "Are you listening?"

I wasn't. I was fiddling with the bar fridge like a kid with a new toy. I was a bit overwhelmed by the opulence.

"Concentrate. I'll tell you what characters we're to play and you'll do your damnedest to please. Our tips depend on it, and Mischa is a very generous tipper if he's pleased. When we finish our act which usually runs about twenty minutes, then it's the host's turn. I know where Mischa will be headed tonight and it'll be your ass. He likes to fuck rough, that's why I stuck the meth suppository up your butt. It'll make your ass tingle after a while. With any luck it will help you when Mischa's buddies tag your ass."

"How many?" I asked with a little trepidation.

Gage shrugged. "Not sure. Not everyone joins in."

Part of me was appalled but another part of me was excited.

The limo trip took about forty minutes until we were dropped outside a palatial residence on the outskirts of the city. I didn't think people lived in places like this except in the movies. Gage led me around the back to what I took to be the servants' entrance. "If we'd gone through the front door we would have been eaten alive," he said ominously.

We knocked on the kitchen door and a waiter in a penguin suit answered. "Hey, Gage, long time no see, man. Come in. Who's this, your son?" The waiter thought that was a great joke and howled with laughter. I thought he must have been sampling too much of the liquor he was distributing to lubricate the party.

"Ted, this is Young Gage as he likes to bill himself."

We exchanged pleasantries.

"How are they?" Gage asked.

"Rowdy bunch, could easily get out of control, especially since Mischa has suggested I be free with the drinks."

Gage looked worried. "That's what I was afraid of."

"I'll go tell him you're here." Ted opened the door to the rest of the house and the noise of excited partygoers was deafening.

"Fuck," I said in awe.

"Yeah, fuck is right," Gage replied. "I've got a bad feeling about tonight."

Before he could explain, Mischa came bounding into the kitchen. "Gage, how lovely. And you are Young Gage. Feel free to help yourself to the alcohol or the party drugs in the room I've set aside for you."

The room in question was a palace. It was so large I could have lived in it. It was set up as a dressing room and, true to his word, there was a glass bowl of multi-colored pills and tablets. Enough to choke a horse. I was tempted to empty them into my bag and send them to Dazza to sell on campus. That way the three of them wouldn't have to live on a diet of pot noodles four days a week. Gage and Mischa whispered in the corner while I set out my costume in preparation.

Mischa's parting words were, "Help yourselves, gents."

I was about to do just that when Gage slapped my wrist hard.

"Don't even go there. You've got enough in your system right now you don't need any more. Besides, you don't know what half this shit is and you're just as likely to pass out only to wake up to find yourself chained in the basement with a pack of ugly bastards drooling over your ass."

"What were you and Mischa whispering about?"

"Okay, tonight's scenario is father/son. I catch you playing with yourself while watching porn. I punish you, and then to teach you a lesson I fuck you. Really hard. Got it?"

"Got it. Why can't the son turn the tables and fuck the dad for a change?"

"Because that's not the scenario Mischa is paying us to perform. You didn't take some of those pills while I wasn't looking?"

I was indignant. "No, I didn't."

We began to get ready. "Keep your eye on me at all times and I'll cover your back," Gage stressed. "Don't go into another room where I can't see you, no matter what they offer."

"You're beginning to take the fun out of the whole enterprise," I complained.

"It's not fun, kid. It's work. In your case, it can be mighty painful work."

I didn't think so. The way my ass was burning you could have driven a ten-ton truck up there and I still would have itched for more. So a party of how many guys? Ten?

Twenty? Thirty? I'd hardly feel it. Who was I kidding? Usually if anyone went back for a third go, I was begging them to come quickly. This insatiable side of me had to be the drugs talking. I knew my cock was rock hard from the feeling of sexual excess in the air. Or maybe it was the Viagra.

"You ready?" Gage asked.

"Ready as I'll ever be."

Gage went to the door and opened it, nodding to someone on the other side. I heard a muffled announcement and a lot of whistling and yahooing.

"Bend over, kid," Gage demanded.

"I thought I wasn't supposed to have any more pills."

I heard the pump action on a large plastic bottle of lube before Gage pulled my briefs aside and his finger slicked my butt hole.

"Take a deep breath. Let it out."

As I did so, he slid the butt plug into my hole. My sphincter clenched, holding it in place.

"You okay?" he asked.

"Fine," I sulked. I was expecting the specials to be a lot more exciting than this.

"Go," he said.

I walked into the living room to applause from the assembled guests who crowded around a small space that had been left for me. I sat in a bean bag which gave me enough elevation to be seen. I mimed watching a dirty movie on TV, sliding my hand down into my briefs until my cock ached so much from the constriction I had to let it free. Milking it slowly, a thin film of precum oozed from the head. I thought I might as well ad lib a little. With my finger, I wiped it off and then tasted it.

"Nasty," someone muttered from the audience.

Just then Gage burst through the door.

"What the fuck is going on here? Are you watching faggot movies?"

I was so surprised by Gage's entrance I did cringe momentarily, unable to speak.

"Are you a fag, son?"

"No, dad. I just wanted to see what fags do to one another. It's disgusting."

He grabbed my cock. "Is that why you're hard, son? Because you think guys that take it up the ass are disgusting?"

I lowered my eyes.

"Time to teach you a lesson, boy."

Gage grabbed me and bent me over his knees, slapping my ass. He pulled my briefs down. "What have we here, boy?"

Sliding his hand between my cheeks, he wriggled the butt plug free, holding it up for the audience.

"My son is a filthy fag. You'll burn in hell, son. I'm gonna have to punish you for your own good."

He slammed his open hand down on my ass again. It stung but it was also kind of pleasant. He leaned close to my ear. "Struggle. Scream. He likes it violent. Like I'm really hurting you."

Slap.

"No, daddy. That hurts. No more, daddy."

"Sniveling fag boy. Shut your filthy cock-sucking mouth."

Gage rammed the butt plug between my lips and I bit down to keep it lodged there.

He slapped my ass a few more times and I wriggled as if I was in real pain.

"There, boy. Has that driven the devil out of you?"

I wiggled my ass.

"Let me feel that little hole of yours, to see if Satan has been driven out."

He inserted two fingers in my ass. Oh God, it felt so good. He fucked them in and out a few times before pulling out to show them to the audience.

"Damn your butt is so tight, son. So hot and inviting. Look, son. You've made your daddy super hard for your faggot boy ass. On your knees boy."

I kneeled in front of him as he slid his jeans off. He'd gone commando. There was his beautiful prick. I'd waited almost a year to get that where it should always have been. Wedged inside me.

"You want daddy's cock. Son?"

I spat the butt plug out and it rolled under one of the chairs.

"No, daddy. That's evil. That's the devil talking."

"Fuck him, daddy," someone called from the audience.

"I'm gonna fuck you real good, son. I'm gonna fuck you every day if necessary until I fuck the faggot right out of you."

"No, you can't. It's a sin, daddy. Your cock is too big, it'll kill me, daddy."

Gage rolled me over on my back, flinging my legs up onto his chest and over his shoulders. He fingered my ass to make sure I was lubricated then rubbed a little of the residue on his enormous prick.

"Here comes daddy's prick, son. Feel every inch of it as it goes into your faggot ass. You feel that, son? Feel daddy's cock inside you?"

I screamed for him to take it out and it was only part acting. His cock really was spreading me wide open. I couldn't believe how good it felt even while I thought I'd be split in two.

"Take it, son. Take daddy's cock. I'm gonna fuck you until you're no longer a faggot."

"No, daddy, no. It hurts too much. You're killing me."

This set up a pattern which was obviously working because I managed to see part of the audience out of the corner of my eye and some of them had succumbed and were openly manipulating their cocks. But what I wanted most was to watch Gage. His eyes were dead. While I loved having him inside me and this playacting really did add an extra layer of perversity, I wanted to see or feel some indication he was enjoying himself.

"Fuck you, son. Fuck you for the filthy faggot you are."

There was a low chant from the audience. "Fuck him. Fuck him. Fuck him." It slowly built.

Mischa was hovering in the background, totally naked, milking his very large purple-headed cock.

As I felt the tempo of Gage's fucking increase, I knew he was on the home straight.

"Fucking fag slut," he spat.

I could feel the tension in the room. Other men began to crowd around us and then…and then all hell broke loose.

Mischa leaned over and began to slide the hoods off our faces. Gage attempted to stop him but the other men held his arms down. The same happened to me. When Gage's hood was totally removed, I was staring into the eyes of my stepfather who deserted me and my mother when I was fourteen.

"Daddy?"

"Oh, fuck. I've got my cock in my son's ass."

Then I saw the light that had been missing before; the light that shone in his eyes as he pumped his spunk deep inside me and I blew my load all over my belly. Some of the voyeurs couldn't control themselves and I felt their cum spatter against my cheek and my chest. It felt good.

Mischa pushed Gage out of the way so he could bury his own hard pick in my guts. I felt every inch of it as it slammed into me.

Mischa snarled viciously as he forced his cock in and out of my butthole. "You filthy little slut. You let your own father fuck your ass. What sort of filthy pervert are you? Lick your daddy's cock clean. Come on, dad. Feed the faggot."

Gage seemed in a dream but, nevertheless, did as instructed. He slid his slimy prick between my lips. It was still hard. "Oh, God. Your mum knew you'd want this one day. That's why I left. That's why when you were at my show last year, I couldn't…"

I wanted to tell him it was okay, it's what I wanted. I guessed from his actions he wanted it as much as I did.

"Suck it, son. Suck it good," he whimpered.

Mischa turned to the assembled guests. "You guys are gonna love this ass. It's so fuckin' tight. It'll be a sloppy mess by the time we've all finished with him."

I concentrated on giving my stepdad pleasure. Somewhere deep inside I must have known who Gage was. It was the only explanation for my obsession. Now that I'd found him, I felt whole. Something I had never felt since he left.

"Get on your knees, fag boy," Mischa commanded.

I struggled off my back and assumed the position. Dad slid his cock into my mouth again as he ran his thumb over my nose and my eyebrows. It felt so good.

Even Mischa was feeding my overwhelming desire for cock. Dad looked down into my eyes as I pleasured him, sucking his cock down my throat, wanting to taste the juice from his balls. My ass felt so good stuffed with cock and I hoped the other guys at the party were going to tag it as well. I wanted my dad to be proud of me.

"Swallow it, son. Swallow me down."

I tasted his pure daddy cum as I gulped it down. I wanted more. But he disappeared and it all became hazy. Mischa dumped his load in my guts before others fought to be next in line. I saw the pride in daddy's eyes as he watched me being used as he knew I should. Then someone stuffed my mouth and I lost sight of him again. Another man pumped into my willing ass. My body was prodded and propped up in so many different positions I lost count. My holes were plugged by so many cocks, my body filled and covered with so much spunk I wasn't sure I'd ever move again.

Finally, though, I felt myself being lifted in warm masculine arms and someone saying, "Let's get you out of here."

I felt a warm rag cleaning my face and body. I felt cool sheets against my skin, but I felt no pain and I felt no remorse. I knew he was gone, but it no longer mattered.

He did love me. My step daddy hadn't left home because he didn't love me. He really loved me. He proved it. Now I was free.

"Hush, babe. Try to get some sleep. You've had a very busy night."

I knew that voice. That voice didn't criticize me for my behavior, even now.

"Did you enjoy yourself?" Jaeson asked, not a skerrick of condemnation in his tone.

"Mmm." I snuggled against his body.

"You want to do it again?"

"Maybe. I don't know."

"What do you know?"

I knew I wanted to go to sleep but I also knew the answers were important to Jaeson.

"I know I'm very grateful for everything you did. I hurt you and I'm sorry. But it's gone now. All gone."

I was drifting off. I couldn't stop myself. Just before I fell asleep, I said.

"I know now that I love you, Jaeson."

Somewhere inside my brain, I realized that was true.

OMG! THE COLLEGE JOCK'S A NUDIST!

*What's the next step once
you've seen him naked?*

"Put your tongue back in your mouth, you're drooling all over your sandwich," Arli said. Then followed my line of sight. "Oh no, Brett, I thought you had more taste. Not Mr. Neanderthal, the school jock?"

I was so pathetic. How cliché is it for the college gay nerd to fall for the popular sports jock? Only Porno 101.

"Besides," Arli continued, relishing my discomfort, "He's got that air-head, Cindy-Lou Harrower hanging off his arm."

"Of course, he's got a girl hanging off his arm, he's the college stud." I sounded petulant.

Arli was deliberately gross. "You wanna get yourself some of his good old country gonad juice?"

"Uh huh." I sighed. That was a dead giveaway.

"Oh, pul-leaze. Tell me you don't want to marry the bonehead."

"I do."

Arli bashed me on the arm. "Wake up to yourself, Brett. It ain't gonna happen. Besides, you're much too young to settle down. Play the field, enjoy yourself while you can."

What she didn't say was 'Like me.'

My best female friend in the world described herself as postfeminist which roughly translated means she treated men as sex objects in much the same way most men treated women. In old-fashioned lingo it meant she was a bit of a slut. It was a descriptive noun she embraced. Not only that, she had all the missionary zeal necessary to get out there and convert men to her way of thinking. I was the lone failure. I neither succumbed to her obvious charms nor to her encouragement to free my gay sexuality from the 'chains of patriarchal conservatism.'

I may not have dipped my wick where so many men had dipped before, but I loved her like a brother. She returned the affection.

I was curious. "Have you ever tried to…you know?"

One thing she disliked about me was my absolute horror of anything vulgar.

"Spit it out, Brett. Are you asking whether I've ever fucked Cro-Magnon man? No, I have not."

I couldn't help but smile.

"I saw that smirk. You don't think I can?"

To be honest, I didn't think she could. Rocky's type was all-too-apparently big-breasted blonde cheer leaders which was the antithesis of Arli's dark, moody, average-sized tits bohemian appeal. This, however, was not the occasion to tell the truth.

"I think you'd have him in bed with the snap of your pussy muscles," I lied.

"Why, Brett, I do believe you just used a slight, very slight, vulgar term for a woman's cunt."

I used it to deflect her attention away from seducing Rocky. You see, we had a pact that we would never sleep (my term) or fuck (her term) with one of our opposite's conquests. If Arli were to cajole Rocky into the sack, then I'd have to find someone else to fantasize about, and men who were as unattainable as the football jock were few and far between.

There was a reason I chose Rocky. Arli was forever attempting to pair me off. Her idea of a suitable partner for me consisted of her male friends who'd confessed to her they wanted to explore their gay side. I ended up helping them discover they had no gay side but a rather silly notion that by sprouting such rubbish, Arli would give them a tumble. More fool them when all they had to do was approach her and ask, 'Wanna fuck?'

More fool me that I played along with so many misguided attempts at match-making, although a small number of them did lead to an enjoyable night of faked passion. Not faked on my side, but definitely on theirs. They were so horny they would have screwed a tortoise that couldn't crawl away fast enough – and I wasn't running. I cut my baby teeth of experience with these guys. I thought that was a generous exchange. They got their rocks off and I got to practice my gay skills, virginal as they were.

With more confidence, came less patience with Arli's interference in my domestic life, or lack thereof. Explaining to her that I needed to learn seduction techniques and also learn to recognize fellow travelers along the winding gay path to relationship satisfaction was insufficient to get her to tone down totally her insatiable quest to drive me to gay slutdom. Now she was merely a pedestrian shoving me in that direction.

The only out I could find to my dilemma was to develop an all-consuming crush on some man, the more unattainable the better. An added plus would be if Arli found my choice total anathema. It was a big ask, but the perfect solution presented himself one day when she and I were finalists in the college diving championships: different divisions, of course. I say, of course, knowing full well that Arli can dive the Speedos off me. She won't admit it, but she's definitely Olympics material. That's not to say I'm not good at it, but I'll never be world-class.

I'd just completed my most difficult dive from the platform and was waiting for the results. I'm no Greg Louganis but I was satisfied with my effort, and it took me to the top spot in my class. Arli was delighted but not so much that she didn't rub my nose in her higher score. We'd both be heading off to the state championships. I guess I was allowed a little time to get my head out of the clouds but it's difficult when everyone is offering a backslap and congratulations, none more so than when Arli and I were traversing the car-park to be stopped in our tracks by a call of 'Hey, dude.'

Arli and I both turned to see Rocky, another of his constant bubble-headed blonde bimbos being dragged along on his arm, striding toward us, his smile a mile wide. "Awesome dives, dude," he complimented me, ignoring Arli who quietly fumed that she'd been relegated to the same level as the gun-chewing bimbo.

What you need to know here is that in the hierarchy of college sports, at least in our college, football is the superstar jockdom category. It then goes in descending order until you reach the swim team, and way down deep inside that is the lowly competitive diver. It's just about the lowest rung before you get to the next college species: nerds.

So, for Rocky to even acknowledge my existence was special enough, if you're into that sort of specious popularity, but to have the sports god actually high five my win, well that was up there with the stratosphere. Unbelievably, he shook off his date to put his arm around my shoulders as we walked toward his car, treating me as jock to jock. The jar of electricity that shot through my body surprised me although he didn't seem to feel it. I'm afraid he did all the talking, mainly about the imperative of keeping your eye on the ball (all his clichés came from his chosen sport), training hard, perfecting skills, and peaking on the day. There was nothing to disagree with and for a brief shining moment, I swam in Rocky's blessed orbit.

Once at his car, he patted my shoulder and said quietly as if he were shy, "I'm proud of ya, mate. Congratulations." And then he and Clara Belle or whatever her name was were gone in the pop of a pink gum bubble.

"What was that all about?" Arli asked, once she'd overcome the coughing attack brought on by the exhaust fumes.

"No idea," I shrugged. "But I think I'm in love."

Arli hated the way she'd been treated. Rocky had not even acknowledged her existence, let alone her win that was superior to mine, so Arli hated Rocky. On the other hand, I had found the man I could use to fend off Arli's further attacks on my single status. I would cultivate an obsession with the jock. He had all the attributes I needed. He was gorgeous. He was straight. He had so many girlfriends we'd all lost count at around the number thirty-five. He had a body that simply wouldn't quit, including an ass that I could bury my face in and die happy. His cock was an unknown but God could not have been so cruel as to cheat him in that department. He was perfect. Did I mention he's gorgeous?

Much as I liked to pretend my infatuation with Rocky was all to do with my ruse to stop Arli interfering in my life, I knew that I was fooling myself as well. I did have a stupid crush on the big guy. Dumb, eh? At the very least I would have changed my opinion of his Neanderthalism from that brief meeting. Yeah, he was still a jock and, yeah, he was still dating cheer leaders, but I couldn't deny the fizz of attraction that aroused my interest and other parts of my body when he touched me. Now he was my jock. At least in my fantasies. That meant it wasn't difficult to keep up my pretense with Arli, although she gave me heaps of shit over it.

After that, I seemed to run into Rocky everywhere. Whether my subconscious was at work, steering me to places I was likely to see him, or whether I just noticed him more now that I had created a fictitious attraction, was open to conjecture. In the past his presence probably didn't even register with me, while now I was acutely aware of the buff beauty.

Something had changed, however. If Rocky saw me in the street, he'd call out, "Hey, Brett, howzitgoin?" Or else, he'd stop and chat about my training and the importance of focus, usually ending with a half-embarrassed half-shy 'I'm proud of ya, man.' His behavior became so pervasive even Arli noticed. She was never likely to actually like Rocky but once he started including her in our brief conversations if she was with me, she thawed from seething hatred to a sort of favorable neutrality.

"For a jock, he's okay," she finally admitted. "I can sort of see what you like about him."

I was heartbroken by that admission because it was a cover for the fact she really did like him. In *that* way. And if Arli liked you in *that* way, then she got you. She wasn't bound by any particular loyalty to me because my relationship with him was all in my head. More importantly, for me, it meant if she did inveigle him into any sort of sexual action, he was off-limits to me. I was realistic enough to realize I was never actually going to get him myself because he was straight, but what it meant was I could no longer use him as a human shield against Arli's matchmaking.

Plus there was the fact I'd worked out Rocky's little game. I wouldn't have been much of a friend if I hadn't explained it to Arli. "Don't you see?" I asked. "That's exactly the reason he cultivated this pseudo-friendship with me."

"Are you serious?" she scoffed. "You think too much."

"Think about it. You're way out of his league," I flattered, although it was basically true. "You're smart, intelligent, great looking—"

"Small tits," she interrupted.

"Don't you see his attraction is to much more than the superficial? He's too shy to approach you directly, so he's doing it through me. He probably knows what you think of jocks, after all you don't keep your opinions to yourself, and he's scared of rejection."

I could see she liked the idea.

"So what can I do to encourage him?"

In the end what she had to do was ask him out on a date herself. Rocky's attraction to Arli was stalemated. His conversations with us remained much the same as they had before. Much to my horror, she needed my moral support which was so unlike Arli I wondered how much she was covering up about her true feelings. She steered us all over campus so we could 'accidentally' run into Rocky and she could ask him out because Cindy-Lou Harrower had gone to Europe with her family and would be away for about four weeks.

"He'll have blue balls by the time she comes back if I don't help him out," she announced. "And I'm a much safer bet, not like those other cheerleaders who'd report straight back to Cindy-Lou the moment she returns if he tried something with them."

I couldn't argue with her thinking but it was another tedious hour of helping her plan her seduction before we ran across the man in question coming out of a fast food outlet, burping up the excess fat and sugar as he tossed the paper wrapping in the bin. For once in his life, he was alone.

"Hey guys," he called when he saw us.

We pretended surprise to run into him.

A painful nudge from Arli was the signal. "You must be at a loose end while Cindy-Lou's away," I said.

"What? Oh, yeah, it's the pits." He sounded totally unconvincing, the idea suddenly occurred to me that perhaps his girlfriend had been whisked away because she was 'in trouble,' to use the old euphemism.

"I know," Arli said brightly as if the idea had just occurred to her instead of having been rehearsed until I wanted to strangle her. "There's a great party on tonight, why don't you come?"

Good touch. A generic invitation. No pressure.

Rocky's face did brighten at the thought. "Cool. Who's going?"

"There won't be anyone from your circle of friends if that's what you're worried about," Arli added.

"Cool," Rocky said again. "Sounds just like what I need. It's always good to meet different people. Broaden your horizons."

His emphasis on 'different' and 'broaden your horizons' didn't escape my notice although it sailed right over Arli's head. She was giving details of where he could pick her up at what time when, casually, he turned to me, "You're gonna be there, dude?"

Arli spoke for me. "Nah, Brett has to spend a night at the library. Essay he forgot about. Due in on Monday." She went on in a similar vein for so long it was beginning to sound forced.

Rocky got totally the wrong idea. "Hey, man, I'm not trying to steal your girlfriend. I thought we could like go on a double date."

Sometimes Arli could be so insensitive I wanted to strangle her. "What? You think Brett's my boyfriend? Get real."

"Everyone thinks you two are…" He was polite enough not to continue the thought.

"Are you crazy? Why would anyone think I was dating a gay guy?"

Way to go, outed by your best friend in front of a man you had fantasies over.

"Dude," Rocky gasped. "You're gay?"

Arli smiled slyly. Had she given away my secret so that Rocky would turn against me and I'd be no competition, or had she revealed my secret as a friend to see if it sparked any interest in him.

"Dude, I'm so sorry. I didn't know." What was he sorry about? The fact I was gay? "I mean, you're so masculine. Who would have thought?"

Could he dig the hole any deeper?

"Enjoy the party," I said, my voice wobbling a little as I attempted to wrest back control of my emotions.

I heard Rocky as I walked away. "Shit! I handled that really bad, didn't I?"

You bet, mate.

I had a stern talk to myself as I wandered miserably around the campus. I had no right to be upset. Rocky was an acquaintance, a very cute acquaintance admittedly, but he had never given me any reason to believe he was interested in me romantically or sexually.

That was totally a figment of my imagination. I had been so carried away, I'd begun to believe my own fantasy. Lethal, *dude*. I just needed time alone to wallow in self-pity and lick my wounds.

I tried staying in, watching telly, but the programs were so abysmal they forced me out into the streets where my feet automatically took me to the one place I felt safe: Saturday night and there I was ensconced in the library with all the other losers who didn't have a date or anywhere else better to be. That was the downside. The upside was that I was getting a lot of future essay work done so I could take it easy over the next few weeks, maybe even actually do something about my personal life to get the bitter taste of rejection out of my mouth.

Good one, Brett. Rejection? You were setting yourself up for rejection from the start. You knew Rocky was straight.

I giggled a little too loudly at the absurdity of my self-pity, trying to swallow it when a number of people glanced my way, which turned it into a hiccup. I was attempting to hold my breath to ward off another explosive spasm of my diaphragm when I felt a chair pulled out from the opposite side of the table at which I was studying. Opening my eyes, I hiccupped even louder than ever, much of it in surprise, for seated opposite me was the hottest man I'd ever seen. Dressed for partying, out of his usual jock gear, Rocky was even more handsome, more desirable.

"Awesome hiccup, dude," he smiled.

Now that he was no longer my boyfriend, even in fantasy, his constant use of the word 'dude' threatened to become intensely irritating. The clock said 10pm.

"Did Arli stand you up?" I can be hopeful, can't I?

"Nah, not my sort of party."

"It didn't take you long to find out, it's only been going an hour or so."

"Look, dude, don't be angry if I tell you something."

He paused long enough to indicate he required an answer. "Okay," I said.

"That Arli. Dude, way too intense for me. She was all over me from the moment she got in the car. Trying to get my tackle outa my jeans while I was driving. Sulked when I told her to slow down. I don't need that sorta shit in my life. At the party she either had her hands all over me, down my jeans, trying to kiss me, showing disrespect, dude, or else she ignored me trying to make me jealous by doing the same thing to other guys at the party. It might work on dudes who are that desperate but, you know, I can get it any time I want."

My feeble response was, "Sorry, it didn't work out."

He laughed. "I'm not. Come on, dude. Let's get out of here. It's Saturday night, no time to be stuck in the library."

I was pretty amazed by the invitation, but even more so by his correct pronunciation of the word 'library.' God, I'm such a snob.

Rocky grabbed my notes and was half-way across the floor before I scrambled to grab the remainder of my belongings and ran to catch up. He was already seated impatiently in his car by the time I'd unplugged my laptop from the power, returned the books I'd been using to the counter, and generally got myself in the right frame of mind to join him. That frame would be studied indifference. Alas, it didn't last long.

"Get in," he instructed as I approached. He leaned over and opened the passenger door for me. I guess he'd at least got out of the car for Arli, but then, this wasn't a date.

I hopped in but Rocky didn't start the car, he seemed to be wrestling with something in his mind. I didn't interrupt, and eventually we drove off, although I suddenly realized I didn't know if Rocky was a homophobe and had designs on slicing off my tackle and shoving it down my throat so I'd suffocate or bleed to death. Nah, too many witnesses saw him in the library. Are killers that smart?

Silence seemed the best recourse and, to be honest, I loved sitting beside Rocky, watching the fierce concentration in the set of his jaw. My mind was already working overtime, weaving its fantasy. We drove east toward the coast and a silent half hour later, we arrived at the empty car park overlooking the path that led down to the secluded beach surrounded by scrub and trees that thrived in the sandy conditions.

Rocky got out of the car without saying a word, so I did the same. He was leaning against the front of the car looking out to sea, the lights from cargo ships that were coming into the port about one hundred kilometers to the south, twinkling on the horizon. I faced away from him because whatever it was he had to say, it was important.

We stood silently for a minute or so before he said, "You really gay, dude?"

I could see no point in denying it. "Yeah."

"You mind Arli saying that about you in front of me?"

I could see it was going to be one of those long drawn-out discussions about being gay. I sat up on one of the picnic tables that dotted the sandy area on the edge of the car park.

"Yes and no. Yes, because she didn't ask my permission to tell you, and also because I didn't know her motive. No, because I'm not ashamed of who I am. It's not like it's a secret."

"Arli said you fancy me."

"She's got a big mouth."

"So, do you?"

"You're handsome as fuck, dude."

"I'm a jock, for fuck's sake. Of course I'm hot." He sounded irritated rather than boastful.

"You ever come here before?" he asked

"This beach?"

"Yeah."

"No."

"You should."

"Why's that?"

"You'll meet a lot of guys like you here. Especially in the bushes."

"Oh."

It hadn't penetrated my brain until now, but this was the notorious Queen's Inlet, the nude beach which was a cruising ground for horny gay guys. Women were welcome to exhibit their attributes but were warned not to wander off into the undergrowth where all sorts of male-on-male coupling took place. The authorities attempted to close the area down on a regular basis but it was too popular with all sorts of men, including those from the college who came to have their dicks sucked if they were horny enough. That begged the question.

"You come here a lot?" I asked

"I like to get an all-over tan."

"I'll bet that's a sight to see."

"You had much experience?"

"Sex, you mean?" He nodded his head. "Nah. Arli keeps trying to match me up with her friends. Never works out."

"Why?"

"They weren't my type."

"Am I?"

I sighed. He just kept staring out to sea like the answer to everything was out there between the breakers.

"We need to get you some more experience, dude," he said. "Come on, let's get back. I got practice in the morning."

He hopped in the car and was keying the ignition while I was still clambering into my seat wondering what that had all been about. I could have understood it if he'd let me suck his dick or if he'd bashed me. But, nothing?

"You doing anything tomorrow afternoon?"

"Nah."

"I'll pick you up at one, drive us out here, get you laid."

Everyone seemed to want to get me laid, though there'd be very little chance of that at the beach with Rocky beside me. What the hell? It was time to live dangerously.

"Okay about the pick-up," I said suggestively, paused a while, then added, "We'll see about the getting laid part."

I had a smile on my face for the rest of the journey. The night hadn't turned out at all like I expected, it had turned out much better.

The trip back seemed to take half the time, probably because I didn't want it to end. I really liked the easy camaraderie between me and Rocky, and if I couldn't have him as a boyfriend, then I think I'd like the guy as a mate.

He dropped me off outside the frat house where I had a room to myself. It crossed my mind for a split second to invite him up, but I thought better of it. Rocky said quietly, "Dude, sorry I didn't handle it real well when I found out you were gay. I think it's awesome."

Before the shock wore off, he leaned over and kissed me square on the lips, and not just a coy lip-to-lip smacker, he went for the tongue. My brain was doing a little dance that the college jock had his tongue wedged in my mouth and had his arms around me. I shifted to give him better access but it broke the mood and he pulled away in embarrassment or disgust or something. He must have felt how hard I was for him, or else I'd mistaken his intention when I opened my mouth.

I mumbled good-night and ran off as fast as I could to escape. I was such a klutz. Now I'd gone and ruined everything.

Safe in my bed, I jerked off replaying that kiss over and over, each time moving Rocky's hand closer to my throbbing hard-on. It made for a very satisfied night's sleep, rudely interrupted the following morning by Arli, eager to spill the beans.

"Good date, was it?" I asked.

"Absolute disaster. I as good as begged him to fuck me but he wasn't interested," she wailed.

"Maybe he doesn't like women who come on too strong."

"That's why he surrounds himself with all those insults to feminism he's always seen with."

"Maybe."

"Anyway, all he wanted to do was talk about you."

"Me?"

"Yeah, whether you had a boyfriend, how much experience you had, when you realized you were gay, all that blah blah shit. Got boring real quick but he wouldn't quit with the questions. Got so I wish I hadn't told him. It must have really done his head in. Must be a real innocent."

"What did you do?"

"Left him to his own questions and went looking for someone else to satisfy me. When I returned for him a little while later, he was gone."

"Sorry it didn't work out." That was the biggest lie ever.

"Worked out in the end, I met Errol…"

She spent the next fifteen minutes boasting about her new conquest who, I knew from experience, would last about three weeks before she got bored with him. I ran my fingers across my lips, remembering Rocky's kiss, only half listening to Arli. It didn't matter, she never asked questions about what she'd said.

I wondered what to do for the remainder of the day because Arli and Errol had a few more positions they wanted to try out, and I really didn't expect Rocky to turn up after my faux pas last night. I had two slices of leftover pizza in my small fridge and decided that was all I needed as a nutritious breakfast. That, and two strong coffees.

Powering up the laptop, I decided it was time for me to get out and live. People I knew could see it, so why couldn't I? I wasn't exactly a virgin, but I certainly wasn't all that experienced and, yeah, it would be nice to have a lover, but until that came along, it was no use sealing myself in my room. Lovers didn't come battering down the door, you had to get out and mix. Now, that, I hated. Especially as I was born without gaydar and couldn't tell a gay man from a straight man, even up close and sucking my dick. No one had bothered to furnish me with an instruction manual so I could plug in the gaydar, or fine tune it or whatever the bloody hell you needed to do to get it to work, I was a dud at recognizing my own tribe. That's why God invented the internet. And gay personals.

I'd been chatting for hours with hot guys who seemed superficially interesting but, when pressed, weren't into meeting face-to-face, probably because their profile picture was ten years out-of-date, or they got their jollies jerking off to dirty screen talk, or…who knew what went on in their minds? All I knew was I was horny and Ma Palmer and her five kids weren't about to satisfy me. That's when my cell phone rang.

I didn't recognize the number,

"Hi, I'll be there in about ten minutes. Meet you downstairs."

"Um, okay."

I think he'd hung up before I could even reply. Shit, Rocky had turned up. I grabbed my bathers, although they weren't strictly necessary, a towel, and dressed quickly in a T-shirt and shorts. I was waiting curbside when he pulled in.

Tongue-tied because of last night, all I could think to say was, "How was training?"

His response was cold and impersonal. "The usual."

He was probably waiting for me to apologize. I'd have to otherwise the afternoon would be crap.

"Look, about last night, when you dropped me off…"

That's as far as I got. He interrupted. "Don't sweat it, I understand."

What did he understand? His response was so enigmatic but I didn't want to push too hard. I let it lie.

"Looks like a good afternoon for the beach," he said.

I agreed.

The conversation went back and forth in this dispirited manner until he reached over and squeezed my thigh. "Really, I do understand. And it's okay."

I relaxed although I was still none the wiser as to what was okay. The fact I fancied the ass off him? That I'd French kissed him? That I had an ache in my groin from just sitting next to him? That I wanted to get down on my knees and worship him? Maybe that last one was over the top.

"Thanks," I said as warmly as I could manage.

"I'm disappointed, dude, but I'll get over it. Today is for you. I want to see a smile on that beautiful kisser of yours by the time we go home this afternoon. Deal?"

"Deal."

And for most of the afternoon, there was a smile on my face as wide as the ocean. Rocky was such fun to be with although I sensed an underlying feeling of melancholy. If he was disappointed in me for what happened last night he was obviously willing to overlook the offense. We managed to get a good parking spot and he unloaded an Esky from the boot.

"Gotta have our sustenance, mate. Man cannot live by surf, sand and sex alone. He's gotta have beer."

"God, Rocky, you are so straight," I joked.

"What, gay guys can't drink beer? Why wasn't I informed?"

We joked all the way down the steps to the beach, which had a fair number of sunbathers already there and a number of towels laid out whose owners, I surmised, were off in the bushes. I shuddered at the thought of doing that myself later. I wasn't sure I had the personality for al fresco lovemaking. There was still plenty of room for us, though, and we made ourselves comfortable, Rocky handing me a cold one. Beer wasn't my favorite beverage but this was one of the new boutique ales that had hit the market and it tasted like the beer you have when you're not having a beer. I could get to like it. Maybe it was the company that was mellowing my taste.

Then the big moment arrived: the unveiling. Rocky had already explained the protocol. Newcomers were allowed to wear swimmers on their first visit, but anything after that required total nudity or the denizens were liable to think you were a voyeur. He skinned off his shorts and tank top to reveal the most perfect body I had ever seen. He had his back to me and I just wanted to reach up and stroke his ass. When he turned I tried to look away but my eyes were transfixed on his pendulous semi-engorged cock. It should be illegal to be this perfect. I'm afraid I licked my lips.

Rocky laughed. "See something you like?"

Like? No way. At that moment I fell ever deeper in love. I'm so shallow.

"Your turn," Rocky said, slapping my ass.

"I don't think I can," I admitted.

"A hot body like yours needs to be seen. It'll draw men to you like bees to honey, dude."

There was only one bee I wanted to attract and he was right next to me. I wouldn't spoil his afternoon by saying it out loud.

I stripped quickly and was naked in no time flat, lying face down on my towel before my cock could give me away. I can't have been quick enough for Rocky whistled like he would a hot chick and I felt my cheeks flame.

"That's some seriously big tackle you've got there, Brett. The natives will be mighty impressed. And your body. Wow. I knew you'd be buff, mate, but you are serious competition."

I know he was trying to boost my ego but he was not helping me to get my cock back to a more manageable size as we were in company.

"No one cares if you get a hard-on around here, especially late in the afternoon when serious action starts. Then it's almost obligatory," he explained, but I was still embarrassed to show it in public.

"I should be careful," I said. "I burn easily. I didn't bring any sunscreen."

"Fear not," Rocky said. "I have everything you'll need in my Magic Esky." So saying he produced a bottle of SPF30+. "I know this will sound like old porn movie dialogue, but you want me to do your back?"

"Would you mind? Obviously I can't do it myself."

"I'll have to do your…uh…butt as well. That okay?"

"Of course." I didn't dare add that I wanted him to do my butt in a very different way to what he imagined.

He straddled my legs and poured the cold oil on my back, making me jump. "You fucker, you did that on purpose."

"Who? Me?" he said innocently.

Before I could complain further he was massaging it into my shoulders and my neck shuffling his body up until I could feel his cock poking at my butt cheeks. I know it had nothing to do with me and was all about nudity and exhibitionism but that didn't help me get my libido under control. I just wanted to thrust my ass up, capture his cock in my warm hole and have him fuck me into the sand. Just thinking about it raised my temperature.

He did my arms, my neck, my upper back, my lower back…then he turned his attention to my legs. We'd both stopped kidding around by this stage and my breath was coming in gasps. I could have sworn that Rocky was panting a little. It must be the heat.

He admired my hairless legs then it was time for my ass.

"Gonna do your cheeks now," he warned, slapping them playfully.

His touch was electric as he squeezed my ass muscles, massaging the oil in until my butt must have glistened. His fingers sometimes went deep into my crack and once or twice his thumb grazed my tight puckered hole. Each time I gasped and Rocky was so apologetic I felt chastened. I loved it, I just wished he'd ram his cock in and be done with it. All too soon it was over and Rocky lay on his stomach expecting me to reciprocate.

I didn't dare straddle his naked body like he had mine so I rubbed in the sunscreen while kneeling beside him. He seemed a bit pissed off at my reticence, complaining that I wasn't doing it properly until I gave in and sat astride his butt. I could have sworn he was pushing up to meet me every time I leaned forward to cream his back and arms.

"Fuck, that feels so good, dude. You have magic fingers. You could have your way with me if you keep that up."

"You shouldn't say things like that, Rocky," I said. "Someone might take it the wrong way."

"Sorry, dude."

I changed the subject quickly. "Where did you get my mobile number, Rocky? When you rang this morning."

"Easy. I rang Arli. She gave it to me."

"Oh."

"Don't forget my ass. It doesn't see the sun very often so it needs special attention cause it burns easily."

I dribbled oil on his cheeks and began to rub it in, squeezing the same way he did me.

"Oh, dude, you could make a living doing this. Sweet."

I couldn't help myself and I allowed a dribble of oil to work its way into his crevice. He shuddered.

"Sorry," I said, not meaning a word of it. "Let me wipe that away."

I parted his cheeks and saw his cute little ass entrance surrounded by about a dozen dark hairs. It took every piece of willpower in my possession to stop myself from reaching over to kiss it. I accidentally on purpose dribbled more oil so it oozed down into his crack and then ran my hand along the canyon and across the hole. He shuddered uncontrollably, moaning as I massaged in the excess sunscreen. I felt his body convulse and I would have sworn he was blowing his load. What had I done? He'd never forgive me.

I lay down on my towel, the two of us passing the time by discussing our past and our futures, like people do on a first date, though ours wasn't a date. It was just dudes getting to know each other better. We both spoke in generalities until Rocky dared ask the first personal question. "What are you looking for? A boyfriend? Casual sex? What?"

"I'd love a boyfriend," I admitted. "Someone to share my life with. You know, moments like these. It's hard on your own. Things are easier now than they were but it can still be difficult. I imagine it is for you, too."

I didn't want it to seem like I thought straight boys had it too easy.

"What's your type?" he said. "Maybe I can keep an eye out for him."

I wanted to scream, *You, you're exactly my type.* Instead, I said, "I'm still looking. I don't know if I have a type yet. What about you?"

"I have a very definite type," he said.

Don't I know it. Big-titted, blonde cheerleaders.

No way would I ever fit that job description. I didn't think even implants and a bleach job would help.

"You ever been in love?" he asked.

This was getting a bit personal.

"Yeah, but I kept it secret."

"That's sad. Why did you keep it secret?"

"He was straight and I didn't want to spoil the friendship."

"Yeah, that works."

"You?"

"Yeah. Hit me hard. Didn't work out though."

"Sorry."

That feeling of melancholy that I'd noticed earlier settled over him once again.

Rocky stood and pulled on his shorts, shoving the sunscreen in his back pocket.

"You feel like an ice cream? That should cheer us both up."

So he felt it, too.

"Where are you going to get ice cream around here?"

"There's always a couple of vans selling sodas and ice cream in the car park."

"I'll come with you," I said.

"Nah, dude. You stay here and see if there are any men that…you know."

The only reason I said what I did was he sounded so damn sad. "Hey, man, we'll still be friends."

"Yeah," he said.

This afternoon was turning into a real downer. I got out my cell phone to listen to music I'd downloaded; that would cheer me up. While I was humming along to my favorite tracks I surveyed the beach for likely prospects. There was no denying there were some ideal candidates but I couldn't help but compare them with Rocky, finding them wanting. The afternoon was fast disappearing and I noticed from the time on my mobile Rocky had been gone for forty minutes. I knew it was a hike to the top of the cliff and the car park but he should have been back by now. Perhaps I should go and look for him. He had my number if something had gone wrong.

Just then my mobile rang. It was Arli.

"You and the boyfriend at the beach?" she chortled down the phone.

I ignored the provocation.

"He's gone to get ice cream."

"That means you're as good as engaged."

"You didn't tell me he rang to get my phone number."

"I thought you would have guessed it was me gave it to him. How many people you give your number to?"

She had a point.

"So, tell me about it. You having the best time ever?"

"I was, but Rocky seems a bit down in the dumps. I guess he's missing Cindy-Lou."

"Hasn't he told you yet?" she shrieked down the phone.

"Told me what?"

"He and Cindy-Lou were never an item. He was her beard. She was in love with this musician that her parents didn't approve of, so she asked Rocky to pretend they were seeing each other to throw mum and dad off the scent. They did approve of a good-looking jock who was almost guaranteed a sports scholarship. So on the nights they were supposed to be out fucking, she was actually with her musician. She's not in Europe, she ran off with her boyfriend. That's so cool."

"So, that's not why he's down?"

"You didn't go and reject him, did you? Don't take any of that Neanderthal shit I used to go on about to heart. It was a joke."

"What do you mean, reject him?"

"Oh my God, you really are that dumb. Brett, Rocky has the biggest crush on you I've ever seen."

"Rocky is gay?"

"You didn't know?"

"Not a clue. And he likes *me*?"

"I think the feeling is a lot stronger than like…"

"Gotta go."

I disconnected, trying to trawl back through my brain for my entire conversation with Rocky. Fuck, the clues were all there, I just didn't see them. He must think I'm an asshole. God, I even made him come. Surely he didn't drive off and leave me here. No, his Esky was still beside me. Think, Brett, think. He put the sunscreen in his pocket. Holy shit! I knew where he was. I ran up the beach toward the scrub and tea trees hoping this was the right spot. That was confirmed almost immediately by the number of men I saw coming and going through a break in the thicket.

I plunged into a world almost as foreign as Alice's Wonderland. Everything was like that segment in a movie nightmare with close-ups of faces laughing maniacally although in this case it was men groaning, men thrusting, men jerking. I pushed my way through the undergrowth, scratching myself on twigs, as I searched for Rocky. I was frantic. This obviously wasn't his first time in the thick of it but if I had my way it would be his last. I had no problem with men openly coupling, openly watching, or any of the other various combinations they engaged in, perhaps one day I would too, but for now I wanted to find my man. I was the reason he was melancholy. He must think I didn't want him.

Calling his name probably would have got me better results but, looking at the activity around me, I thought it was something to save till the last.

Men reached out to grope me as I passed by, issuing invitations to join them for all sorts of lascivious pleasures. I might have been tempted had it not been for my single-minded pursuit of…Rocky! There he was, down on his knees in the midst of a group of men, an elderly gent plugging his mouth while a younger, around his own age, plowed his ass giving a running commentary to those watching.

"Rocky," I cried out.

He took his mouth off the old cock, turning toward the sound of my voice. He looked beaten, humiliated.

"Shit, it's the boyfriend," I heard someone whisper and the crowd began to disperse quickly. The older gent tugged on his cock a few times and his slime squirted across Rocky's face while the young man increased his pace until he slammed into Rocky's ass and remained stock still grunting as he shot his spunk up his ass.

"Piss off, fucker," I said to the young man who pulled his still squirting dick from my boyfriend's ass.

Rocky couldn't look at me, collapsing on the sand in misery.

I slithered down beside him, putting my arm under his body, turning him over. He shielded his eyes with his arm, afraid to look at me. I put my lips to his and forced my way inside.

"Don't," he said, attempting to push me away.

"I don't care," I said, and tried again. This time he grabbed me, latching onto my mouth so my tongue tasted the sperm that various strangers had deposited there while he'd kneeled in the sand. I caressed his hair as our lips remained locked until he believed me. Eventually we were forced to break apart just to breath.

"I couldn't bear you didn't want me," he said. "That's why I came up here."

"But I do want you. It's all been a misunderstanding."

"Then why did you push me away last night when I was kissing you?"

"Push you away?" I thought about it, and laughed. "I was shifting in the seat to get more comfortable, I wasn't pushing you away."

"Really?"

"Of course. I thought I'd pissed you off by coming on too strong. I thought you were straight."

"I'm so confused, I don't know what I am any more. Except for one thing. I fuckin' love you, dude."

"The feeling's quite mutual, dude. Now, on your back."

"Yes, sir," he complied.

I pushed my fingers into his ass to make sure he was sufficiently lubricated. I don't know how many there'd been before me but it must have been quite a few because his ass was as leaky as an old boat.

"Sorry," he said. "You wanna wait till later?"

"No way," I panted. "It just shows what good taste other guys have that they want to fuck my boyfriend."

"Boyfriend?"

"That's if you'll have me."

"Fuck me hard, Brett."

I pushed into him and even though I had only ever done this two or three times before with other men, this time it felt so right. Rocky clamped his ass muscles around my cock as I slowly rocked in and out of his sloppy hole, lubricated with sunscreen and other men's cum. When I'd marked him with my possessive spunk, I expected he'd only put out for me. In return he could brand my near virginal ass. We'd begin as I meant us to go on.

OMG! PUT SOME CLOTHES ON!

Naked ain't always pretty.

It was the biggest, longest, thickest cock I'd ever seen. And the ugliest. It appeared gnarled and angry, purple with frustration, as if it hated the world and everyone in it. It was brutal and unforgiving. It also belonged to my boyfriend's dad.

"For God's sake, dad, put some clothes on!" Ryan sighed as he saw what had stopped me in my tracks. "You're not at home now. You could scare the neighbors."

"Looks like I scared that little fag boyfriend of yours," Zef muttered as he pulled the towel back around his waist. "I thought the slut would have seen plenty of cock in his time."

"Da-ad!" Ryan warned.

Ever since he'd arrived, Zef had been baiting me in front of his son and, even worse, behind his back. I'd complained about his obnoxious taunts but the sternest reprimand Ryan ever managed was to split the word 'dad' into two syllables. My boyfriend was so piss weak sometimes.

Up until now it had been verbal abuse, displaying his cock was something new. Okay, it appeared like an accident, his towel falling off as he walked back to the guest bedroom while I was coming along the hall, but I suspected it was an effort to belittle me with the size and girth of his schlong. If Ryan hadn't come along right behind me, who knows where it might have led.

I don't mean physically. Zef repulsed me. In his fifties, he looked more like a battered suitcase than a middle-aged man. His body was wiry and muscular, from his job as a landscape gardener, his hair peppered with some gray around the temples, but it was his face that seemed lived in. The wrinkles were more than skin deep, they seemed to be scored right into his soul and, with his piercing brown eyes, I always felt when he looked at me he was looking into depths of my soul that I didn't know existed. His constant sneer coupled with the unshaven stubble on his cheeks and chin gave him an otherworldly appearance. I hesitate to say he always appeared the personification of 'evil' because I don't believe in the concept, but he definitely had a nasty quality to him.

That he was also an arch homophobe who constantly belittled me and his son's relationship meant his stay was a visit from a hell. Fuck, why not say it? Zef was the personification of a suburban Satan.

So I wasn't surprised when his prick looked like something from the paintings of Hieronymus Bosch.

I'm studying art history at university, a useless subject according to Zef, who is far from pleased his son is supporting me while I study. He thinks I'm a gold digger because Ryan has a small business that allows us to live comfortably although, with the downturn in the economy forcing him to let half his staff go, he has had to put more hours in. That, in turn, means more time alone with his dad. I was on summer vacation and even though I could spend time at the uni library or visiting friends, I wasn't going to allow Zef to force me from my own home.

Extra worry was the last thing Ryan needed as he worked hard to pull the company out of the doldrums, so I kept the more outrageous examples of Zef's barrage of abuse from him. I'd handle it myself although the slurs had become so monotonous and so irritating on a couple of occasions that I'd bunched my fists up in preparation for a physical solution to the problem. That had merely encouraged Zef to smirk. "Bring it on, fag boy. Think you stand a chance against a real man?"

"When I see any real men around here, I'll let you know." My response was hardly the stuff of Oscar Wilde but it put him in his place. For a moment.

Then he laughed. "I hope you don't mean that ball-less wonder that's my son. The fag lover who won't even stand up for his boyfriend."

That one hurt. Ryan was just sweeping it all under the carpet hoping it would go away. Well, it wouldn't. Zef, however, would eventually depart. He was staying with us until his wife forgave one of his periodic transgressions. She'd caught him with his conscienceless dick up a neighbor and had thrown him out on his ass. Landscape gardeners were in even less demand than the goods Ryan's company produced, so with no money and no job, Zef ended up in our spare room with an open-ended invitation to stay.

Ryan took me aside after the unveiling of the ugly family jewels, pleading, "Try and get along with dad please, Grant. I just don't have the time or the energy to deal with all that shit right now. Okay? He's just angry over being out of work and how things are with mum."

I agreed, promising to try harder while knowing that Zef's antagonism was much more deeply ingrained. All I had to do was hold on until uni returned after the break and I wouldn't be forced to live with his macho superiority day in and day out.

After I waved Ryan off to work from the front door, our daily ritual, I went to the kitchen for a coffee.

"For God's sake, Zef," I complained when I saw him seated at the glass-topped breakfast table still dressed in the towel that was now flopped open to reveal his cock in all its hideous glory. He scratched his balls as he drank his coffee and read the morning paper. "Put some clothes on."

"Why, fag boy. Does the sight of my big juicy cock turn you on?" he sneered.

"Hardly. I've had much bigger than that for breakfast."

"Not from my fag son if what I've seen is anything to go by."

He was right. Ryan's cock was considerably smaller than his dad's but was still ample for me. And it was not ugly like his dad's. "How would you know?"

"I've watched you two fuck. I've seen you blow him."

I was horrified. "When?"

"You don't think I hear the noises you make when he fucks you like a pig slut? You're both too engrossed in your little fag games to hear me watching through the crack in your bedroom door."

My stomach did a violent turn. I would have thrown up my breakfast if I'd had any.

"Get your rocks off, did you?" I replied as I helped myself to coffee.

"No more than you do."

"What's that mean?"

"It means I know you have to get yourself off with your toys after my fag son's fucked you. Not satisfying, is he? Small dick. Told you, you need a real man's cock."

I walked right into it. "Like yours, you mean?"

Smug bastard actually smiled.

"So that's why you showed me your ugly dick this morning?"

"I knew it would turn you on. You fags are all the same. Hungry for cock. Bet you're out getting that hot ass of yours boned every opportunity."

Did he just say 'hot ass'?

"I know why you're angry, fag boy. I'm cramping your style. You can't have your fuck buddies over to fill your slut hole in case I tell Ryan all about you. Well guess what? I don't give a shit what you get up to, how many toys or cocks you ram up that ass of yours, but you'll never get your hands on mine. I know you want it. You haven't been able to take your eyes off it since you've come into the kitchen. So much for loving my son. I bet you'd be down on your knees with your mouth around it if I let you. No way, fag!"

With that he pulled the towel across his lap hiding his tackle from view.

He was right; I had been staring at his cock. Yeah, it was ugly as sin, if I believed in sin, and nasty as hell but it was thick and long with a yummy mushroom head.

I slapped myself mentally. Whoa, boy. This is your boyfriend's dad you're thinking about. Plus he's a frothing-at-the-mouth homophobe. Don't even think about it.

I hadn't been consciously aware of any of it. It was my natural propensity to fantasize when confronted with a cock. My common sense kicked in and I was revolted by where my libido was leading me. I really did have dick for brains.

I found the whole episode disturbing, so I went into town to take in a movie but I couldn't concentrate. I was anxious, pent up and for a few seconds considered going to the adult bookshop to get relief through one of the glory holes in the porno booths. Nah, Ryan and I had been faithful during our two years. I didn't want to jeopardize that relationship, but I also didn't want to go home and beat off to internet porn as gratifying as that sounded.

Fuck! My life is a mess.

If I couldn't have promiscuous sex then at least I could have a drink to calm my agitation. There was a gay bar nearby and I ducked in for a beer but the atmosphere inside was so cool and calming, I stayed for a second and then a third. The bar was fairly dark and I sat alone in a corner luxuriating in the fact I wasn't being hassled by my homo-hating father-in-law. I could have remained here until Ryan got home later tonight but I knew I had to face up to whatever demons were awaiting me at home. One demon, at least.

I chugged down the last of my warming beer and was getting my act together to leave when a new brew was slammed down on the small wooden table at which I sat. The bartender looked me over then dismissed me with a curt, "We don't appreciate hustlers in this establishment." He nodded toward the gentleman seated at the bar who had obviously paid for my drink. Raising the bottle in salute to my benefactor, secretly delighted the barman had mistaken me for anyone who could possibly attract a paying clientele, I knew Ryan would get quite a chuckle out of the misunderstanding. Until I realized Mr. Generous was making his way to my table.

I may have thought he was a gentleman from a distance but as he plonked his portly body on the chair opposite, I saw that he was very much a blue collar worker. I'm no snob but this guy was all love handles, stubble and beer breath. If he lost one hundred and fifty pounds and got himself some decent clothes he'd pass as pretty respectable rough trade. As it was the word he conjured up was 'slob.'

"What's a good-looking boy doing in a place like this in the middle of the day?"

Oh, brother.

"Just having a quiet beer before I head off home."

"Ned." He offered his hand.

His grip was cold, clammy and limp. "Grant."

"What do you do, Grant?"

I kept my answers brief. "I'm a student."

"You must be in need of money," he said, leering at me.

"Not really, I have a wealthy boyfriend." I hated myself for saying it and it sounded much worse than I imagined.

"A sugar daddy, eh? He knows you're out talking to strange men in bars?"

"As a matter of fact, he does," I lied.

"Doesn't mind you making a little extra on the side?"

He grinned like he was onto a good thing. I almost looked forward to disappointing him.

"I think you have the wrong…"

"Oh, I don't think so," he said, startling me when I felt his hand creep up my thigh to cover my crotch.

I was so surprised I stood up, knocking my beer over so that it spilled across the table and onto the floor. He looked around the few other patrons in the bar at this time of the day as if he might be identified. He opened his wallet and pressed a card into my pocket. "There, that's my number. When you change your mind, ring me. I've got a dick that'll make you cross-eyed," he boasted as he fled the bar. I wondered if he was someone famous or important. I examined his card but his name was not familiar.

I headed for the exit as the barman came over with a cloth to mop up the spill. As I passed him, he muttered, "You guys are always trouble."

On the scale of abuse I'd received recently that was so mild as to not even register.

I cursed myself for not using the back entrance in case Ned was waiting for me outside but once my eyes got accustomed to the glare, he was nowhere to be seen.

On the bus on the way back home I wondered what I had done to deserve my life the way it was going. I was incredibly frustrated. It was unbearable at home with

Ryan's dad and his snide comments all the time, his presence also inhibiting my personal life as Ryan didn't want to rub 'our lifestyle' in his old man's face.

"For Christ's sake, Ryan," I screamed at him one night after he'd turned me down yet again over sex. "You'll never please the old buzzard, I don't know why you even try. If he was my dad, I would never let him disrespect you the way your dad does me. He'd be tossed out on his ass quick smart."

"Ah, you don't understand what it's like to be brought up in a family that's half-Italian. We have more family loyalty."

I seethed over his continual excuses for his dad's vile behavior.

"Being half-Italian doesn't excuse rotten conduct in anyone's culture."

Zef must have overheard our argument because he had a triumphant smirk on his face for the rest of the day. Bastard!

Sex had been an occasional rushed option for three weeks now, squeezed in when we thought Zef was out. It seems we were wrong. I was going crazy. To my mind it's not unreasonable to expect that, in a relationship, sex should not be furtive and should occur on a regular basis. If Zef remained at our home for much longer, forcing Ryan into continued guilt-ridden hair-trigger coupling, I would have to seriously consider a blow-up doll or rampant infidelity. Or else I would crack.

My determination to have my wicked way with the reluctant Ryan was thwarted in the worst possible way when I got home. It wasn't just that Zef was slobbing all over the couch in the living room still clad only in a towel which did nothing to cover his cock and balls, or that the coffee table was littered with empty beer cans, it was mainly his message as I came through the front door.

"Hey, fag boy," he yelled so that it was impossible to sneak in and avoid him. "You missed Ryan by about twenty minutes. Said he couldn't wait any longer for you. Bit upset he was. Thought you should have been home instead of out whoring that pretty little ass of yours all over town."

There was no point in contradicting him so I let it slide.

"Is there a problem?" I asked, worried that Ryan may be sick or injured.

"Only that my son is a faggot and his boyfriend is a cock slut."

I sighed loudly enough that he even someone as thick as him would get the hint.

"Said he had to leave town for a week to ten days. Got a heads up on a great new product that will mean big bickies for the company and untold wealth for the two of you."

"Did he say where he was going?"

"Nope. Just that he'll ring you from his hotel when he gets there. He's given his employees the week off so whatever it is, it's gotta be big. Unless he's just out getting himself some fresh faggot ass."

I thought he would have got sick of all the fag references he was making constantly but I noticed the more he used the word the more blood seemed to pump into his hideous prick. It was like some somnambulistic creature slowly waking from its doze. It was at once horrifyingly repellent and hypnotically seductive.

"Like what you see, fag?"

"Put some clothes on," I snarled, tearing my eyes away from his engorging cock. If I thought it was large when I'd seen it semi-tumescent earlier that day, I was amazed at how much it grew when fully aroused as it was now. I couldn't imagine anyone taking it for pleasure.

"Makes your eyes water just thinking about it, doesn't it?" he suggested as he gave it a half-hearted tug, smearing the slippery pre-cum across the knob with his thumb.

"It might if I did give it a moment's thought," I replied.

He was so fucking superior I wanted to smack him. "Oh, you will. In fact, it'll haunt your every waking moment and then it will invade your dreams until you're begging me for a taste of it."

My laugh sounded false even to me.

Wondering if I could persuade Zef's wife to forgive him and take him back, out of my hair, I dreaded spending the next week or so alone with him. Ryan wasn't much of an intermediary but he was a hell of a lot better than none at all.

It wasn't fair. I was horny as fuck and I'd have to rely on my small collection of sex toys and my fantasies to get off. I was constantly on edge sexually, not helped by Zef's ugly genitals on open display. Not that I wanted them but when you're not getting any even the ugliest examples on view add an unwelcome temptation.

That, of course, is what Zef was after. How could I be so dumb as not to have seen that before? Zef wanted me to make a play for him so he could report my slutty behavior to Ryan and split us up. Whether he thought I was a passing phase and he could then turn his son straight I didn't know but it was the sort of devious plan he would come up with. Either that or provoke me to the extent I moved out or, even better, physically attacked him.

Paranoia was not a good look. I shook the conspiracy theories out of my head and, in an effort to mend fences, cleared the beer cans from the coffee table. He replaced them with his feet which meant the towel flapped open even wider.

Deep breaths. Don't look at his prick. Don't look at his prick. Oh, crap, I looked.

He didn't have to say anything, I heard him chuckle. That was enough.

"You want something for dinner?" I asked.

"You cooking?"

"Yes."

"Faggot food or real food? I can call for pizza if it's faggot food."

I gave him a rundown on what I intended. He appeared genuinely surprised.

"You can cook that?"

"Try me."

Try my cooking he did although he didn't exactly dress for dinner. He merely wrapped the towel around his waist a little more tightly before he sat down at the table. To my surprise, he managed a compliment.

"I gotta hand it to you fags. You know how to suck cock and you know how to cook."

Well, it was sort of an insult compliment but it was the last time he used the F word during the meal for which I was grateful. However, that could have been because he hardly managed to string a coherent sentence together while we were eating. I think, like me, he sensed the game plan had changed with Ryan's absence and he hadn't quite worked out a strategy. I was sure it wouldn't be long before he did.

It was difficult not to stare at the bulge in his towel and when he noticed he managed to open a flap so his cock dangled tantalizingly in view. I'd made the mistake of having the meal in the kitchen at the glass-topped table and as he was seated directly across from me I had limited choice as to where to look: my meal, his face, his cock. In my frustrated state it was obvious where my eyes would tend to focus.

I wondered why he hadn't passed on the thick cock gene to Ryan. I'm not a size queen and Ryan's cock is a comfortable assfull but a boy sometimes likes to have his horizons stretched and Zef's monster would certainly do that.

Shit! I need to have a good wank and get the idea of cock out of my head.

It was around eight o'clock when we finished the mainly silent meal and I was stacking the dishwasher when the phone rang. I raced to grab it, pleased to hear Ryan's voice on the other end. I walked upstairs with the hands free to take the call in the bedroom hoping he might like to indulge in a little phone sex which was a better prospect than doing it solo even if he were countless hundreds of miles away.

I lay on our bed, shucking my jeans and undies down to my knees to play with my dick while I listened to his explanations. Sometimes I wished he loved money a little less and me a little more but that was ungrateful as he was doing it to secure our future. Then his curiosity turned to why I wasn't home when he'd come back to pack a bag for his trip.

There was no use antagonizing him further about his dad so I lied and told him I'd gone to the library for research. I already had my courses lined up for the new semester and I wanted to get a head start, I told him.

"I dropped into that gay bar near the movie house, you know the one," I explained. "I had a few beers to help clear my head and guess what? This fat guy at the bar sends over a free beer, then comes over to my table and offers me money for sex. He thought I was on the game. So did the barman."

We both had a good laugh at the idea of me as a sex worker although I found it much less amusing than Ryan who used sex for relief while I used it for pleasure. He was strictly vanilla, whereas I was not averse to a walk on the wild side. I loved cock while he didn't like anything near his ass, not even my tongue. It made lovemaking with Ryan a very one-sided affair.

"Guess what I'm doing while I'm talking to you?" I purred down the phone.

He didn't have the imagination to guess or the wherewithal to understand why I would need to be doing what I was. The idea of stroking his cock while I talked dirty to him on the phone was a concept so alien I gave up trying, my cock withering under his lack of understanding. Yep, I did beg, telling him of my needs but it made no difference. He didn't comprehend sexual needs.

I could have jerked off just to the sound of his voice but he was sprouting such inanities it was counter-erotic.

He said he'd ring me when he could but he expected to be incredibly busy for the next week or so, asking me to be patient if I couldn't raise him on his mobile phone. I wasn't to worry as the deal was so hush hush that he couldn't afford any of his competitors to get wind of it. It was all gobbledygook to me as I don't have a mind for business so I didn't take it all in. I was bored now. If he wasn't going to help me out and he was going to be almost certainly uncontactable in the Twilight Zone for the best part of a week then I was on my own.

Zef would make a big deal out of it, suggesting all sorts of nightmare scenarios of infidelity, but I knew Ryan's appetites almost as well as my own and he was never hungry enough for sex to go to such a subterfuge. Besides, he'd done this sort of thing before.

"I'll miss you," I said.

"Me, too." He sounded sad.

"I love you, hurry back."

"Love you, Grant."

Sighing, I gave my limp dick a few dispirited tugs but it refused to get hard again so I tucked it away. A sound in the hallway outside the bedroom disturbed me and I wondered if Zef had been listening to the phone conversation. Fuck him! What did I care?

Pulling the bedclothes over me, I thought I'd try to nap. There was no way I wanted to spend the evening downstairs with Ryan's dad, the butt of his jibes. Besides, I was more exhausted than I thought. The stress of holding my natural sarcasm in check, plus the attempt to be friendly to Zef had taken it out of me and I fell into a deep sleep. I didn't dream of Zef's cock in particular but my head was full of suggestion so that when I awoke a few hours later, my cock was hard.

The house was still and I heard no sound from downstairs. I reckoned it was safe to get myself a juice to quench my raging thirst. If I was quiet enough I might watch a bit of telly undisturbed by Zef's inane comments about the state of the world today and how young people are taking the country to the brink. The brink of what, he never quite explained. I used to respond to his goading but now I just let it wash over me like a polluted ocean tide.

Soft groaning coming from the living room made me hesitate on the stairs. Had Zef brought home a sex playmate? He was game as I could easily let the information slip to his wife and she'd keep him banished for longer. Ah, I could see now why he thought I wouldn't report him. I sneaked toward the open living room door to peek at what was going on. The lights were out, the room's only illumination coming from the flat screen mounted on the wall but it was enough for me to see a fully naked Zef stroking his prick slowly as he watched a porn movie, recognizing it straight away as one of my favorites, a bisexual gangbang movie in which a young couple is ravished by a gang of burglars who break into their house on their wedding night and proceed to have their way with both bride and groom.

Don't get me wrong, I'm as gay as Disco but straight men in porn are so hot particularly when they are eager for wet holes and don't care who they fuck. I guess I identify with the women in gangbang porn and fantasize about taking on a tag team.

Ryan found my taste in porn movies rather distasteful, he was probably jealous that one of him wasn't good enough to satisfy me. I tried explaining it was all in my head and that it would be bloody uncomfortable and quite painful in real life but that sometimes the good old missionary position just didn't do it for me when I was handling my own tackle. On those occasions I wanted the full Monty: widescreen, Technicolor fantasy with as many hot men I could conjure. Ryan admitted he never fantasized. Not about sex anyway. I expect when he wanted to get hard he dreamed about money.

Wait a second.

I kept my fetish material in a special drawer in the bedroom so as not to rub Ryan's face in my unfulfilled fantasy. How the fuck had Zef found it? He must have been going through the house when I wasn't home. What the fuck?

Now, of course, was not really the time to confront him as I had my own real-live porn experience happening a few feet from me. I was watching a scraggy middle-aged man working over his meat but in my state of frustration his wiry body and taut musculature was as desirable as anything Hollywood could create and his ugly prick was a mouthwatering beauty that I wanted to feel up my ass.

By standing in the darkened hallway I could watch Zef working his stiff rod, eyes glued to the movie, his breath catching in his throat. I hauled out my own dick and milked it quietly while I watched the scene unfold before me, Zef encouraging the tough fuckers in the porn to 'rip the bitch open' and other profanities that made my balls tingle.

Who would have thought I'd be jerking off over the sight of a jerk jerking, a homo wanking over his homophobic dad-in-law's purple-headed prick? I almost chuckled, wondering how Zef would act if he knew he was being used as fantasy fodder by a fag. I didn't need to wonder because I knew: he'd feel so fucking superior he'd be unbearable.

My attention was equally divided between the screen and Zef pleasuring himself but as time passed and Zef seemed in no hurry to bring on his climax I began concentrating on his cock. If I tried to be objective, ignoring the bastard's hatred for all things gay, it was a mighty impressive piece of meat. On anyone else, I would have been tempted with Ryan away and having not had my lips, anal or facial, around anything even approximating what I was watching in…well… ever.

Now that I looked, really looked, examining his prick from a distance with forensic impartiality, I could see why women found Zef desirable. His craggy good looks, his tight slim body without an ounce of fat, and that mammoth appendage – what's not to like?

The moral part of my brain kept intruding with the obvious answer: his poisonous personality.

I slapped a lock on morality and just wallowed in the sheer excess of what I was watching. It was almost too much and I had to stop tugging on a number of occasions I was so close to losing my load, prolonging the delicious ache in my balls. Zef's breath was more ragged, his instructions to the actors on the screen more violent when he jumped to his feet, thrust out his hips and blew an arc of spunk across the coffee table.

OMG! I thought his squirts would never end. He was in danger of drowning a small Pacific island with the amount of spooge his balls produced. Unconsciously, I poked out my tongue as if to catch the drops to taste for myself.

Shit, I was a sick and faithless fuck.

I fled back to my bedroom, my cock bursting, my ass twitching. I slammed open the drawer beside the bed, greased up, and inserted my favorite dildo in my ass before I lost the image of what I'd just witnessed.

I tried to imagine it was Ryan's hand on my cock and Ryan's dick in my ass but Zef's image kept swatting him aside. The battle was brief and Zef won out in the end, fantasies can't be cheated. I relaxed into it, wondering what Zef's weapon would feel like wedged in my butt, my dildo a poor excuse in comparison.

I erupted all over my stomach and chest, murmuring 'Fuck me Zef' as I slammed the rubber cock as far up my anal canal as it would go, my sphincter clamping it in place.

Wild. Fantasy rocks.

I heard movement in the hallway again and wondered if someone had been watching me. Someone? I was becoming paranoia central. The only other person in the house was Zef and he must be downstairs cleaning up his messy spunk from the coffee table. Before that image could make me hard again, I brought my morality shield back up and fell asleep superior in the knowledge that what happens in your fantasy, stays in your fantasy. It doesn't encroach on real life.

Right! What a smug bastard I was. And how ripe for a fall. Not long in coming either.

The next morning I awoke to the delicious smell of coffee wafting from downstairs. I bounded out of bed prepared to take on the world, anxious to give Zef the opportunity to turn over a new page. Forget it. He as good as took the whole volume and ripped it to shreds with his greeting, "Morning, fag," as I entered the kitchen. He was dressed, if you can call it that, in another towel which somehow seemed even skimpier than the one he wore yesterday, his cock and balls dangling below the hemline.

I shook my head to dislodge the image although it clung on tenaciously.

"Put some clothes on!" I snapped.

"Snappy fag, this morning. Missing our boyfriend, are we?"

"I don't know if you're missing yours, but I'm missing mine."

Touché. A goal to my team.

Or it would have been, had he understood the semantics. He looked at me blankly. It wasn't worth explaining to him.

"And just where is the man who rocks your boat?"

I wish I knew.

"He never tells me," I admitted reluctantly. "It sounds awful, but I don't have a head for business. I ask to be polite but I'm really not very interested. Just as he's not interested in my field, so it balances itself out. You probably know more about his dealings than I do."

"Nah, we don't talk much, him being a fag—"

"And you being a fag basher."

He ignored the putdown.

"He'll ring me when he gets a chance. Meanwhile, I've got his mobile number if there's an emergency at home. It's usually turned off because he's in meetings but I can leave a message."

"What if there's an emergency at his end?"

"I guess he'd phone."

"What if he can't? How would you know what had happened?"

"Way to bring a guy down, Zef. I'd ring Derwent if I didn't hear from him. Derwent is his personal assistant."

I saw the beginning of a smirk twitching at the corners of his mouth. I felt the need to squelch it.

"Don't even go there, Zef. I trust Ryan. Before you ask, Derwent is the cutest young twink you're ever likely to lay your eyes on. Ambitious as fuck and has come on to Ryan on numerous occasions but Ryan always tells me about them." I played my ace. "Besides, Ryan is not that much into sex." Oops, I played my Joker. I wanted to slap myself for blurting that out.

"That must be why you can't take your faggy eyes off my cock."

I'd had enough. "Look, I don't like you or your fuckin' comments—"

"You just like my cock, eh?"

"On anyone else I'd be on my knees sucking it so hard his brain would cave in. On you…" I spat.

"So you're with Ryan for the money?"

"You can find something nasty in everything, can't you?"

"That's not an answer."

"Truth?"

He nodded. I wasn't about to let him get under my skin.

"You can turn your little recording device on or take notes now if you want. I have nothing to hide from him. Yes, of course, the money is good. I'm a fuckin' student for Christ's sake. If I hadn't met Ryan I'd be sharing a room with some cretinous fag basher half your age…" I looked him up and down and put the boot in, "A third your age, on campus and working my ass off in a burger joint just to have enough to barely survive. I didn't have much experience when I met Ryan—"

"And you still don't by the sound of it. This is definitely one case of unlike father, unlike son. Maybe you need a bit of training…" He grabbed his cock, waving it in my direction. I noticed it was semi-tumescent.

"If I need training, I'll hire a professional."

"Save your money, go straight to the best." He opened his arms wide as if advertising his credentials.

"Think I'd need a few references before I took your word for it."

He handed me his mobile phone. "Call any of them. They'll vouch for me."

I attempted to squeeze as much sarcasm into my voice as possible. "Think I'd prefer a reference from a male if it's all the same to you."

He grabbed his phone back and scrolled through his phone book, selecting a number before handing it back to me. I was so tempted to dial.

"Go ahead. Test me."

I put the phone down on the table. "I thought you didn't like fags as you persist in calling them."

"It turns some guys on. Calling them fags. Know what I mean?"

Before I had a chance to stop it, my head was nodding. Shit! I'm so transparent.

"You, too, eh?"

"In some situations," I admitted. No use attempting to lie my way out of it now.

"Now you haven't answered the question."

"My cock has no problem at all with fags."

"But you wouldn't want your son to marry one?"

He shrugged. "His mother and I did have other plans for him."

"How about you?"

"Me what?"

"Would you marry a fag?"

"Nah," he said. He got up and headed for the door, informing me he was going to take a shower. He turned at the last minute to add, "Wouldn't marry one but I'd sure fuck one, especially if he was as cute as you."

Then he was gone.

I sat down in surprise, so many conflicting emotions running through my head.

He has an amazing cock.

But he's your father-in-law.

He said he'd fuck me.

He's Ryan's dad, are you listening?

Remember, he said your ass is hot.

You're in a relationship.

I wonder what it would be like to be trained…fucked by a guy who really knows what he's doing?

You think his cock is ugly.

Not when you divorce it from his personality.

You're in a monogamous relationship.

I need more experience to please Ryan.

Sex isn't everything.

With Ryan, it's close to nothing. I want to see if I'm missing out.

And if you are?

I'll rethink my relationship.

Fidelity is more important than good sex.

Did you hear what you just said?

You think he's a dog.

You're beginning to repeat yourself.

The argument in my mind took a matter of seconds and I knew if Zef were to come on to me, my hold out would be extremely short lived. Amazing how the prospect of a big cock up your ass can make someone look more attractive than you first thought.

I wandered into the living room to have my coffee stopping, open mouthed, when I noticed Zef had not cleaned up his mess from the previous night. It was enough to make me forget how much I was attracted to his cock until I noticed he hadn't cleaned up his spunk either. It was no longer a puddle of man juice but had dried out leaving a small scab of spooge adhering to the table.

Seething, I went to the kitchen to get a garbage bag for the cans and other rubbish he'd left after I'd cleaned up the first time, plus a cloth to wipe away the tell-tale deposit. I'd give him a piece of my mind when he was out of the shower. I left the dried sperm until last, careful to clear the detritus from around it. Had you asked me why, I would have been hard pressed to answer. I kept glancing at it, there seemed to be so much, wondering what his slime would taste like.

When I dumped the bag of rubbish in the kitchen I went back to clear away all traces of his solo action. It had the appearance of a salt slick as I kneeled with my damp cloth determined to erase all trace of his appalling behavior. I bet he wouldn't have done it if Ryan had been home.

Ryan. I suddenly felt guilty because I hadn't given him much of a thought since I'd been seduced by the sight of Zef's cock. Unconsciously, I ran my finger across the slick and then tasted it. Damn. Not enough of it adhered to my finger to have a flavor. I stared at it as if mesmerized. Again, I don't know what made me do it but I leaned forward and ran my tongue across the subject of my fascination.

Mmm, salty on my tongue. I stared at it again, determining whether to sample it again when I was interrupted. "That's it, boy, lick it all up."

Startled, I was about to jump to my feet but Zef held me in position on my knees.

"Don't waste it, son. Good spunk is hard to find and this is the best, dry or not. Lick it up!"

I resisted but he forced my head down onto the coffee table, rubbing my nose in the dried patch.

"You know you want to lick it all up like a dog. Go on, boy. No one will know. I won't tell Ryan you sucked my dried spunk off the coffee table. Or what a disgusting little fag you are."

The feel of his powerful hand around the back of my head plus the close proximity of his towel-wrapped body heated my blood. I could always say that he forced me if the story ever got out. I justified it on the grounds that it was against my will even though I had willingly taken the first taste.

He yanked my head back by the hair, making me look up into his nasty eyes, flecked with what I read as the most disgusting, the filthiest thoughts imaginable. This was his method of letting me know his orders were not to be toyed with, that I was in real physical danger.

I flicked out my tongue in compliance and he patted me heavily on the head. "Good faggot, I knew you were nothing but a gutless slut."

He pushed my head back to the coffee table rubbing my face in his dried spooge until the smell filled my nostrils and my tongue licked the surface clean, all the while he abused me as 'filthy faggot,' 'cock whore,' 'cum slut,' and much worse. I was strangely aroused by the verbal humiliation and Zef's dominant personality, more excited than I ever had been with Ryan. Maybe I was all the names Zef called me.

When I'd finished cleaning up his mess, Zef yanked my head back and, without hesitation, I opened my mouth as instructed. I wondered at my obedience. Zef tilted his head forward and spat into my open mouth. Under normal circumstances I would have been disgusted and spat it out immediately but I was so aroused I swallowed, perilously close to shooting a load in my pants.

"Good faggot," Zef cooed, and I was exhilarated by his compliment.

He pushed his thumbs into my open mouth, stretching my lips, opening my jaws before pushing three fingers as far into my throat as he could. I gagged. I tried to push him away, but he was stronger than me.

"Arms by your side, boy. Don't try to fight it. Relax and you'll be okay. Struggle and it will be much more unpleasant."

I did as I was told.

"Good slut."

Why am I trying to please this man?

"Do as I say, boy. Open your mouth wide, as wide as you can. That's it. Now just relax, don't fight it. Be a good faggot, do as daddy tells you. Open wider."

My jaw ached but I did as commanded.

"This is what you want, isn't it, slut?" He removed his towel, his cock standing deliciously close to my face. "You want my cock, boy? You want to feel your boyfriend's dad's big juicy prick in your throat, sucking all the spunk out of his balls? That's right, hold still. I'm going to ride your mouth, boy. Fuck it like it's nothing but a cum dump. All you have to do is keep your mouth open and take everything I dish out. Don't try to suck my cock, don't try anything at all. Got it?"

I nodded my head.

"Good boy."

He pushed his cock roughly into my gob. "Take a deep breath, fag."

I just had time to gulp in a lungful of air before he grabbed the back of my head and rammed his cock all the way in. I felt it reach my throat muscles before it forced its way through until he was buried up to his balls. My eyes must have opened in sheer terror as my oxygen supply was cut off.

"Don't fight it, boy. That's the worst thing you can do. Just let it happen. I'll take care of you."

He was so reassuring, I knew he wouldn't let me choke to death on cock although the idea of having that on a death certificate was somehow appealing. I couldn't relax completely so he withdrew his prick far enough for me to take another breath at which point I was so relieved I did relax. That must have been his signal because he rammed back in pushing the tardy breath into me as he blocked my throat. Zef pushed in and out slowly until my gag reflex gave up in disgust and his mammoth weapon felt comfortable.

"This is it, boy. You're gonna get the face fuck of a lifetime. I bet my faggot son doesn't ride your lips like I'm gonna. Your pretty face was made to be fucked like a whore's cunt."

Did he just call me pretty?

Oh, shit!

He held my head so firmly in his grip it was as if I was totally constrained. He'd lulled me into such a passive state I took the first few slams comfortably, and then my panic reflex kicked in. He was fucking my face like it was just a hole for his entertainment, of use only for his cock to spew its junk in. That was confirmed by the tirade of abuse he heaped on me.

I couldn't help but gag as he pierced my throat savagely time and time again until his cock was covered in drool, long strands of gag juice dribbling from my chin attached to his slimy cock as he pulled it from my mouth to give me seconds to breathe before he plunged back in again.

It was intense, and it was frightening. Why was I so turned on? This ugly man could use my mouth for anything he wanted because, among the demeaning epithets he threw at me, there was also a stream of encouragement and compliments. The small part of my mind that wasn't concentrating on the mouth battering I was receiving did a quick calculation on how many compliments Ryan had given me over the years we'd been together. For all his supposed care and love, Ryan had never once offered even the most basic acknowledgement of my worth to him while his dad, regardless of the brutality of his fuck, was treating me with more humanity than his son.

He was also unleashing something inside me that had lain dormant all my life.

I was so aroused by his sexual humiliation that I ejaculated into my trousers. I didn't fucking care. I felt so liberated as I took Zef's cock down my throat, overjoyed I could please this ugly man and his even uglier prick. If I could have smiled around his engorged cock, I would have.

It seemed like hours, but it must have been less than a minute or two that Zef stopped his violent face fuck, allowing me to breathe normally although my throat was coated with gag slime and felt as raw as a whore's ass. I gulped in air, coughing up phlegm as Zef smeared the excess off his cock across my upturned face. That evil smile seemed a lot more benevolent than it had previously. He was breathing deeply as well.

"Fuck, boy. You sure can take punishment. I knew the first day I saw you that you were a natural."

A natural what?

"Wowee, that was some ride. You're a fuckin' Grade A fag. No wonder Ryan keeps you around."

He had to go and spoil it.

He must have seen the look of disappointment cross my face.

"Hey, fag, I'm no snitch. I won't tell your boyfriend," he said by way of placating me.

He didn't get it.

When I didn't smile, a cloud crossed his face.

"That's not it, is it? I know you're a fuckin' slut so it can't be the language. I know how much you enjoyed that. I know you love cock. I know Ryan doesn't treat you like you should be treated. Like you want to be treated. Dominated. So you must be getting it outside the relationship or else Ryan is bringing home extras for you."

I guess my shock registered.

"You and Ryan don't play around?"

I shook my head.

"Let me guess, you don't play up on the side?"

I shook my head again.

"Fu-uck. Then Ryan is truly no son of mine. If you were my fag you'd be on your back taking cock all day and night."

I couldn't believe I moaned at the thought.

"I knew it. If you were one of my boys, oh the fun we could have."

His boys?

As if to demonstrate, he slid his cock over my tongue allowing me to pleasure him, suck, lick and nip his huge shaft as he poked it gingerly into my tormented throat.

"Mmm, you do gentle just as good as rough," he said, a slight whimper to his voice.

I licked and sucked his balls as he towered over me before returning to his cock, taking it all the way down.

"You can't get enough, can you, boy? That's it. I want you to taste my nasty cock phlegm. I want to see that pretty face of yours covered in my spunk. I bet you'd love to drown in ball juice."

He increased the pace but not enough to cut off air flow and I matched him all the way. I forgot everything except pleasing this man.

"Shit, I can't hold off," he panted just before he pulled his cock from my disappointed mouth and aimed it at my face giving it a last few tugs. The first squirt spattered across my cheek and forehead. I opened my mouth wide and was rewarded with a warm string of spunk which tasted like nectar as I swirled it around on my tongue. I was sticky when he'd shuddered to completion, opening his eyes to look down on my spooge thickened face, rubbing his cock across my cheek and forehead and then feeding me his cum-coated cock to clean.

He shivered a few more times as I ran my tongue around the still leaking head of his prick. When he withdrew he lifted me to my feet, ran his hand down the side of my face and suggested a shower was in order. I wanted to beg off because I would have gladly worn his dried cum on my face all day as a badge of honor.

In the bathroom, I peeled off my clothes, contaminated with my infidelity. Ryan wasn't likely to be home anytime soon so I dropped them on the floor. I'd put them in the wash when I'd cleaned up. Turning on the water, I scraped some of the drying cum onto my finger and sucked it clean. My cock twitched. Ryan had never had that effect on me. Then again, Ryan had never shot his wad all over my face; he was too much the neatness freak.

As I stepped under the warm spray, hoping Zef would join me, I wondered what this would do to my relationship. Relationships? How would this impinge on my marriage to Ryan? What did Zef expect now? Would we return to our old sparring? Would he want a repeat of what we just did?

Yes, please.

Would he want to take it further?

Dear God, please.

It didn't escape my notice I was concentrating on my relationship with Zef rather than his son. If I wasn't still basking in the glow of my sexual indiscretion, I would have realized I had a serious problem.

Zef didn't join me in the shower. In fact, he gave me a wide berth for the next two days. There was no antagonism which I actually began to miss. I didn't like the new introspective Zef. He was a bore. I'd look up sometimes and catch him staring at me across the table or the room. Not a nasty stare because I'd learned by now the sneer and the Mr. Nasty were an image. Sure, they were an exaggeration but still part and parcel of what went to make up Zef's complicated personality. I won't say there was a teddy bear underneath his gruff exterior but there was a rather nice man beneath the several layers of aggression if you just peeled them away.

I was so frustrated with Zef's lack of follow-up I began to act as slutty and accommodating as possible by following his example and wearing a revealing towel around the house as often as possible. He surprised me by snapping, "Put some clothes on," after I'd paraded near nude for only a few hours. He had gone back to wearing street clothes as soon as we'd finished our short oral escapade.

Something was wrong.

By the fourth day after our bit on the side, I was screaming for it. He was as agitated as fuck, prowling the house like a caged panther. I decided to go out just to get some air. I felt in the pocket of my trousers for my keys and my fingers touched something familiar. I extracted the card. It was the bear from the bar. My butt twitched at the thought of ringing him. Zef must have been watching me because he reacted angrily.

"Just where do you think you're going?"

"Out!"

"Going to see one of your boyfriends?" His sneer was like a bug being wiped across a car windscreen.

"Up until our little adventure, I was totally happy with Ryan. Totally monogamous as well. No outside boyfriends. And if," I emphasized the word, "if I was to have a boyfriend, you'd be first choice."

I slammed the door on the way out. It was only later when I was seated in a café that overlooked the main shopping street of the town that I realized what I'd said in a moment of pique. Many a truth and all that.

Yes, I had been happy with Ryan in our cozy suburban existence but less than half an hour of Zef's aggressive form of lovemaking showed me the bubbling dissatisfaction eating away at my soul. But had I really told an ugly old man that he was my ideal boyfriend? Shit, I was in so much trouble. My life was unraveling faster than I could stitch it back together again.

I needed a fuck and I needed it now. I hadn't heard from Ryan in almost a week. That was unusual enough on its own. The thing that worried me was that I didn't care. He'd treated me in such a cavalier manner for so long now that I'd finally woken up to it, I was seething. But not enough to go on the hunt for a revenge fuck. Maybe later. I had one man in mind and I would give it my best shot. I'd show him how much I wanted him in case it was my relationship with his son that was giving him pause.

If I wanted to be treated like a slut then I'd have to act like one. I conjured up a number of scenarios by which to seduce Zef, though seduction was not quite the word. I wanted a rough, aggressive fuck from a very large cock that would have me whimpering. Once satisfied with Ryan's lazy fuck, now all I wanted was to be thrown on the floor and ravished. I snorted my derision. I was acting like the heroine of the trashy romance erotica everyone talks about.

When I arrived home I was disappointed that Zef was not about. There was plenty of evidence he had been as drawers and cupboards had been opened and pillaged, their contents scattered like innards at an abattoir. What on earth was he looking for? Surely it wasn't porn, as he'd already found my stash. I know he didn't need money because Ryan had offered, Zef turned him down. He'd seemed more concerned with lack of contact from Ryan than I did which was odd considering he continued to call him 'my faggot son.'

I wondered at Zef leaving the evidence of his anger, obviously uncaring of my discovering his snooping, unless he intended tidying up before I returned. I had come back much sooner than I'd intended.

His being out took care of seduction scenarios one through five. I'd get myself ready for number six so I could be in position on his return. As time dragged on, I began to lose impetus. If he was much longer, I'd have lost it altogether. I tidied up the bedroom. Zef could tidy up his own mess downstairs although I despaired that he'd ever get around to it. I did clear the living room, because that was the center of operations for my scenario, piling the mess of papers, DVDs and books on the dining table. Maybe the mess was a blessing. Now I would be forced to go through the accumulated junk and toss out anything we didn't need or hadn't used for a year or more.

When I heard his car pull into the driveway, I was so fucking nervous I was shaking. Shit! I'd left one of the major essentials upstairs. No time to get it, I'd have to improvise. I clicked the DVD on, ran to the kitchen and grabbed the first thing I could find, before throwing myself onto the couch. Still shaking, I reached for the Dutch courage, hoping to time this right. I snorted two hits of the poppers I kept hidden at the back of the drawer under the flat screen, the only drug I used now and then to help me get off while watching porn once Ryan had finished unloading in me, leaving me unsatisfied.

Shit, he was taking too long; the effect of the poppers was wearing off. I doubled the dose and soon I was flying. The visuals on the screen plus the sound of hard group fucking addled my brain. I pushed the zucchini I grabbed from the fridge crisper into my pre-lubed ass. It was cool but it felt so good. So good, in fact, that if Zef resisted the temptation I could still have a whole lot of fun on my own.

I had to slow down; I was in danger of bringing myself off too soon. I had admitted to myself long ago that my ass was the center of my sexual universe but no one had ever taken that claim seriously, planted a flag so to speak. I was hoping Zef might show me the way.

I had the sound level on the porn loud enough to attract Zef's attention but it also meant I couldn't hear him enter. I had to continue my self-pleasuring so he could catch me. Third time lucky, I hoped when I sniffed the poppers again, anchored my legs over my head on the lounge and began the relentless pounding of my hole with the very large vegetable.

When he did announce his presence by coughing loudly at the door to the living room, I was genuinely startled, turning crimson with embarrassment but also hyped up enough that after my initial reaction I went right back to what I was doing. There was no way I could stop even if he'd brought Ryan with him. He hadn't, he was alone. I was pleased to see a bulge filling in his crotch.

He just stood watching, his eyes flickering from the screen to my live action performance. He was going to make me instigate the first move.

"See something you like?"

He shifted uncomfortably. "I see lots of things I like," he said, nodding toward the screen and toward me. "You like that sort of porn shit?"

"It's my favorite."

Group of rough auto mechanics working over two gay lovers whose car has broken down in Nowhere, USA, and who have to give up their asses and their mouths as payment. I always pictured myself in the film, though never Ryan.

"You like group stuff?"

"Never had it," I replied.

"You like your slut fag ass worked over though?"

Good, he was using the F word again. Meant he was getting into the mood.

I thought I could afford to sneer for once. "What's it look like?"

"Didn't get enough from the friend whose name is on this card?" He held it aloft. It must have fallen from my pocket and he found it.

"Just some old cunt even uglier than you who tried to pick me up in a bar. Thought I was hot enough he wanted to pay me."

"Looks like I was right about what a whore you are."

"I only take payment in cock and spunk."

Was this really me talking?

"You had me fooled for a while," he said stripping off his clothes. "I thought that routine about loyalty to Zef and the happy homo life was genuine. More fool me. That's why I haven't touched you again. But now I see you're just a cheap fuckin' hole for cock, well, who am I to pass up such an inviting invitation?"

"You like to work over fag sluts, eh? Makes you feel like a real man, eh, you ugly fuckin' old cunt. Think you can get it up long enough to fuck me, old man?"

He ripped the substitute cock from my ass to replace it with three of his fingers. It burned as he plunged them in and out, twisting and turning as if he were kneading dough. It hurt like fuck.

"God, you're so tight, I don't fuckin' believe it." He looked at me uneasily. "You really a slut?"

"Believe it," I boasted bravely.

"Hmm, I know a few guys who would really love to work you over like those whores in the movie. How would you like that?"

"Bring it on, fucker," I swore, excited to the point of orgasm by what his fingers were doing to my ass.

"You man enough to take my cock? Lots of fags think they can handle it but scream when they find out how big it is stretching their guts. Once I'm inside you, slut, I won't be stopping for begging, pleading or seismic seven earthquakes although that's what you'll think has hit you when I've finished with your ass."

"You think you're man enough to satisfy me?"

The dare was on.

I wasn't stupid, I'd left a plastic bottle of lube on the coffee table so he could grease up his weapon before he lunged into me. Zef flicked the lid while he still had his three fingers in my ass, drizzling the gel along his shaft, then rubbing it in with his free hand.

"You want foreplay? I can take it gentle till you're comfortable."

"Skip the foreplay," I said. "I've had bigger and not even felt it."

"Oh, you'll feel this you little fuckin' slut. I'll make sure of it."

My mouth was running away on me. If it didn't shut up soon, it'd be responsible for doing me a serious injury.

"You might like to take a hit from your drug bottle there because when I meet a real fuckin' slut whore like you, I like it extra rough."

Okay, there's brave and there's stupid. After a promise like that it was wise to tread on the cautious side. I took an extra-large sniff or five and placed the bottle back on the coffee table. Before I had even let it go, Zef had extracted his fingers from my stretched ass and positioned his cock at the entrance. He waited until he saw I was away with the pixie fumes before he slid his mammoth cock right down to his balls in one smooth action. I watched as it entered my asshole, stretching me wider than I ever dreamed possible until I took every inch of it.

"Holy fucking Christ!" I moaned.

Zef's cock filled every available space in my bowel. I felt so full I never wanted him to pull back even though the burning pain of my ass muscles stretching to accommodate him screamed for mercy. He was having none of it. Pausing just long enough to see I was still conscious I presume, he withdrew the full length and plunged again. The friction against my sphincter was intense but I could endure it, even get to like the way the bulbous head of his prick scraped my prostate.

"You fuckin' little cock tease," Zef sneered as his face loomed over me, doubled up on the lounge, my legs in danger of snapping. "I've wanted to bury my fuckin' pole in your ass since that first day, fuck you into oblivion like you deserve. Shit, your ass is so tight, I could fuck it forever and never get sick of it. I love your whore's ass, want you to be my cock puppet. Want to breed your sloppy asshole, son. Steal you away from my useless fag son, treat you like the slut you are. Farm you out to all the ugly old fuckers who want to breed your raw ass. You like that idea, boy?"

"Yes, daddy. Anything to please you. I'll be your whore, your slut, your fuck hole, your cum dump."

"What about Ryan?" he said, momentarily bringing reality into the sexual equation. It almost threw me until I realized he wanted permission to cuckold his own son.

"Forget him, daddy. You're ten times the man he will ever be."

"Slut!" He grabbed me by the throat and squeezed so that I opened my mouth to cry out. He spat savagely on my face, some of his spit dribbling into my mouth. "Fuckin' whore. Take it like the back alley slut you are. You're not good enough for Ryan. You're just a common cock craving cunt, like all the other fags. Your ass is there to be fucked and abused, I told Ryan what sort of crude fag you are. He didn't believe me. If he could just see you now."

Zef kept up his rhythm as he screwed me into the lounge, grabbing my mobile phone from the side table to film us fucking. I didn't care. I knew he wouldn't dare send it to his son because it would implicate him as well. I decided to make sure of that.

"Fuck me, Zef. Ram me with that pole between your legs, split me open, Zef. I'm a slut for your cock. Fill my ass with daddy spunk till I can't take any more."

Zef kept one hand tight round my throat while he banged my butt filming as much as the mobile phone would take. Then he put it down to concentrate on getting his rocks off. If Ryan had little regard for me and my needs, Zef was much the same, concentrating on his cock in my hole. He watched it slide through my ass lips admiring the vision. I know because he verbalized his appreciation. The major difference between father and son was that Zef could keep the action going long enough that it brought me to the edge.

With a string of expletives that were way outside even a sailor's league he slammed into my guts one more time and I felt his spunk flood my anal passage. It set me off and soon my cum was spurting across my belly, my ass twitching to clutch the cock embedded inside me.

"Fuck, boy," he panted, struggling to catch his breath. "Fuck."

He pulled out, sitting on the coffee table as I lowered my legs, my back aching from the cramped, doubled-over position, his cum dribbling out of my ass.

"I need a drink," I said standing unsteadily, heading to the kitchen. "You want something?"

"How about some juice?"

I didn't bother to dress as I hoped there might be some cuddling or even a repeat involved. I took my mobile with me to see the action that he'd shot. I was engrossed in the footage of Zef in my ass, cursing me, while I poured a juice for the two of us, when I noticed he'd sent the video to two numbers in my address book. I shuddered. He'd sent evidence of my infidelity to his own phone, maybe to upload it to X-Tube, and also to Ryan. I was fucked. Well and truly. I was about to storm into the living room when I was stopped by loud knocking on the front door along with the constant tone of the bell. I heard Zef swear vehemently as he scrambled for his clothes. Whoever was at the front door was impatient and the hammering did not let up.

Zef yelled, "Hold your horses, I'm coming."

As he passed the kitchen he tossed my clothes in to me. "Here, get dressed quickly."

It almost sounded as if he knew who our visitors were.

I wiped my butt on a cloth in the sink and quickly pulled on my trousers. I was just slipping into my shirt when two belligerent looking men appeared in the doorway asking for me by name.

"That's me," I said

They identified themselves as police and asked me to accompany them to headquarters for questioning.

"What's this all about?" I asked as they manhandled me toward the door.

One of the men snorted. "As if you don't know."

They didn't give me much choice in the matter of accompanying them as both of them held an arm each. I looked to Zef for help but he merely put his finger to his lips which I assumed meant keep my trap shut. About what?

"Is Ryan all right? Has there been some sort of accident?"

"I'd like to come with him," Zef said.

"Afraid not, sir," one of the cops replied. "This could take quite a while."

The last I saw as I was driven away in the police vehicle was Zef watching from the front door, his mobile in his hand.

I'm normally the calmest of people when up against authority. There's no point antagonizing people who hold all the aces, so I was mute for the car ride to the city, wondering what had happened to Ryan and why Zef had encouraged me to be silent.

I've never liked cops, except as sex partners on an irregular basis, not that I've done that but it's a fantasy to fulfill in later life. If I have one.

I was put in a room and told to wait, all the cops beginning to blur in my mind, their hostility was of such similarity. When a cop opened the door to the interview room and I looked out, I saw a group of them with my mobile phone watching the screen. I didn't need to hear my voice begging to be fucked to know it was me they were watching. Their comments were ribald, vulgar and homophobic although one cop said, "Shit, I'd fuck him. He's a cute slut and look at the ass and the lips on him. Bet he's be better than most of our wives, eh?"

He looked up and his gaze met mine. He winked while his mates gave him hell.

I forgot Zef's instructions as soon as the taped questioning began.

"Has something happened to Ryan?"

"You tell us," one of the cops said.

"Well, I haven't heard from him for a week."

"Isn't that unusual?"

"Yeah. When he's away it's normally only a day or two before he calls."

"But you weren't worried?"

"Sure, but…"

The cop questioning me turned to his mate and chuckled, "But you had other things on your mind. Or should I say in your ass."

The cops would tell me nothing but it obviously had to do with Ryan and, from what I gathered, he had to be alive as they were chasing his whereabouts. I didn't know where he was any more than I knew the maneuverings of his company. They didn't seem to believe me. My answers mainly consisted of 'I don't know,' until an older gent turned up informing the cops I would no longer answer any of their questions and if they had any evidence they should charge me.

Tom Gadd was my lawyer it seems although I had no idea who hired him let alone how much he would cost, but by the looks of his expensive suit and accessories he was way out of my league.

"Who hired you, Mr. Gadd?" I asked as soon as we were out of earshot of the cop questioners.

"Not permitted to say, lad. The Good Samaritan wishes to remain anonymous."

"Thanks for getting me out."

"Not a problem, though I suspect they'll be on to you again. Just give me a call when they are. We'll sort it all out. Above all, don't say anything at all without me there. Got it?"

"Got it."

As he returned my confiscated mobile phone, we both looked up at the sound of shouting coming from one of the offices along the hallway. We couldn't make out the exact words but the tone left no doubt as to the anger involved. We did hear the barrage of expletives as the door opened and, to my surprise, Zef walked out screaming at the person inside, 'He's got nothing to do with it,' before slamming the door so hard the pictures on the wall in the corridor rattled precariously.

"Well, good day to you, Grant, I hope I don't see you again but the chances are that I will."

I watched Tom Gadd walk toward the front door and if I hadn't been watching forensically I would have missed the curt surreptitious nod of recognition that Gadd and Zef gave each other. Why would he hire a lawyer for me after his brutal betrayal? Curious.

Zef indicated that I should follow him and the foul tempered look on his face brooked no argument. Besides, I wanted to get to the bottom of what was going on.

"Did they give you a hard time?" he asked when I caught up with him.

"Only over a certain video which seemed to amuse them."

He laughed. "It'll probably reap rewards for you in future now that…"

I finished the sentence for him. "Now that Ryan's not coming back any more."

He appeared surprised. "You knew?"

"I took an educated guess. I may be a faggot slut, but I'm not stupid."

"Listen, about that."

"Save it until we're away from here, then let me give you my few surmises and see how good I am at playing detective."

"Okay."

"Then you can tell me where I fit into all this in relation to you."

He didn't seem quite as pleased when I said that.

On the car trip back to the house, Zef attempted to start the conversation but I shooshed him. I was still formulating it all in my mind so by the time we entered the house, I had half a good idea about what was going on. We picked up pizza and beer on the way back because I did not feel in the mood for cooking or even brewing a coffee. What I wanted to do was talk.

We settled in on the lounge, the one we'd fucked on earlier, the accoutrements of that explosive sexual adventure still evident as was the cum that occasionally oozed from my butt. We sat at opposite ends, careful to avoid contact. I was sorry because I genuinely liked Zef. Liked him more than I'd ever liked his son.

"Tell me what you think you've worked out," he said patronizingly. I hoped we weren't going to go back to the fag references.

I took a swig from the cold stubby bottle. "First up," I said, "I think Ryan's got himself involved in some scheme that's gone wrong and he's skipped the country so no one can find him. Maybe money, maybe drugs. I'm not sure, but whatever he was involved in, it's big. Now, you either assumed it was my doing and not Ryan's or that I'd led your little boy astray and that's why you turned on the, and I quote here, 'little faggot slut whore.' The whole homophobic redneck was an act because you were angry at me for my perceived involvement in whatever was going on. Don't interrupt. You can apologize all you like when I finish. If you knew about what was happening that makes you either a cop or a private investigator."

"Or one of the bad guys," he interrupted. "Did you ever think of that?"

"You're too fuckin' ugly to be a bad guy," I teased. "I couldn't work out why you were spending so much time in the house instead of going out looking for work. A guy like you doesn't bludge off welfare. When you played that DVD I knew you'd been through the house searching for something. It couldn't have been money because Ryan was always careful not to leave any large amounts lying around. I checked the closet in the bedroom and, sure enough, things had been moved, rearranged. Ryan was an anal retentive when it came to his drawers and his closet. Everything had its spot and I'll give you credit, you almost got it right. But I have a trained eye for any slight variation, it comes from living with him and his meticulousness for two years. I knew you'd been searching through the house."

"Not bad for an amateur," he smiled.

"When Ryan didn't ring again, I started to worry. I hadn't seen him come home, I had to take your word for it. I had to assume he hadn't been taken away by the cops or whoever the bad guys are and forced to make that first call where he couldn't get off the phone fast enough. You would have been a little upset if Ryan had been disposed of. It stands to reason then, he'd done a bunk. I came to that conclusion much later. I couldn't work out what you were searching for, except maybe some sort of evidence to connect me to whatever he'd done though I would have thought it obvious that I'd have gone with him if I had been involved.

"When Ryan left and you searched the place but couldn't find whatever it was you were looking for, that's when you tried the really dirty tricks. You were convinced I was a slut so you decided to get me onside by treating me like one. Maybe get me to fall for you and reveal any little secrets that you thought I could divulge. That's the one thing I can't forgive you for."

My voice cracked and I stopped to clear my throat.

"Look, I'm really sorry for the abuse and the slut business. I can't apologize enough."

"That's not what I can't forgive you for," I said, my eyes clouding. "I thought you liked me. That's why I played the slut for you."

"Played? You're not what you said you were?"

I laughed. "I thought the inexperience would have given me away. I wasn't kidding when I said Ryan was vanilla. When it comes to positions, he's a missionary man. Poke it, jiggle it about, blow a load, go to sleep."

Zef looked aghast. "Shit, man, I'm so sorry. I didn't mean to hurt you."

"You didn't hurt me, at least not like that. I loved it. Every rough fucking moment of it. I wanted you to keep on doing it. Through you, I finally learned something about myself."

"How did I hurt you then?"

"I was starting to develop feelings for you." I wondered if I should correct myself. "Am developing."

"Oh, shit. What a cunt I am. I pulled away after that incredible blow job because I thought you were a good kid and I didn't want to hurt you. It was only when you admitted to being a whore and a cock slut that I took advantage of you."

"My fault then."

"Listen, there's something I've got to tell you," he said looking at the clock. "Um, I don't know quite how to say this, but…"

He was interrupted by loud knocking at the door.

"They haven't come to arrest me, have they?"

"No," he admitted. "Look, I'm sorry, it's my fault. I told them you were easy. Let me handle this."

He went to the front door and I could hear arguing. The visitors sounded slightly drunk so I went out into the hallway to see if I could help. I recognized the cops at the door from the station as they pushed their way in carrying a slab of beer.

"There he is," the first cop shouted. It was the guy who'd winked at me while he was watching the video of Zef fucking me.

The second cop looked me up and down before he added, "Yeah, sweet cock sucking mouth."

Zef looked appalled, trying to drag them back to the door but there was no way they were taking any notice of him.

"Come in, guys," I said, to Zef's obvious discomfort. "Make yourselves comfortable in the living room. Break out the beers. Let me get a porno I'm sure you'd like and we can make a night of it. Hey, Zef. Grab the leftover pizza and see if our friends want any. Get them in the party mood."

Zef grabbed me by the arm and took me into the kitchen while the other two yahooed as they made themselves comfortable in the living room.

"I don't think you understand," Zef said.

"I understand perfectly. Those two in there are here to fuck me. What I can't work out is whether it's a present or a punishment. They're cute fuckers, I'll give you that. And I did say I liked groups even though I lied. I've never been involved in one."

"I'll send them home," Zef said.

"I doubt you'd get them to leave now. Besides, I may not have ever had the pleasure of three guys to gang bang me, but the idea certainly has appeal. Too late to turn back now, even if I wanted to. But I don't."

"Three guys?"

"You don't think I'm letting you off the hook."

I piled the pizza boxes into his arms and led him by his shirt front back into the living room where I shoved on a bisexual gang bang movie that most straight guys seem to love and away we went. The small talk continued for a little while after the movie began but eventually everyone's breathing slowed, trousers tented and the sexual frisson in the room was such you could cut it with a knife.

"Any of you guys mind if I make myself comfortable?" I asked as I stripped off my shirt and began to unzip my trousers.

There was mumbled assent.

"Why don't you guys get comfortable as well? We're all guys here. Nothing to be embarrassed about."

There was a flurry of activity as Hal, the good-looking cop who winked at me, and his mate, Neil, peeled off their shirts and their jeans, sitting back down in their jockey shorts. I was seated on the floor between them, my head at cock height. Zef reluctantly stripped but I yanked down his briefs before he could sit down. His mammoth hard cock sprang free.

Hal and Neil were too frightened to start anything so I was about to make a move on Zef's gorgeous schlong when Hal picked up the bottle of poppers that I'd left on the coffee table.

"What's this?" he said unscrewing the lid.

"Careful," I said. "That's mighty powerful stuff. If you sniff it, it breaks down all moral barriers. Makes you so horny you would fuck anything that moved."

"You mean I might want to stick my dick in Zef there?" Neil laughed.

"It's not that powerful," I joked. "But if there was a sweet cocksucker nearby you might find you want to stick it in his mouth or his ass even though you're one hundred per cent straight."

God it was tedious playing games with straight men.

"So, what you're saying is, if say Hal and me take a sniff then we'll be so horny we might want to fuck your face or your ass?"

"Yeah."

"And you'd like, um, let us?"

"Hell, yeah, especially if I took a sniff or two. You guys are hot. Any fag would love to get his mouth or his ass around your hard cocks."

I looked over at Zef who was looking at the ceiling in wonder.

"It, um, won't turn us gay, will it?" Neil asked.

"Nah, it just makes you super horny for a while. No side effects. Helps you enjoy yourself."

"I want to try that." Neil held it to his nose and sniffed.

I kneeled between the two men to show them how to do it and Neil tried again. It wasn't long before he reddened in the face and sank back in the lounge.

"Oh, fuck. Sweet."

I took advantage of the state he was in and pulled down the front of his jockeys, his cock was already a nice seven inches hard and wet on the tip. The window of opportunity was short so I leaned over and took him in my mouth.

"Holy Mother of God," he stammered.

Hal watched then he, too, took a giant hit from the bottle waiting for it to kick in. When it did he lifted my face off Neil's cock and pushed it on to his. He closed his eyes, muttering some incoherent prayer to the deity of cocksucking, I assumed. Neither of them was expert, having a tendency to shove their cocks roughly in and out of my throat rather than allowing me to do the work.

Zef took charge. "Guys, let me show you how it's done, okay?"

They didn't look too pleased to have their cocksucker taken away from them.

"Watch this, guys. I guarantee you'll never have another blow job like it. Okay, boy?"

Zef gave me time to take a giant hit before I licked my tongue along the underside of his shaft to his balls, sucking them gently before making my way back to the head. Licking it to taste his pre-cum I opened my mouth wide, sheathed my teeth and began to slide along his hard thick pole until I felt him hit the back of my throat. I withdrew a little to take a lungful of air then continued to push his cock down my throat.

"Shit, he's taking it all," Hal said admiringly.

"I don't believe it. This guy is one cocksucking genius."

"He deep throats," Zef said. I noticed a certain amount of pride in his voice.

I bobbed about on his cock until I needed to come up for air.

"There you go guys. Let him do all the work. You just sit back and enjoy it."

"Why don't you direct the action, Zef? You know what you're doing. Don't hold back." I hoped he got my message.

"The little fag loves spunk down his throat, all over his face and in his ass," Zef encouraged.

"I don't think I could do his ass, that's faggot stuff," Neil said.

"You don't have to do that if you don't want to. But one sniff and I bet when you see Zef plug my butt you'll want a piece of the action."

The look of wonder on Hal's face said it all. "You're gonna take that up your ass?"

I wanted to encourage him without scaring him "And yours as well. If you want."

"Fuck, yeah. That stuff has really turned me fag for the night. I'll even let you lick my ass."

Hmm, a little bird told me Hal was no virgin when it came to gay sex. The little bottle of poppers had done the trick. Feed a bi-curious guy any sort of bullshit to cover his behavior and he's into it. Neil would take more convincing but I was fine with just blowing him if that's all I could get. Couldn't be too greedy for my first group grope.

"Why don't you grab your ankles, hoist your legs in the air, Hal, let the fag eat your shit hole now."

Hal didn't need to be instructed twice. He had his legs hoisted in the air, his sweet mouthwatering butthole on view. He pulled his ass cheeks apart to give me better access and I lapped my tongue from the end of the crack up past his hole to his balls. He squealed like a stuck pig as I reversed direction, taking my time to slip my tongue into his tight hole.

"Man, you have the kiss of an angel," Hal said. "You should get him to do you, Neil."

"No one gets near my butthole," he griped.

"You don't know what you're missing, dude."

Zef judged Neil was the weak link in the activity and commanded me. "Give Neil a taste of your mouth, slut. Suck his balls dry."

"Yes, sir," I said with too much enthusiasm to be submissive.

I didn't think Neil was into the finer points of fellatio, he seemed more a dump and go man. I swirled my tongue around the knob, then placed my mouth over his shaft and moved down toward his balls. He bucked as my tongue slid along the underside, tickling his sensitive prick. I didn't want him to come too quickly but then Hal said those magic words, "We both took Viagra earlier."

That was all the encouragement I needed. I went all out to show Neil what a good cocksucker could do and soon he was writhing beneath my mouth like a time bomb ready to explode. Hal had lowered his legs and was slowly stroking his nice sized prick that I definitely wanted to feel in my ass. Neil was not a stayer and soon his cum was bubbling up his shaft shooting into my mouth. I took it all, keeping it on my tongue, vacuuming every ounce of the warm salty fluid. He pulled out when the sensation got too much, stumbling out of the room telling us he needed to take a piss.

"If it had been anyone but Neil, I would have told you to drink his piss, slut. Would you do that for me, boy?"

I nodded my head eagerly. Nudging Hal that I wanted another go at his ass. He obeyed instantly and I shoved my tongue in as far as it would go opening him up.

"That's it, fag boy. Eat my fuckin' asshole. Suck it clean."

I opened up to show them both I still had a mouth full of Neil's spooge. Zef got the idea at once.

"Shit, boy, you sure have a vivid imagination. He hoisted Hal roughly so he was almost on his back, his asshole upright, then he tried prizing Hal's ass lips open so I could dribble the spunk down inside him.

"How's that feel, mate?" Zef asked.

"Well, I'd rather the spooge belonged to someone other than Neil but God, it feels so good. Why don't you put a load in there as well fag boy and you can suck it out later."

"You heard him, fag."

I was grateful for the release because I wouldn't last much longer. I aimed my cock at the stretched opening and started to jerk off.

"Don't even think about putting your cock inside me, fag. I don't do that."

Not at the moment, maybe, but give it time.

It didn't take long for me to blow a huge load most of which oozed into his bowels. I pushed the remaining spurts in with my finger, taking the opportunity to push inside Hal's butt. There was no complaint, just the firm grip of his sphincter muscles. I cleaned him up by licking away any of the traces of spunk that still spattered his crack.

Hal flexed his legs for cramp as he lowered them. "This fag is one in a million, Zef. Where'd you find him?"

"Around," Zef said smiling. "Just around. I'm training him."

"Doesn't sound to me like he needs much training."

"It'll take a lot for him to match me when it comes to sex," Zef boasted.

"I'll do anything, sir." I said modestly.

"We'll see, son," Zef said, ruffling my hair.

Neil looked a bit sheepish when he returned.

"Ah, look guys. I think I might head off. Wife's expecting me at home so…"

"No problems mate," Hal said. "And what we did here tonight stays here, okay."

Neil looked relieved. "Yeah."

"See you tomorrow," Hal called.

"See you, Zef." Then Neil was gone.

"Let the real party begin," Hal said pulling my face down onto his cock.

By the time Hal finally left some three hours later, I'd eaten two loads out of his ass, drunk his beer piss, swallowed a load of his cum and taken two up the ass. Zef had been no slouch either but I'd copped just a mouthful of his juice.

"I'm saving some for later," he whispered.

Hal was very eager for a return bout.

"How about it, fag?" he asked as he dressed after wiping his ass and his cock on my face.

"You'll have to ask Zef. He's the boss."

I could see Zef was taken aback. I wanted to see Hal again, I enjoyed his twisted sex needs but I wasn't about to step out of line.

"You serious?" he asked.

"Definitely," I replied.

"Any time you like, Hal. Just let me know."

"Will do. You want I should bring some other guys who are, um, more into it than Neil?"

I looked at Zef.

"Yeah, why not?"

"They can be rough."

"The fag loves it rough, don't you?"

"Yes, sir."

After Hal left I went into the kitchen to make coffee for the two of us.

"That was a test, wasn't it?" I called.

Zef brought the empty pizza boxes with him, crunching them in his strong hands until they fitted in the garbage.

"And a present. It was never meant as punishment. How do you feel?"

"Like a new man," I chirped.

"How about an ugly old cunt?"

"I guess that'll have to do."

I rode his cock for almost an hour in his son's bed, until my asshole felt like it had been rubbed raw. I would be sore tomorrow but for now I was content, full of warm cum that I wished I could siphon out of my ass with my own mouth.

I had lots of questions still unanswered but they would have to wait, I was too tired. I lay down and Zef held me in his arms. I wondered what he thought of me. As if anticipating the question he turned me over and clamped his mouth against mine, pushing his tongue between my lips, tasting the salty spunk of the men I'd sucked tonight.

Ryan had never kissed me like that.

I fell asleep, Zef spooning me, hoping it was not all a dream.

When I woke up, Zef was gone. It may sound dramatic, but my heart broke a little. I choked but forced myself out of bed, put on a pair of briefs and headed downstairs for a heart starter. I smelled coffee. Fresh coffee. My heart did a little skip and I raced down the remainder of the stairs, bursting into the kitchen where Zef was reading the paper, the usual towel around his waist.

"Morning, sleepy," he said without looking up.

"Morning," I replied in as neutral a tone as I could manage but as I went to the bench to get myself a drink I leaned over and pasted my lips on his. I didn't try to tangle tongues, just a lip smack that lasted longer than a good morning kiss.

He grabbed me and sat me sideways on his lap. "Someone's frisky this morning."

I squeezed his hard-on which was poking through the towel against my butt. "Does this thing never go down?"

"Not when you're around," he smirked.

"How long will you be around?" I asked, unsure whether I wanted to know the answer.

"Depends on you," he said.

That was what I wanted to hear. Then he spoiled it by adding. "I don't have a home to go to. Ryan's mother threw me out for good. Doesn't want me back. Found herself a younger feller who loves her and won't play around on her like I did."

"Oh."

"And there's one distinct advantage to staying here."

"We won't be. I can't afford it."

"That was the one nice thing my bastard son did before he went on the run. Not that he meant it as a nice thing, just protection for his financial ass. The house is yours. Has been for close on two years. He cooked the books so it looks like most of the money came from you. Somewhere along the line he would have got you to sign it back to him but, legally, the house is yours."

Fuck. I'm landed gentry.

"What was it? Drugs?"

"Nothing so glamorous. Just plain embezzlement. He was taking all the money out of the company without supplying the goods people ordered. Close to three million dollars' worth. There'd been rumors for about a year that the company was about to go under but he kept up the pretense, sucking every dollar out of his contractors that he could."

"He didn't do it alone, did he?"

"What do you mean?"

I shrugged. "When I went out that day, I thought it was time to check up on Derwent. When the message on his cell phone said the number was disconnected I went over to where he lives. Dead giveaway really when there's a For Lease sign on the front lawn. Neighbors said he left a month before."

Zef hugged me. "Cops think Derwent left early to smooth the way for Ryan."

"They were fucking, weren't they?"

Zef admitted it reluctantly. "Yep."

I waited to feel the sting. When it arrived it surprised me by its mildness. However, the sliver of pain must have shown on my face.

Zef commiserated. "You'll get over it. Give it time."

"Yeah," I said. "Give me five, ten minutes. That should be enough."

He laughed. I liked it when he laughed.

"Cop or PI?"

"Ex-cop. True, I'm a landscape gardener now. Had enough murder and mayhem and being a gardener gets me a lot of pussy and ass. Hal told me the cops were investigating Ryan. I couldn't believe a son of mine would be so corrupt and so stupid, so I decided to do a bit of investigating on my own. That's why I turned up here. You know the rest."

"Not all of it. Bi-curious or bi?"

"You want the truth?"

I nodded.

"I'd fuck anything with a hole in it."

"You sure know how to make a fag feel wanted."

"I'm way too old to change, even if I wanted to, which I don't."

"I was joking, grandpa." I had to ask. "Why did you send Ryan the video of us fucking? That puzzled me."

"Two reasons. One, I thought he might get so fuckin' angry he'd call and we could at least trace what country he's hiding in. Two, to show him what a fuckwit he is leaving you behind."

Did I dare spoil my mood? Yeah, I've always hated uncertainty. "So, where does that leave me now?"

"On the end of my prick, I hope."

"Not much of an answer."

"I'm a selfish cunt," he said.

"Check."

"As old as Methuselah."

"Check."

"Ugly as an asshole of piles."

"Double check."

"That's not enough?"

"Nope. When are you gonna start listing your bad points?"

"Okay." He took a deep breath. "My tastes are not what you'd call mainstream."

My eyes opened wide. "Really? I never would have noticed if you hadn't told me."

"You don't know just how far from mainstream."

"Do they include any of the usual illegal activities we read about in the paper?"

"God, no," he said. "I'm not a pervert."

"That's good enough for me. I'll try it, if I don't like it you'll have to look elsewhere for those jollies."

"You don't want exclusive?"

"Fuck. No. How boring is that?"

"Stupefying," he laughed. "Mate, you could be just the fag I'm looking for."

"Mate, you could be just the dominant I think I need to broaden my horizons."

"I can be a bastard," he warned.

"So can I."

"What's say we try another little test?"

"Like yesterday's?"

"Much worse."

"Bring it on. As long as it's not another Neil type, nice as he was."

"Exactly the opposite. No, this will really test your limits and your commitment. This is real nasty."

"You want to see me be a nasty fag for you, Zef? I would love to do that for you. I'm up for it."

"Make or break?"

"Make or break."

"Right, you asked for it. Three o'clock this afternoon. On your back on the coffee table, legs in the air, ass greased and ready, no poppers, I have to see that you can do this without being off your face. And that means no alcohol either. Your ass should be facing the front door. You should have a pillow under you head to watch as I enter. You can change your mind and back out up until the moment I'm naked. Then it's too late. Understand."

"Uh huh."

To change the subject, he asked, "What do you want for breakfast?"

In answer, I kneeled under the table, unwrapped his towel and took his cock in my mouth.

Zef went out an hour or so later to clear up a few loose ends and to have his mail redirected to his new home. We hadn't discussed the sleeping arrangements but Zef had his own room for when he entertained others and I had the same. Yes, there was a twinge when he suggested it but he did protest it was more likely than not, me that would be taking advantage of the arrangement as I was young, hot, and up for anything. As well as having the best ass he'd ever fucked. That was enough to make the twinge subside.

I was nervous all day, wondering how gross the test would be. I was prepared for just about anything. I ran some of the most gross ideas through my mind from family pets to masquerading as a human toilet. I was amazed how many times my cock got hard. Seems I did have a few qualms so I just hoped they weren't on the agenda that day.

As the appointed time approached, my stomach did a few flips but I was more aroused than apprehensive as I lay naked on the coffee table as instructed. I loved the idea of being slave to Zef's whims, to laying myself open to whatever he wanted of me. I heard the key in the door, pacing my breath so I wouldn't have a panic attack. Hoping it was going to be something along the lines of the group experience of the previous night, I suspect my face gave me away when Zef came into the house, hesitating on the threshold of the living room.

"Hey, fag," he called. "You remember Ned?"

The grotesque slob from the bar who'd given me his calling card lumbered into view, a lewd grin plastered across his face. My stomach lurched and I was in danger of upchucking my lunch.

I can do this. I can do this. I can do this.

Zef was obviously into humiliating his partners. Okay, the guy was grossly overweight but I'd concentrate on his cock. After all, he told me it was so large it would turn me cross-eyed. Slowly, I turned my disgust around by concentrating on the positives. Not too slowly as Zef was awaiting my response. Hell, two giant cocks, I'd be in paradise. Maybe they'd do my ass together.

I smiled widely.

"What are you two waiting for? For fuck's sake, get your clothes off."

OMG! MY UNCLE'S A FAIRY!

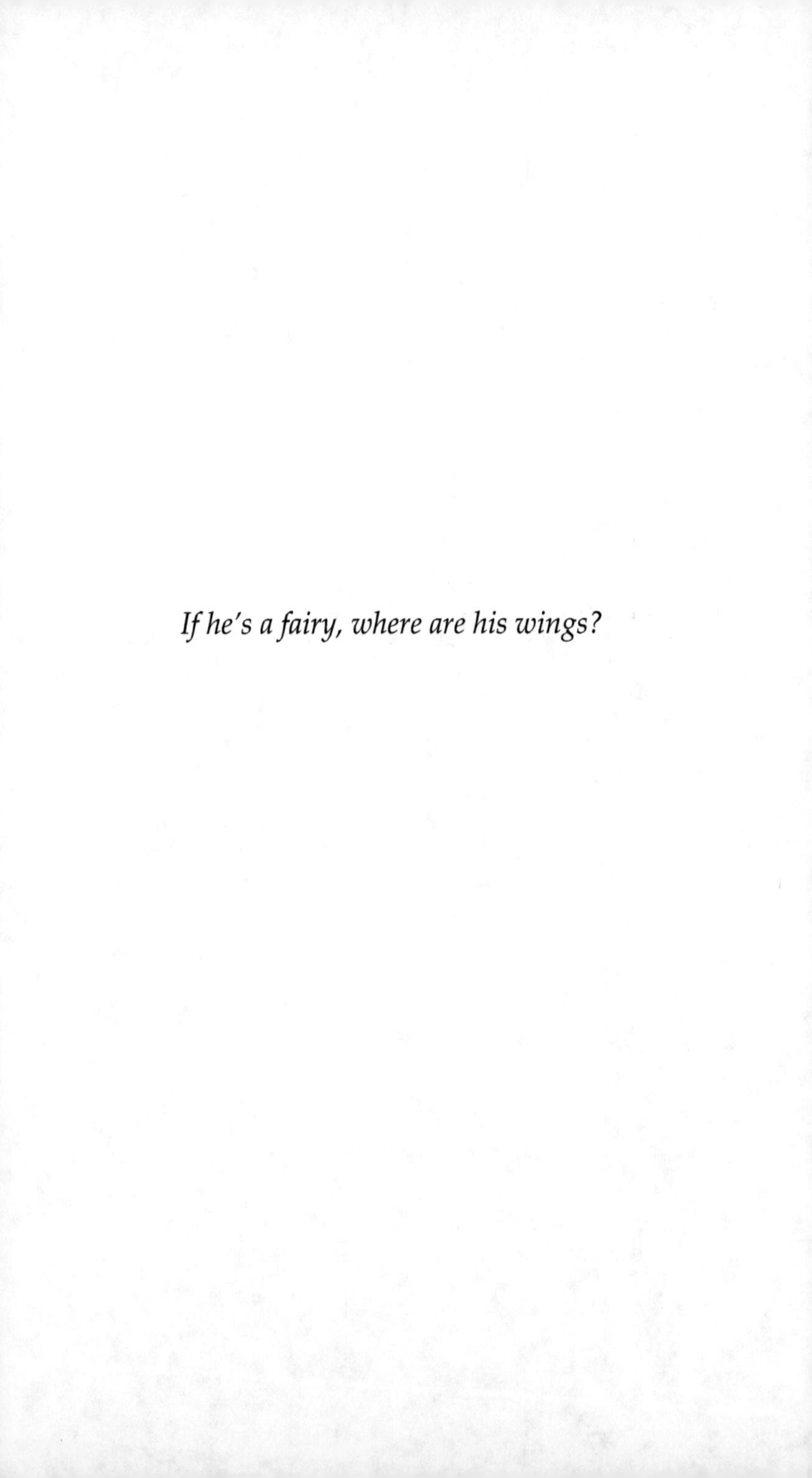

If he's a fairy, where are his wings?

I was ten when I found out my uncle was a fairy. I overheard my dad and mum arguing about Uncle Jeb. "He's a bleedin' fairy, Eileen. I don't want him hanging around Jason."

"It's not something you can catch," my mum laughed. "It's not like the common cold that can be passed on in sneezes."

"And that mate of his, Hal. He's a fairy too."

"Jason adores both of them," Mum said, her voice icy. "You going to tell him he can't see his favorite relative anymore?"

My dad grumbled like he does every time he loses an argument to my mum. Then he always has to have the last word. "It's not right. They spend far too much time over here. They're a bad influence."

I wandered out into the backyard to throw ball with Daz, our ageing Jack Russell terrier. He looked at me, as he always did whenever I kicked the bald tennis ball for him to fetch, as if to say that he was way too old for this sort of energetic behavior. Nevertheless, he would always waddle away obediently and fetch, then slump over the ball, growling if I attempted to retrieve it.

I realized he was getting old, his reflexes not as sharp as they once were when he would almost beg for a game of fetch. Age was a foreign concept to me. I knew my nanna was as old as Daz. She used to nap every afternoon as well.

I was too hyperactive to ever want to rest, something that drove my mum and dad spare so I'd go outside when I felt over-stimulated.

Like now. Finding out Uncle Jeb was a fairy. I wouldn't have believed it just on my dad's say-so because he was prone to exaggeration. But mum, that was a different matter altogether. She had never steered me wrong. She told the truth when I asked if Santa Claus was real. When I questioned my dad about what I'd heard at school, he merely looked guilt stricken, telling me to 'go ask your mother.'

So if my mum said Uncle Jeb was a fairy, then I believed her. Trouble was he was such a big guy. So was Hal. I always thought fairies were girls. And they were tiny little things like in cartoons on the telly. They hopped around on flowers and rode on the backs of bees and that sort of thing.

Jeb and Hal were my favorite people in the world. They didn't treat me like a little kid. They listened to what I had to say and gently steered me to draw my own conclusions from what I'd observed. They never told me I was stupid even when I said the dumbest things. They also had the coolest stories because they'd been places I only ever heard of on the news or looked up on the computer when they talked about them. They always encouraged me to seek out knowledge if I was interested in where they'd been after they returned with little wooden gifts or colorful stamps, or unusual postcards they brought from exotic locations. I kept them in a cardboard shoe box underneath my bed and, sometimes, after my dad had grizzled about 'It's all right for some, but I have a family to support,' I'd take them out and place them all over my bed and dream of being like Uncle Jeb.

It wasn't likely though because I had what the doctor diagnosed as a nervous disorder which later he changed to something with initials, something like ADHD. He prescribed tablets which I took every day. When my uncle found out he and my dad had a shouting match about my health. Uncle Jeb shouted that there was nothing wrong with me.

"Jason is just a kid. He's a bundle of energy. He needs to play, Tom. Instead, you drug him to the gills. Turn him into a zombie so he doesn't interrupt your cozy lifestyle. If you feel that way, why did you ever have a child?"

"Because Eileen wanted a kid, that's why."

That did it. I kissed goodbye to ever having a baby brother or sister. I'm not saying it didn't hurt. Although it left a residual gut punch, it was not something I angsted over. I had more important things to discover: like were Hal and Uncle Jeb really fairies, for example. I couldn't wait until next time we all went to the beach. Dad never came with us; he preferred expending his energy in thumb sports: clicking the remote control on the television to change channels between the different codes of football or, depending on the season, cricket, or basketball. He was the ultimate sports fanatic: lounge chair brigade.

It was the first warm weekend in October, a few weeks after the conversation about fairies, before mum packed a picnic lunch and we headed to the beach at Clovelly. There were a few early summer souls braving the temperature of the ocean but they were mainly in wetsuits riding boards. The breeze off the water was cool enough that Jeb and Hal didn't remove their shirts. I was getting frustrated.

"Don't you want to sunbake, Uncle Jeb? Get a tan before anyone else?" I almost begged.

"What's got into you, Jason? Leave Uncle Jeb alone. If he doesn't want to take his shirt off, that's his business," Mum said.

She looked at me strangely and I had the sudden thought she may think I wanted to stare at Uncle Jeb's body. I blushed. Hal nudged Jeb and they both pretended not to notice my embarrassment.

The two guys did have great bodies. It wasn't just me thought so. You couldn't help but notice. They both looked like the guys on the front of those men's health magazines I kept under my bed, even though Hal was as old as my dad.

"I guess it wouldn't hurt to get a few rays," Hal winked.

"You want to oil our backs?" Jeb asked, handing me the sunscreen.

"Just don't tell your father, Jason," mum warned.

What was there to tell?

Uncle Jeb removed his shirt and both men stood flexing their muscles, showing off. Mum lowered the sunglasses on her nose to stare at their carry on. "Ah, what a waste," she said returning to her novel. I didn't know what she meant.

I squirted the thick cream onto Jeb's back and he shivered because it was cold. I took a good look but I couldn't see any sign of wings and everyone knows fairies have wings. I started to spread the cream taking every opportunity to feel for wings that he may have folded up under his skin. I pressed the bones in his spine thinking that might free them or at least give me an idea where he kept them when he was on the beach. I supposed they could always be detachable so he could leave them at home so people wouldn't stare. But where did he screw them in? I looked under his armpits and right down to the top of his swimsuit.

"Jason, what on earth are you doing?" mum said as she watched my erratic behavior. "It's like you've lost your mind and you've gone looking for it."

"What is it, mate?" Jeb asked kindly. "What are you looking for?"

I didn't like them making fun of me so I huffed up my chest as best I could before spilling the beans. "I heard daddy say that Uncle Jeb and Hal are fairies, so I'm looking for where they keep their wings."

The three of them looked at one another before they burst into hysterical laughter. I stamped my foot in a temper. "Stop it! Stop laughing at me."

Jeb grabbed me and wrestled me to the sand. "We're not laughing at you, Jason. We're laughing at your dad."

"I suppose he's old enough to know," my mum sighed. "He'd have to be told eventually."

"Told what?" I asked.

"Can you keep a secret?" Hal asked.

I was indignant. "Of course."

Jeb explained patiently that my dad was being nasty and that he and Hal weren't real fairies but that was a name people used to describe men who liked other men.

"Don't you like girls, Uncle Jeb?"

"Yes, I like girls, Jason, I just don't want to… um…kiss them."

I know now he was explaining it simplistically so I would understand.

"So you and Uncle Hal like each other the way me and Marcie Haines at school like each other?"

"Yes," Uncle Jeb said.

"You must like Uncle Hal an awful lot then."

He ruffled my hair which I've noticed is something grown-ups do when they get emotional. In this case I didn't mind because he and Uncle Hal treat me as a grown up when they talk to me. I like that.

"So which one of you is the man then?"

My mum decided that was enough explanations for the day. She didn't want to tire me out. "I think we'll leave that discussion for a later time, Jason."

I was disappointed but it could wait. "Okay, mum." I turned to Jeb, "So no wings, huh?"

He smiled. "No wings."

For my next birthday, Uncle Jeb and Uncle Hal gave me a skateboard.

My father just looked at them and snorted. "Don't think I don't know what you're doing," he said before heading back to his home office, the spare room he converted into a place where he could go so mum and I didn't disturb him. That was pretty much all the time when he was home.

Jeb and Hal took me and mum to a skate park near where they lived. They wrapped me up in a helmet and pads so I felt like an alien from outer space, then they helped me on the little kids' section. Jeb and Hal took turns holding on to me as I slid down the concave ramp.

Without warning, Uncle Jeb released me about half way from the bottom. I panicked, and fell. Mum was up out of her seat where she'd watched and clapped every time I'd made it to the bottom without injury. Jeb put his hand up to stop her. She sat down again but I could see the concerned look on her face as I picked myself up.

"Did that hurt?" Uncle Jeb asked.

It did a little bit but I pretended it hadn't.

"You want to try again?"

I nodded, knowing if I didn't I would never get on the skateboard again.

Jeb let me go at the same spot as before. I wobbled a bit, mainly because I tensed up in expectation, and fell off again. And again. And again.

My mum cringed but didn't turn away.

"Relax," Hal said as he took over from my uncle. "I won't let you go like Jeb did. I'll hold you all the way down, till you get your confidence. Okay?"

"Uh huh," I squeaked. I knew if I fell a few more times I would give up. If I can't do something then I'll try something else. I didn't want to appear ungrateful for the birthday present, especially as I could picture my dad smirking and shaking his head if I came home defeated.

I was at the top of the ramp, which was not even as tall as Hal, and I was relaxed, as ready as I ever would be to shoot down the slope with him holding on to me protectively. Except he didn't. Even higher up than Uncle Jeb, he let me go. I wasn't expecting it. Time seemed to be in slow motion and I had all the time in the world to realize I could panic or I could ride my way to the bottom confident in the way I was standing. I saw my mum's face; she was gasping and rising in the seat. I saw Uncle Jeb's huge smile, and I bent my knees slightly and I rode the bugger to the bottom. Okay, my landing wasn't graceful. It wouldn't get points in a competition but I didn't fall off. Well, not on my ass at any rate. I stumbled off but didn't fall.

Some of the bigger guys who were sitting about waiting their turn on the bigger guys' ramps applauded. So did mum and Jeb and Hal. They all High Fived me like pro sportsmen do. It felt so good. I tried it again. Not so good that time, but I kept right on at it until no one had to hold on to me at all. I was scratched and bruised but I was proud of my achievements. One of the big guys wandered over, ignoring my family, and said, "Hey, little dude, name's Scratch, here let me give you a few pointers." He draped his arm across my shoulder to guide me away from the adults. I looked at mum but Scratch gave her a look which she must have interpreted as 'Back off' because she remained where she was.

The grown-ups watched as Scratch, who must have been about fifteen or so, gave me a quick lesson in stance, aerodynamics, and skater etiquette. He watched as I tried a few moves on my own, gave me some further advice, watched again, and then gave me the thumbs up. "Later, dude," he smiled as he wandered away. I knew I'd see him again.

When we went home late in the afternoon I was so buzzed even my dad's comment that 'skateboarding's not a real sport like cricket or AFL,' couldn't dampen my spirits. I went to my room, hugging the skateboard to my chest. Somewhere in my dreams of sporting glory I wasn't hugging the skateboard any longer, I was hugging Scratch. I developed a serious case of hero worship.

And I stopped taking my medication.

I just kept the pill in my mouth and spat it out when no one was looking. Then I learned how to palm it so that it was never in my mouth in the first place. Mum looked at me quizzically from time to time but dad never noticed any change in my behavior – if there was any – apart from my enthusiasm for my new sport which he began to encourage mainly, I suspect, because it got me out of the house and from under his feet. However, he still had a problem admitting it took any great skill.

When I began bringing home the odd trophy from small-time competitions, dad's sneering about 'real sports' got even worse. Uncle Jeb, who turned up at every competition with Hal, told me not to worry because Tom, my dad, was jealous of my success. He said that I shouldn't attempt to try to impress him because nothing ever would. It was the way of the world, he said. The only person I should do it for – is myself. Not him, not Hal, not mum. Myself.

"Not that we aren't proud of you," he added. "We are. Very proud. But do it because you enjoy it. When it becomes a chore or you're not enjoying it any more, then walk away. It's your life, live it for yourself."

It took a few years, and a few more attempts to impress dad with my bigger and better trophy wins before I knew Jeb was right. When I let that go, there was no stopping me. Although she worried initially, Mum came to terms with my medication free regimen. Dad still didn't notice anything. Not even when I began to develop. I was a late bloomer.

I grew hair around my dick and under my arms. My voice cracked like a screechy eggshell and, suddenly, I began to have feelings. It was Scratch who helped me out in that department. He explained about wanking, which he called 'masturbation.' Not only did he explain how to do it, he demonstrated for me. After I got the hang of it by practicing at home, learning which stroke was best and where to position my fingers like my dick was some sort of musical instrument, Scratch and I would sometimes belt out a load or two when the desire got too great to be contained in our balls.

It wasn't queer, and we never thought of it that way, it was a dude-to-dude thing, helping out a mate. We hung out together, we ate pizza together, we skated together, and we jerked off together. Natural progression, right?

We double dated girls together but my experience was restricted to copping a feel of her tits, pushing my tongue into her mouth and, once, fingering her pussy at the movies. I was too young to go all the way, although Scratch had bloomed and was laying every chick he could get his hands on. And he liked to do it with me watching. He promised me an extra special birthday treat when I turned sixteen.

That became moot under the circumstances.

I was getting better and better at skateboarding and even persuaded my parents to let me go to the national championships as I was one of the top five contenders in my age category. Mum was keen for me to go, but my dad was adamant I was staying home. I would have to travel interstate for the tournament and my dad was down on Scratch as a chaperone. He thought he was a very bad influence on me as my grades at school were suffering. Plus I gave the old man lip whenever we got to that broken record rendition of the old family favorite, "What are you doing with your life? You need an education to get ahead in the world." That same old/same old shit that parents always give their kids. Especially when it looks as if that kid is likely to make more money than the old man who doesn't understand the modern world and its culture.

Like skateboarding. Dad didn't acknowledge it was a sport even after I got a few small paid gigs modeling skateboarder clothes or the boards themselves. I was paying mum board while I was at school; something she pointed out my dad never did for his parents. He'd just snort and head to the security of his office whenever the subject came up.

It's not like I was paying board all the time but whenever I made good money I'd always put my fair share in the kitty. The rest I put aside for a 'rainy day' like the championships. After weeks of arguing about going to the championships interstate, the problem was solved when Uncle Jeb called in and let it drop that he and Hal were driving to Adelaide for a short break to visit friends. I guessed mum had engineered the whole thing.

Dad still put up a brave fight but he was outnumbered and out-maneuvered.

In the end, mum got her way, me and Scratch hitching a ride to the championships with Jeb and Hal. Scratch knew them well enough from the times they'd turned up to cheer me on. He was only about ten years younger than Jeb but, surprisingly, although they were miles apart socially and culturally, it was he and Hal who got along so well that he joined him in the front seat when he was driving while I shared the back seat with Uncle Jeb.

Jeb and Hal alternated as drivers every two hours although they never allowed Scratch to take the wheel no matter how much he pleaded, and I was still too young to drive. We split the trip by stopping overnight at a motel in some forlorn country town that looked as if predatory white ants had chewed all the hope out of it. The woman behind the front desk merely raised an eyebrow when Hal asked for a double bed, but said nothing; wise decision considering the motel and its greasy spoon café seemed to be a haven for every sexual indiscretion the area attracted, including the long-haul truck drivers and their youthful runaway pick-ups.

After a surprisingly good meal in the café, we decided to call it a night. There seemed to be little attraction in the town apart from a boisterous pub that appeared unlikely to welcome two skateboarders and two gay guys. Besides, we wanted to get an early start in the morning.

Scratch and I were looking forward to a few ZZZs but the activity in the room next door, separated from ours by walls that were obviously as thin as cardboard and about as soundproof, kept us awake. We lay in our single beds, discussing tactics for the forthcoming championships trying to block out the orgasmic screams of some young woman being pounded by a truckie. At least that's what it sounded like to us. No amount of banging on the walls could get them to turn it down a notch.

On the other side were two men going at it just as eagerly, but Jeb and Hal were definitely less vocal in the sex department. Eventually, having run out of conversation, Scratch and I decided to call it a night. I pulled the pillow over my head in an effort to block out not only the sounds but the flashing neon light from the motel's street sign that flooded the room through the tissue thin curtains, threatening me with a bout of epilepsy. I did eventually fall asleep but woke early in the morning needing to piss. Scratch's bed was empty so I thought he must have gone to the bathroom before me.

Switching on the light so he could find his way back to his bed without tripping over the frayed carpet, I waited in vain for his return. I got up to find he wasn't in the bathroom at all. I shrugged. Not my responsibility he went walkabout in the middle of the night. Perhaps he couldn't sleep. Perhaps the sounds of sexual coupling had turned him on and he needed to relieve himself though I wondered if that were so, why he didn't just whip it out and whack it off. We usually had no qualms about that sort of thing.

I did my business and was back in bed with the light off, staring at the ceiling when he crept back into the room. He smelled of booze and sex so I assumed he'd wandered into town and picked up a chick at the pub. Good luck to him. Next thing I knew it was morning and Hal was banging on the door telling us to hurry up, we were making tracks.

The shower, shit and shave ritual was pretty perfunctory, we spent more time having breakfast, before we took off on the last leg of the journey, arriving in Adelaide in the late afternoon. We'd been in no hurry as competition registration didn't begin until the following day. Unbeknown to either Scratch or me, Jeb had booked us into a classier motel than the dorm accommodation we'd been contemplating. We were both grateful, as the walls were thicker, the beds more comfortable, and the motel's neon away from the windows which were, at any rate, double-backed curtained to keep out light.

We did a recon of the championship venue and got in a some practice runs with a few of the local guys who made us welcome, especially after Scratch demonstrated his radical moves which he then proceeded to teach them. The moves were purely for showing off and played no part in his championship routine but they usually broke the ice around other skateboarders protective of their turf.

When we got back to the motel, Jeb invited us to a restaurant for dinner and as neither Scratch nor I had much in the way of spare cash to throw around for anything other than Maccas, we gladly accepted. We were on our best behavior although our daggy gear was definitely out of place in our fine surroundings. We knew it was all class because the waiters treated us as if we were royalty. It helped that Hal knew the guys and they fussed over him like a returning hero. They also fussed over Scratch but he was oblivious to all the flirting. I guess he was focused on his chances in the competition. If he came in the top three in his class, he was assured of enough money to turn pro. That was his dream.

In the end, he came second so, chuffed at his achievement, he partied hard.

By the middle of the week, it looked as if I had a real chance as well. Jeb rang mum and offered to fly her and dad down for the finals in my age event. Mum accepted with alacrity but, she told me later, dad grizzled as usual. She arrived the night before my big contest but I was so on edge psyching myself up that she went out to dinner with Jeb and Hal. It wasn't the end of the world if I didn't win, but it would be confirmation to my dad that his son was a loser even though I had a shelf of trophies at home. This, too, was a shot at the big time. Well, as big time as skateboarding gets. It doesn't quite rate up there with cricket, football, or even women's netball in TV coverage or paid product endorsements.

Without going into detail, let's just say I nailed it. It was touch and go for a while but I scraped over the line, a few points ahead of a local hero who was gracious enough to acknowledge my triumph was well deserved. Jeb and Hal were there to offer their congratulations while mum had tears in her eyes but held back from being too clinging and effusive because the other competitors were around. I heard a couple of guys comment that mum was a total MILF and I had to wash my brain to purge the image from my mind.

Scratch was there to cheer me on but I could read in his eyes that he wished I hadn't done quite as well as I had. He was jealous, but he did a good job of covering it. He declined an invitation to come out and par-tay with me. The runner up had invited me to a celebration. It was at his home so it promised to be alcohol and drug free. I didn't believe that for a moment, neither did mum who proceeded to give me a lecture on the evils of narcotics and booze. Rich, coming from a woman who smoked dope in her younger years and still managed to guzzle her way through a wine club selection each month.

I didn't have to remind her though, Jeb did that for me. As it turned out, the party was pretty tame in the illegal (to under-age me) sense. Sure, there was the scent of a particular 'weed' in the air, but it was not all-pervasive, and the alcohol was light beer which we drank sparingly. Still, it was a great night discussing the finer points of skateboarding with likeminded guys. Scratch probably would have enjoyed himself.

It wasn't late when I got back to the motel, so I wasn't surprised to discover Scratch was still out. He'd made new mates while in the city and had even talked about relocating but I knew it was a spur-of-the-moment thing as they didn't have the breadth of facilities and opportunities that our home city had. I popped in on mum who had a room a couple of doors down from mine for a good old natter about my win, about dad, and about my future. I went to bed feeling very pleased with myself.

In the morning, Scratch still hadn't appeared. I wasn't too concerned because we'd made no set time for our return journey and, anyway, he never went anywhere without his mobile phone.

To thank them for their support, I decided to drop in on Jeb and Hal. I was still coming down from the euphoria of my win and the hero worship at the party so, after I knocked at the door to their room, I just barged my way in as it was unlocked. Not a good idea. The triumphant grin on my face disappeared quickly.

I lost it. Big time. My grin. My euphoria. And my temper. For there on the bed, Hal was doing things to Scratch that I had only ever seen in porn movies. My mouth acted without waiting to connect to my brain. They were as startled by the vitriol that poured from my mouth as the calmer part of my brain was. If the tongue lashing I gave them had been with a real whip, they would have been covered in welts.

It didn't help that my shouting brought Jeb out of the bathroom, unsuccessfully adjusting a towel over his nakedness. That merely spurred me on to even wilder accusations and name calling. At one stage, I seem to recall yelling, "Who else you got in here? My mum?"

I let fly at Scratch for his treacherous behavior before turning my attention to my uncles. I was only part way through all the things I had stored up, when Jeb snapped, "That's enough!"

I had never heard him utter a harsh word before in his life, not even when goaded by dad, so his tone immediately silenced me. He'd been throwing on clothes while I'd vented, so he was now fully dressed. He told Hal and Scratch that he was taking me for a walk to help me calm down and that they should pack the car up ready to roll.

We walked the streets in silence until we found a park, deserted except for a few solitary individuals jogging or on their way to early starts at work. We found a bench away from prying ears. I expected a verbal tirade about my behavior which I would return in kind. Instead, Jeb asked quietly, "What was it that upset you, Jason?" I went to answer without thinking but he held up his hand. "Don't give me the first glib answer that comes into your head, think about it."

Realizing I was about to answer automatically, I closed my mouth. After wrestling with my conscience for a few moments, I had to confess, "I don't know Uncle Jeb. I thought I did but…"

"That's good," he said.

"Is it?"

"We can work from there. If you gave me a typical bullshit answer there was nowhere to go. That would have proved you'd closed your mind. This way we can work it through. Were you upset with Scratch that he was having sex with Hal?"

"Partly," I admitted. "I thought he was my friend."

"He is your friend. More than you know. You're only fifteen, Jason. In the eyes of the law, you're a birthday shy of consent in this state."

"Why didn't he tell me he's gay," I complained.

"He doesn't know that he is, Jason. He's still testing his wings. Plus he didn't know how you'd take it. It's a very different thing having a gay best friend to having a gay uncle."

"I thought Hal was being unfaithful to you."

Jeb took a deep breath. "It wasn't the ideal way for you to find out, Jason, but Hal and I share."

"Everything?"

"Everything."

"Even other men?"

"That, too."

"Wow."

"It's not something they teach you at school but you can like a lot of girls or boys or whatever it is you're into at the same time. I'm not prying Jason, that's your own business. There's a difference between love and sex. Hal and I love each other but sometimes we like a bit of variety. Neither of us loves Scratch but he's a very accommodating playmate for a night or two. Some people don't understand the difference; some people aren't capable of sex without love. I'm not saying that our style of living is for everyone, but it suits us.

"It's like Hal is my meat and potatoes, Scratch is the salad on the side."

It was a lot to take in. A lot of social conditioning to question. "I think I understand."

"You had breakfast?" Jeb asked.

I shook my head.

"Come on, let's go and have something fattening and sugary and you ask me any questions you like no matter how embarrassing, okay?"

I had a million things I wanted to ask. Suddenly the world was a bigger, scarier, but more interesting place than I'd ever imagined. Uncle Jeb rang Hal back at the motel and told him where to meet us with the car in about an hour, and that he should pick up mum as well.

I bombarded Jeb with enough questions to fill an encyclopedia and, as he said he would, he answered truthfully, to the extent I embarrassed him a number of times so that he turned as red as the raspberry Slurpee I had with my breakfast. We talked some more while we waited for them to pick us up. When they were half an hour late and Jeb had finished his third coffee, he rang Hal's mobile.

It was answered by the police.

The funerals were a forlorn affair. Dad blamed me for mum's death, but blamed Jeb even more. It seemed to me that he was just looking for an excuse to ban my uncle from the house. I still snuck out to see Jeb, especially to join him at Scratch's funeral, and to support him at Hal's. We both cried our eyes out, holding on to each other for support.

Later, back at his home, with a few of his closest friends, I told him he had every right to hate me just as my dad did.

He was puzzled. "Why would I hate you?"

"It's my fault Hal is dead. That mum is dead. That Scratch is dead."

"Is that what you believe?"

"Yeah. So does dad."

"Your dad is a fool. I expected better from you. The accident had nothing to do with you. It was because some idiot ran a red light and careened into Hal's car."

"But if I hadn't thrown a wobbly, they wouldn't have been on their way to pick us up."

"No, the chances are we all would have been in the car heading back home and you and I would be six feet under along with the others. Stop beating yourself up over it."

"I can't stop feeling guilty," I said.

And I didn't. Life changed. Jeb took himself overseas for long periods attempting to find the missing part of him in out-of-the-way spots where he found beauty but little solace. I saved his postcards like they were little pieces of a Jeb jigsaw waiting to be put back together. I chucked in skateboarding believing it was what had caused all the problems in the first place. Dad was pleased that I concentrated on my education but every time I passed someone on a skateboard my stomach flip flopped in a peculiar way.

Two years passed. It wasn't like I put my social life on hold. I dated women. I masturbated with men. I experimented, but none of it was fulfilling. Maybe I was one of those people who needed to be in love to find satisfaction. I wished I had Jeb to talk to. I could discuss these sorts of things with him without embarrassment. My dad was not the go-to guy to talk about feelings and sexuality. He was always pleased when I brought a girl home to meet him but equally accusatory when, as inevitably happened, we split up. It was easier to tell him I was too young to settle down and that I was still 'sowing my wild oats.'

Trouble is I had no oats, wild or otherwise. Dad and I barely tolerated each other's presence. Had I enough money to support myself, I would have moved out.

Then, just before my eighteenth birthday, Jeb wrote to say he was returning home for good, his wandering days over.

Dad's attitude hadn't mellowed in the intervening two years. "Don't think he's coming here to visit. I don't want the faggot anywhere near you."

"You don't let him visit, then I'll go over to his place," I smart-assed back.

"You'll do no such thing. While you live here you'll obey my rules."

"No matter how stupid they are."

I was at that stage of youthful rebellion I was prepared to risk everything. I won my point by suggesting that if dad was so concerned that Uncle Jeb would try something 'faggy' on me wouldn't it be better Jeb visit me at home where dad could keep an eye on him. "Just about anything could happen if I go to his place." I made it sound so sinister I almost burst out laughing. Uncle Jeb simply wasn't like that but it paid to feed dad's paranoia so I got my way.

Jeb came over for dinner. I cooked, one of the suspicious non-masculine tasks I was good at, much to my dad's chagrin. If I hadn't been, we both would have been living on cardboard microwave meals, and takeaway.

The conversation revolved around his trips overseas which sounded full of adventure and exoticism although I could see he was pulling his punches as he related stories humorous and stories dangerous. I wanted to hear stories outrageous and stories sexual which he merely hinted at.

"I don't know why everyone is so keen to head off overseas," dad whined. "This country is good enough for me. You won't find any better no matter how many places you visit."

Jeb smiled and let him have his way, never contradicting dad's parochial rigidity. The dinner continued peacefully, the truce holding until Jeb mentioned the new skateboard that was the buzz in all the magazines and newspapers. I must admit I'd pored over the articles, dreaming what I could do with the new sleek design. But I was rusty. Sure, I'd sneak out sometimes just to keep my skills up, but I had no intention of returning to the circuit. That was my penance for what I'd done.

"What if I told you I could get my hands on the new design?" Jeb said a little too casually, like he'd rehearsed it to be a surprise.

My heart started palpitating at the mere chance of it, giving me away. I sighed at how easily manipulated I was. Then my mouth ran away from my brain again.

"If you do that for me, Uncle Jeb, then just maybe I'll let you fuck me."

I watched as coffee shot out of Jeb's nose. My dad spat his across the table. They both looked at me in amazement.

Dad bellowed. "What the fuck did you just say?"

That sort of belligerent screaming might have worked once but I was up for defying the alpha male of the household. Jeb jumped in before I could repeat my outrageous offer.

He didn't rise to the bait though. "I'll see what I can do, Jason, but I can't promise anything."

"In that case, neither can I," I winked as I got up and left the room, hesitating outside the door to eavesdrop.

Dad was still purple with rage. "Calm down," Jeb said to stop him having a heart attack. "He's just baiting you. It's what young kids do."

"The hell they do," dad fumed. "I always knew he was a faggot. That's your influence."

"He's not gay. He was using the only ammo he has to needle you and the fact you're a rabid homophobe, he pushed all the right buttons."

"I'm not …"

"Don't give me that shit. When it comes to being down on gays you're at the head of the line."

Dad ignored the charge. "You wouldn't, would you?"

"What?"

"Fuck your own nephew. Your sister's boy."

"Well, he is mighty tasty for his age."

"You fuckin' pervert," he yelled.

"See! That's how easy it is to get you all riled up. Of course, I wouldn't touch him. He's family. I don't do that.

And he's far too young. I'm old enough to be his dad. Unless he prefers older men."

I snickered quietly at the way Jeb was manipulating my old man.

Truth be told, a lot of gay guys did fancy me. I inherited my old man's jock body and granite physique but my mom's looks. I guess I'm cute rather than rugged but I learned young to compensate for that softness by developing a personality so masculine you could almost cut it with a knife. If testosterone had a personality then it would be like mine. That kept the faggot baiters at bay. Except for my dad. As a result, I'm popular with guys but even more popular with girls who I attract like flies to honey.

I was amused that from the conversation with my uncle earlier in the evening he assumed I was bedding ten times the number of women that dad was. It simply wasn't true. Dad had become the troll since mum's death while I'd become… well…more particular.

Jeb was still lecturing dad. "If you listened carefully instead of flying off the handle like you always do you would have noticed Jason said 'just maybe' so you have little reason to think he's going to jump into bed with me."

Perceptive bugger.

"Besides, he's straight. I've seen the chicks hanging off him at the skate park. He's a stud like his old man."

That was pouring it on so thick it was making my stomach turn, but dad seemed to be buying it.

"If I thought for one moment he was a fag he'd be out on his ass," he said.

Jeb dug the knife in one last time. "And don't think there wouldn't be a lot of offers to help him up off that pretty ass of his either."

The next day I met Uncle Jeb for lunch.

"I hope you don't mind," he said, "but I've already lobbied on your behalf. I met Karl, the designer of the new board, while I was in Switzerland."

"Hmm," I grinned. "Exactly how well do you know him?"

Jeb told me. I wasn't shocked. I loved it when he thought enough of my maturity not to hold anything back.

"I know it's none of my business, but it's such a waste of talent to give up your sport," Jeb said. I kept mum as I guessed what he was doing. He was using the new design to get me back into the sport I'd once loved so much and out of the funk in which I found myself. "I showed Karl film footage of you in action, skateboard action, Jason, get your mind out of the sewer. He was very impressed."

I thanked him for intervening on my behalf, but I could never afford the extravagant purchase price for the prototype. Still, I did appreciate his interest. He was all smiles when he turned up at the skateboard park three days later. I'd phoned to ask for a lift but also coincidentally to show him that his pep talk was having results. I was working my old skateboard – just for the exercise, I told myself – when I noticed Jeb watching me. He waved. Some of my buddies who remembered him from years back went over to chat to him, knowing he was not some old dude who turned up to perv.

"Hi Jeb," I smiled. I stopped calling him uncle except around my dad who did not encourage familiarity with 'fags.'

"You've still got it," he said. "A skateboard Nureyev."

I imitated my father's voice. "Wasn't he a fag?"

We both laughed. It was so comfortable being around him. I felt like a total shit because I couldn't invite him home. He popped the boot of the car so I could stow my skateboard, then said like he'd forgotten, "Oh, this is for you,"

I didn't say anything. I couldn't speak. I examined every inch of it, ran my fingers along the contours, sniffed it, and licked its new surface. I held it to the light and, when I finished my forensic examination, I held it to my chest and exhaled.

"I owe ya," I beamed.

"Go on," he said, nodding in the direction of the park. "Try it out."

I ran to show my mates. I thought Jeb would hang around but he must have believed he'd done his bit. Plus he was a good guy; he'd know that gratitude is one of the hardest things to get right.

I knew he wouldn't expect me to bend over and part my ass cheeks although most of the guys at the park would have done it gladly for a chance at the new design. Knowing my dad's mind was just a culvert away from a sewer, I kept the new design hidden from him, but he must have suspected and gone searching through my room because I came home one night to find him waiting for me, the skateboard on the table.

He launched straight into it. "So, did you let him fuck you?"

"Don't be ridiculous. I don't do that."

"What? Let men fuck you for money? Or a new skateboard? Or let men fuck you for pleasure?"

"All the above," I said in disgust.

I turned to walk away but dad grabbed me by the arm.

"Don't you walk away when I'm talking to you."

"You're not talking to me, dad," I said. "You're yelling at me. Like you've yelled at me all my life."

"I don't think there's a day I haven't wished you were in that car instead of your mother."

I only just made it to the bathroom before I heaved. I gave him the benefit of the doubt, knowing he was still hurting over mum's death, but I no longer had any respect for him. Wiping my face on a towel, I went to my bedroom to throw a few personal items into a backpack, grabbed my skateboard and headed for the door.

I heard the growl before I felt the punch to my back which laid me out. "Where the fuck are you going?"

"As far away from here as I can get," I snarled as I got up, facing him.

"Get back in your room. You're not going anywhere. You'll do as I say."

"Not any more. You forfeited any rights you had over me when you said what you did."

He made baby noises. "Did daddy hurt his little fag boy's feelings?"

Ignoring him, I walked to the door but he grabbed my hair dragging me into the kitchen. I struggled, punching him in the chest.

"You ungrateful bastard," he yelled, smashing my face down onto the table.

He kept yelling and pummeling me until my lip split and blood smeared the table top. He hesitated when he saw it, giving me enough time, groggy as I was, to push him over and make it to the door to escape into the night air where I knew I would be safe. He screamed obscenities from the doorway but didn't come after me.

To this day, I don't know how I made it to my uncle's place. When Jeb opened his apartment door and saw me standing, shivering, he wrapped his arms around me and led me inside. While he bathed my bruises and cuts, gently pressing my split lip to stop the bleeding, he gave me a strong brandy to dull the pain, not of my physical injuries but the mental scars that would take many months to close up.

When I could barely make coherent sounds because of the alcohol he'd encouraged me to drink, he tucked me in bed in the spare room where I cried myself to sleep. Once or twice through the night I woke up gasping in fright but he was there to soothe me, sleeping fitfully in an old armchair in the corner of the room, keeping watch over me like a fairy godfather. Maybe he is a fairy, after all, I thought as I slumped back into oblivion.

The following day was a series of blurred images. I remained in bed, barely able to think coherently, eating when Jeb told me I should eat, sleeping when he told me I should sleep. The third day I awoke, feeling battered and bruised but able to face the world, I discovered the rest of my clothes and other items in the wardrobe.

When I queried their appearance. Jeb grinned. "I told your father that you needed them more than he did. It took a bit of persuasion but he finally came around to my point of view. I hope I didn't assume too much, but I didn't think you'd be going back."

Over the next week, I talked and talked and talked until I was sure Jeb was sick of the sound of my voice. I told him my dreams, my fears, my successes, my failures. And he listened. I opened my heart to him, inviting him in. He was shocked at first, but admitted one of his reasons for staying away after Hal's death was because it had become increasingly difficult for him to deny his growing feelings for me.

"You don't have to anymore," I said leaning over to kiss him. I was admitting to myself and to him that I'd loved him most of my life.

He hesitated at first, probably wondering if the kiss was platonic, or something deeper.

I broke away, looking him squarely in the eyes. "You asked me once why I was so upset when I walked in on you and Hal and Scratch. The answer is because when I saw what was happening I wanted so much to be Scratch. To be in his position."

The next time I kissed Jeb, he kissed me back.

OMG! SATAN WANTS A BLOW JOB!

Halloween brought out the devil in him.

"Good guys come last," Aiden Batterby was told as a teenager. It was his dad's credo. It wasn't just bullshit either; his father really lived by that one rule. He'd always put the boot in when his opponent was down, both literally and figuratively. He was always the first to plunge the knife between his enemy's shoulder blades before he saw it coming. "No point in a so-called fair fight, Aiden, when your antagonist has all the advantages. The whole idea is to win, not play like a gentleman, give the other side a sporting chance."

Aiden, however, had leaned more toward his mother's philosophy that 'bullies are cowards.' She believed Gandhi's passive resistance was the way to go. He agreed with her because it involved the least provocation. In fact, it involved nothing so much as just doing as Jesus advised and turning the other cheek.

Of course, that rationale resulted in broken ribs, black eyes, skinned knees, public humiliation, and generally speaking, a lot of visits to the doctor who asked him at one stage whether he suffered physical violence at home, threatening to bring in Community Services, until Aiden told him about the bullying at school. The doctor's solution then became quite simple, "You need to man up, Aiden. No one likes a sissy," slapping him in the stomach with the back of his hand for emphasis. Dr. Mackenzie may have been well-meaning but his slap merely increased the pain from the bruises that ringed Aiden's belly and reinforced the perception in Aiden's own mind that somehow or the other he wasn't a real man.

His dad never said anything about masculinity, never criticized his prowess at sport or his pursuit of hobbies less manly. No, he would merely reiterate his abiding philosophy, 'Good guys come last,' gently hinting at methods Aiden could use to stop the bullying. Not that Aiden wasn't tempted when faced with his dad's look of disappointment every time Aiden came home from high school with his nose bleeding or his clothes dirty where he'd scuffled with his tormentors, but the solution was not to be found in the barrel of a handgun as his dad suggested. Not unless he wanted to spend twenty years in prison as the bitch to some huge bald tattooed punk.

The fantasy did have a certain amount of appeal which, of course, was part of the problem. Aiden was attracted to tough guys. As the bullies punched and kicked him he got hard. At least they were paying him attention. On a number of occasions they'd even forced him to suck their cocks, until his throat and face were coated with their spunk then, when they'd finished, they delivered what they thought was the ultimate humiliation and pissed over his face. If he'd known how to phrase it, he would have suggested they fuck his ass as well to teach him a lesson.

That night when he arrived home smelling of stale spunk and defeat, his father said nothing out loud although the look on his face spoke volumes. While Aiden showered, his dad had chosen the heaviest iron bar from the garage and had gone to the park where his son had been humiliated. When his dad returned about forty minutes later, Aiden was seated in the living room watching television sipping a hot chocolate his mother had made him. His father's knuckles were raw and bleeding, the iron bar coated with a thin layer of blood and clumps of matted hair.

His dad washed up and came to join him watching re-runs of *Baywatch*. It was obvious why his dad watched it, all those slow motion titties jiggling in their swimming costumes or T-shirts as the babes ran along the beach, while Aiden was busy watching the boys' shorts and bathers for signs of unanchored male privates or else chiseled male chests that he wanted to lick all over.

He knew his dad sometimes watched him when the tits disappeared from the screen to make way for testosterone. On those occasions he tried so hard not to get that catch in his breath or resort to heavy breathing as he felt blood pump into his cock. Yes, it was true what the bullies said about him – he was a pillow biter, a fudge packer, a shirt lifter, and other names much, much worse. He also knew his dad knew but never once harassed him about it.

That was ten years and a whole different world ago. He'd moved to the city from the industrial town where he'd grown up as soon as he'd finished high school, peeling the grime and soot and despair from under his fingernails and giving his brain a thorough scrubbing although he still hadn't managed to remove all those residual memories. He was glad, though, when his parents moved away from their old home to make a new start near his younger sister when she and her husband began producing grandchildren. His mum and dad had long since given up the idea that Aiden would be responsible for anything other than the demise of the family name. They had never berated him for it, accepting his choices in life.

Aiden was moderately successful. He had a middle management job in finance which he enjoyed because he was good at it. He had a solid, albeit small, group of friends. He had the occasional boyfriend even if the relationships didn't last very long, his partners always claiming 'it's not you, it's me' although Aiden knew bloody well it was him. He was too vanilla, too boring, too bland. His friends were too polite to tell him, but he knew it nevertheless.

Surprisingly, Aiden was a looker. He'd inherited his mother's superior bone structure and blond hair plus his dad's cheeky good looks. It was a lethal combination when Aiden was out at a gay bar, especially coupled with his taut body which he kept in trim once he'd discovered the joy of solo workouts at his local gym. He visited three times a week to ward off the threat of a pudding tummy which he'd noticed one day as he stood on the scales in his bathroom, the muffin top beginning its inexorable spill over the elastic band of his boxers.

It was enough warning that he knew he had to do something about it otherwise he would succumb to a heart attack at a ridiculously early age like his Uncle Charlie. High cholesterol, blood pressure and clogged arteries didn't just run in the family, they galloped; one of the reasons Aiden's dad had given up his stressful job in the factory after his first heart attack at forty-seven. It was the catalyst for his parents' move to a quieter life near his sister.

The problem for Aiden was that he was so attractive men believed he was a narcissist. Nothing was further from the truth. Aiden was shy, almost pathologically so. At the pub he gave off an aura of unapproachability, so only the most adventurous or submissive of men ever dared begin a conversation. When they got him home they found him so unlike the image they'd conjured up that they found him a bore.

"What is your problem?" his best friend, Graham, asked, after the latest boyfriend dumped him after just three weeks. "You have everything going for you. Good looks, hot body, nice personality. So, why can't you keep a man? You do want to keep one longer than it takes you to wash out your cum towel?"

Aiden grimaced at the use of the word 'nice' to describe his personality. It was a wishy-washy word, and Graham had hesitated ever-so-slightly just before using it as if casting around for the right word so that he didn't sound negative.

"What do you mean by 'nice'?" he asked, keeping the snide out of his voice.

Graham had that startled look of someone caught out. "You know," he mumbled. "Nice. As in…um… pleasant."

Kittens and polar bears were nice, pleasant; Aiden didn't want a personality that equated with fur. How do you change your personality? he wondered.

"You just need the right man to release the real you," his other best friend, Rodney, soothed when he noticed Aiden's distress. It didn't help.

"How will the right man know what the real me is when I don't know myself?" Aiden moaned.

His friends quickly grew weary of this conversation, Graham lost patience and turned on his friend. "Quit complaining. At least you don't have to eat dog food every day."

Aiden was shocked. "Where did you read that platitude? The side of a cereal box or one of those calendars with a feel good message for every day of the year?"

"It's from Brent Corrigan's Facebook page," Graham corrected, grinding his teeth.

"Oh, what, so now you live your life according to what some twink porn star writes?"

He'd almost had a complete falling out with the group that evening as he spiraled deeper and deeper into the black hole that was in danger of swallowing him whole. It had been getting larger and more appealing over the previous few weeks, so that Aiden had begun to think of just letting go and embracing the peace and calm of it.

He'd gone home early from the bar not because he'd picked up, but because he, or his friends, were in danger of saying something that was so cutting neither side would forgive or forget. As it was, he was raw from a few home truths he'd been offered; home truths much more lashing than having a 'nice' personality.

The weeks passed uneventfully, Aiden staying home to lick his wounds, his friends calling with perfunctory enquiries as to his state of mind. They were giving him space. He didn't need fucking space, he needed a boyfriend.

No one had invited him to dinner, a party, or the bars in five or six weeks so he'd remained at home, taking out his sexual frustration on a box of tissues and a tube of lube as he watched movies of men who seemed to have no problem getting it on with other men. He would have given anything just for some hot, man-on-man sex; he didn't always expect a lifetime commitment. Hell, an hour would do. Thirty minutes at a pinch.

Aiden sometimes wondered if he were going insane. Perhaps it was being on his own too much; his life having become work, home, and wanking. Graham had popped in initially but his visits became less frequent and it had been a good two weeks since he'd last seen or heard from any of the gang.

To ram the point home, Halloween was coming up shortly and no one had invited him to any of the huge parties that were one of the highlights of the gay calendar. His group usually had swags of invitations. It was the one night of the year he could guarantee he'd get laid because his personality, although not his ripped body, was covered with some sort of grotesque mask or make-up. Aiden threw up in his mind at the thought of it before swearing vehemently at his friends.

He had received one invitation to a party but he had no idea who'd sent it as his friends denied any knowledge. It may have been legitimate, but it may just as easily have been a piss take. Aiden had relegated it to the rubbish bin in the bedroom.

Sick of Good Guys coming last? Feel like you're life is a living hell? the colorful invitation read, illustrated by the devil engulfed in flames. *Join us for the Halloween Party of the year and learn secrets about yourself and how to release the inner You. Cost: One small sou̶l.*

Aiden snickered at the joke. Someone had a sense of humor. If they didn't want his soul as the crossed out 'l' suggested, then where would he get a sou? That question was answered when he picked up the envelope to bin it and a small metal coin fell out. A sou.

Wondering if it was worth anything to a numismatist, Aiden put the money between his teeth and bit down to test its strength. He was unprepared for the shock that passed through his body. It wasn't electrical as such; it was more akin to a flood of warmth beginning in his teeth, spreading quickly to the top of his head and down the full length of his body to his toes. His cock hardened from the flood of heat and his ass spasmed as if he'd eaten too much chili.

The sou was definitely some sort of metal but it was also enchanted. Aiden had a romantic bent to his nature although oft-times he kept it in check because in this electronic age, science or religious fundamentalism were the opposing gods people worshipped. He wished that science, like religion, could be playful enough that it included a few unproven fanciful ideas; Satan, for example. Not that he believed in the all-consuming Christian Satan who punished people by spit-roasting them in perpetuity. That version never made any sense. If the Devil managed to seduce you to his side wouldn't you expect to be rewarded rather than barbecued for eternity? God might want to stoke the fire starters and the charcoal but Satan would roll out the booze and the steaks carved from those irritating moralistic angels' buttocks. Nah, Satan would be hot in the sexual rather than the environmental sense.

As if to pander to his fervid fantasy, the Halloween invitation had a preening Satan of such amazing looks and body that Aiden retrieved the invitation from the bin on a number of occasions to use as visual stimulation as he jerked off. He always threw the card back where he knew it belonged but never crumpling it or tearing it in pieces. Nights upon which he pleasured himself using the card, his dreams were populated with weird creatures copulating ferociously as he watched, eager but unable to join the mass sexual free-for-all. The dreams were basically the same each time although he became aware of that fact only once he'd awoken, his body sticky with his ejaculate.

In sleep, he waited for Satan himself; at least, Satan as portrayed on the invitation. Not the 'real' Satan in whom he had no belief anyway. He didn't think it was necessary to believe in the existence of something to find it arousing. Just look at all that erotica about vampires, and they didn't exist.

Up until the last minute, Aiden fully expected his friends would invite him along on their usual Halloween pub crawl. When it wasn't forthcoming, he took the unusual step of ringing Graham in the week leading up to the big event, dropping hints that his best friend ignored. In the end he'd been forced to ask, "What's the gang got planned for Halloween this year?"

Graham had responded with, "The usual," and left it at that. No invitation, no details. Aiden was a bigger pariah than he thought.

Fuck 'em. I can have just as much fun on my own.

He knew he couldn't but if he didn't put on a show of bravado, even if it was just for himself, he might have cried. On the afternoon of the big day, he determined he'd get himself one of those Brent Corrigan porn movies he'd seen advertised in various gay magazines. Brent may not have been the Jean-Paul Sartre of platitudes but he was one hot twink. He did something to Aiden's insides even if his ideal man was more along the lines of Charlie Harding. His cock got so hard at the thought of Charlie ploughing Brent's perky posterior. At the adult book store where he'd gone to stock up on movies and replace his ageing anal toys, he found they had his favorite 'room deodorizer' back in stock and bought two bottles to store in his refrigerator for future use. He would have stumped up for an 'e' or two if Graham hadn't been his contact for his occasional foray into recreational substances. He never touched the heavy stuff.

The flirtatious middle-aged guy behind the counter suggested Aiden might like to test ride the dildo before purchase and that he, the shop assistant, would be more than happy to help him. Aiden was so close to accepting until the shop assistant farted and the idea of rimming him or even putting his dick anywhere near the assistant's fundament was so repellent he thought he'd have to dry clean his brain.

Of course, he didn't say anything quite so rude, merely thanked him for his generous offer and begged a prior engagement. Noël, the shop assistant, handed Aiden a business card for the shop on the back of which he'd already written his name and phone number. Aiden made a great display of looking at it, nodding his approval, then secreting it in his wallet before handing over his credit card for the purchases. Noël looked at the card, then at Aiden. "Ah," he exclaimed, smiling so that his mouth looked like the jaws of some carnivorous animal ready to pounce, "I think I have something for you."

Aiden was bewildered but intrigued enough to stand his ground while Noël consulted a clip board with a list of names. Finding what he sought, he turned to Aiden with the instruction, "Wait here." The afternoon had turned a little weird but nothing he need be afraid of. Noël went to the back of the store, pushing open a door marked 'Staff Only.' Aiden heard him rooting around, cursing as the sound of cardboard boxes hit the floor. A few minutes later he emerged carrying a large package which he handed to Aiden with, "Here, this is for you."

"I didn't order anything," Aiden said, too surprised to open it.

Noel tapped the list on the clip board, "Says right here that you'll be calling for the costume. That's all I know."

"How much do I owe?" Aiden was concerned this was some sort of scam that would cost him hundreds, if not thousands, of dollars.

"All taken care of," Noel said, tapping the side of his nose as if Aiden were in on the secret.

This was all very strange, he'd obviously been mistaken for somebody else, but Noel was adamant he would not take the package back, showing him that his name, Aiden Batterby, was on the list. With bad grace, Aiden accepted the 'gift' although he knew there would be a price to pay eventually and scampered out of the shop, eager to get home and open the surprise, half expecting it to explode in his face or contain a hissing and very angry poisonous snake.

When he got inside his apartment, the first thing he noticed was that his invitation to the Halloween Party was not where he'd left it in the bin, but was propped up on the buffet in his living room. What's more it seemed to purr as if it were a living, breathing entity. And it glowed. "Stranger and stranger," Aiden said to himself. He picked up the invitation to examine it more closely, believing it was the light or the angle at which it was placed that gave it the strange glow. The card felt warm as if it had a source of heat, the top of the buffet cold to the touch, the heat only in the card itself.

Aiden turned it over, almost dropping it in surprise, because the devil had a much more lascivious leer on his face than Aiden remembered. Just holding the card was giving him a decided tingle in his crotch. When he ran his finger across Satan's very sexy face, he could have sworn he felt a tongue lick the back of his finger, and when he caressed the devil's horns the card seemed to moan in pleasure.

Aiden was not a superstitious man so this phenomenon intrigued him. Right now, though, he had a package to unwrap. He tore the paper off, daring it to be a hoax, almost ripping the costume inside. He held it up. It was the most exquisite set of angel's wings he'd ever seen. The feathers felt so real, so ethereal, he wondered what bird they'd come from for they were real feathers; the purest white he'd ever seen. Accompanying the wings was a feathered cup that fitted perfectly over his genitals.

He stripped naked, clasping the modesty cup to his semi-hard cock, shucking the wings onto his back, holding them fast via the clasps that circled his shoulders. He stared in the full-length mirror in his bedroom, almost unrecognizable even to himself. He looked amazing. He wished he knew where his friends were so he could flaunt himself, rubbing their noses in his beauty. Spinning around in an effort to see himself from all angles, the wings stuck into his shoulder blades painfully.

Aiden took them off to see if he could get them to sit better because there was no way he could stand that pain all evening. Now, why did he think that? He wasn't going anywhere. He was staying home to watch porn and maybe use the new dildo on his ass.

The feathers seemed attached to a thin bone, so intricately interwoven he hadn't noticed it at first. Now that he examined the costume wings more closely it was as if they had been manufactured to look like they'd been wrenched from someone's back, right down to the flecks of blood and the remnants of gristle where the bone joined his back. That join was the cause of the sharp pain that jabbed into him.

He put his arms into the harness one more time, adjusting them as best he could to minimize the discomfort. As he did so, he noticed something reflect the light from the edge of the package in which the wings had been wrapped. He'd been so engrossed in the intricacy of the costume he had explored no further. He put his hand into the parcel and found a small jar with a note attached.

He smacked his forehead for his stupidity. The note informed him of the wings propensity for stabbing wearers in the back, suggesting they rub the attached unguent on the end of the wings which in turn would prevent pain and actually numb the shoulder blades. Aiden quickly applied the salve to the bone and for good measure rubbed a little on his bare shoulders. It couldn't hurt. Within moments, his back felt ablaze with fire. No longer could he feel the sharp jabs of wing bone although there was definite friction in his back as he moved around the apartment.

He felt amazing. Picking up the invitation, he wondered if he should go to the party after all. He wouldn't know anyone but looking the way he did, it wouldn't be long before he had them lining up, considering his ass, one of his best attributes, was bare as a billiard ball for all the world to see.

He grimaced as he felt something cut into the left-side of his back, the pain worse than anything he'd ever felt before. He staggered as another blow of pain tore through his right shoulder blade.

What the fuck was in that ointment? he wondered.

He fell to his knees, futilely attempting to divest himself of the costume. It wouldn't budge and he felt weaker and weaker with every passing moment. He was reaching for his cell phone to call for help when he passed out from the sheer intensity of the pain.

He had no idea how long he'd been unconscious when he awoke. The apartment was dark now, the only light emanating from the glow of the invitation. He was relieved that the pain had subsided. Flexing his shoulders he felt the wings move with him. Odd. He would have to ensure the salve he'd used had not done him damage. It had felt like the most intense liniment and it may have left a rash on his back. Feeling for the straps that held the wings in place he was unable to find them in the dark.

Aiden felt his way to the light switch, illuminating the room. Something was wrong. Turning his head to the side he saw the wings spread behind and above him. He marveled they could fan out in such a magnificent display although they were definitely putting pressure on his back. He clenched the muscles in his shoulders and the wings fluttered.

He moved to the mirror. The straps holding the wings had fallen off; they were nowhere to be seen. He turned his back to the mirror, peering over his shoulder as best he could. At first, he thought it was an illusion because, well, it was impossible. He flexed his shoulders again and the wings moved. Tentatively he moved his hand back feeling his skin as he worked his way toward the wings. His heart beat rapidly, scared that he would confirm by touch what his eyes already told him.

There. He reached it finally. The bone structure that held the feathers so gloriously was now protruding from his back totally unsupported by straps.

Holy fuck! he thought. *The wings are part of me now. I'm hallucinating. It's that ointment; it has psychedelic properties. How is any of this possible?*

It was Halloween. He was really in a bar downtown and someone had spiked his drink. The joke had gone far enough.

Unconsciously, he flexed his wings, knocking the light shade from the ceiling and scattering books and his plastic bottle of drinking water off the bedside table.

His wings felt cramped, in need of spreading their full width.

He needed fresh air. Grabbing a bum bag to store the invitation and the keys to his apartment, he headed down the stairs to the street below, avoiding the elevator because he knew deep down his wings would not fit. Once on the pavement, he relaxed, flexing his back until his wings unfolded to their full width. Passers-by stared at him, not for his near nudity but for the sheer magnificence of his costume; but it wasn't a costume, it was part of him.

Moving the muscles in his shoulders and back he could manipulate the wings, flapping them like a bird. They lifted him off the ground, catapulting him onto the roadway in front of oncoming traffic. He tried again and managed to get himself airborne before any of the vehicles hit him. He was flying – of a sort. It was like learning to walk all over again.

A few people stopped to gawk; an awestruck child dressed in a vampire costume tugging her tired mother's arm to tell her to look at the angel. Most bystanders thought it was a trick, but Aiden was too preoccupied with learning the basics to care. He headed for the wide-open spaces of the park where he would be able to practice without fear of colliding with cars and buses; there his only danger would be from trees and people walking their dogs.

Aiden was not an impatient man under normal circumstances but this evening the circumstances were anything but usual. If he were to get an explanation to his predicament, he would have to attend the Halloween Party and the only way he could think to get there was to fly. His skills in that direction, even after some painful practice, were rudimentary at best and he was angry with himself. He was so far out of his comfort zone he was sure he was going to need extensive therapy when it was all over.

After almost breaking his leg attempting to land, and a savage dog attack from a startled pit-bull, Aiden hit upon an idea which was so outrageous he thought it just might work. Why not? Nothing about the day made any sense at all. Retrieving the invitation from the pouch he wore around his waist, he addressed it directly, "Take me to the party. Take me to the party. Take me to the party." He thought three times was enough as it sounded like an incantation. However, nothing happened. Feeling like an idiot, he added, "Please." Whoever was responsible for his predicament was obviously a stickler for good manners because no sooner had he uttered the magic word than he shot straight up into the air until he was almost nauseous from vertigo, expecting to plummet straight down to his almost certain death. His wings, however, had a mind of their own.

He watched the city far below him twinkling in the darkness as he headed into the less crowded density of the outer suburbs where the houses had more room to expand. He just hoped that he wouldn't wander into the flight path for inbound planes headed for the airport away off to the left.

Up ahead he caught a glimpse of a grandiose stately home atop a small hill but sufficiently high enough that it dominated the surrounding countryside. Curiously, there seemed to be a number of creatures like himself headed in that direction. On closer inspection they weren't all that much like himself, in fact, they weren't human at all, their wings not feathers but membrane stretched like canvas, ending in small sharp claws.

His wings deposited him on the front lawn of the house which was lit up like a Christmas tree although there were no children padding up the long path to the front door to shout 'trick or treat.' Perhaps that was because there were no houses or apartment buildings for miles that he could see. Or perhaps it was because the house sat at the pinnacle of a cemetery, surrounded on all sides by gravestones and mausolea. Aiden had come too far to go back now. The only way was forward.

He rang the old fashioned doorbell expecting it to be answered by a member of the Munsters or the Addams Family. It was somewhat of a surprise to be greeted by an attractive older man wearing nothing but an evening jacket, his cock stiff as a rod. He ushered Aiden inside with, "You're expected, come this way."

It was hard not to be impressed by the sumptuous decoration inside the old mansion. Tapestries and ancient wall hangings adorned the walls between aged oil paintings of macabre creatures that looked like kin of the Devil himself. On closer inspection, the tapestries were woven with obscene mythology that hardened Aiden's cock so that his feathered jock did little to cover his immodesty.

People dressed as creatures from the Inferno danced in the center of the enormous ballroom while other creatures with the heads of eagles but the bodies of sculpted men chatted in corners and alcoves. Smaller creatures scuttled about the floor like vermin except they were naked and erect as far as Aiden could tell. The smell of sex pervaded the air.

As he entered the ballroom all eyes turned in his direction. Aiden felt naked although he was wearing a great deal more than many of the revelers who made no attempt to hide their excitement or their debauched behavior.

"I guess I'm not in Kansas anymore, Toto," Aiden muttered to make himself feel a little braver.

As he was led across the vast room people stopped to stare, even the musicians whose music was a strange combination of the funereal and the salacious. He wished they would go back to their dancing and their copulation because the way they stared at him made him feel uncomfortable.

"Pay them no heed, sir," the butler advised. "They are jealous."

Aiden wondered, jealous of what? He noticed that whereas he was clothed, as far as he could be classified as clothed, in the purest white, everyone else was in hues of black or blood red. No wonder he stood out.

The butler led him to a group laughing in one of the more private corners of the room. A large man with horns protruding from his head and with his back to Aiden was obviously entertaining those around him with humorous anecdotes. The laughter seemed genuine rather than sycophantic.

The butler signaled for Aiden to stand his ground as the man mountain finished another story to shrieks of laughter, then the butler coughed discreetly. The storyteller turned and Aiden buckled at the knees. The man was gorgeous. Admittedly he was also red but that enhanced his good looks rather than detracted from them.

In keeping with the Halloween theme, the man was introduced to Aiden as Satan. Aiden was so tempted to ask, "Do you mind if I call you by your first name, The Great?" but a quick glance around the group put paid to that. Many of them were looking at him with undisguised hostility. He wondered whether his fly was undone or what he could possibly have said or done to attract this level of hatred.

Satan excused himself from his acolytes, putting a protective arm around Aiden's shoulder. "I'm glad you could make it." His voice had the depth of black pits and his breath smelled of sulfur and sin. It was a heady mix and Aiden wished the man, whoever he was, would just sweep him up in his arms and carry him away.

"I don't know who invited me," Aiden admitted. "I don't think I know anyone here."

"I invited you, of course," Satan said.

"Why?"

"You are repaying your father's debt. I invited you here to corrupt you."

"Corrupt away," Aiden laughed.

Satan sighed. "It's not that simple. I wish it were."

"Tell me what I have to do."

"All in good time."

Satan took him around the room, introducing him to various guests some of whom took a genuine interest, some of whom oozed envy, others pretending a friendship that belied their antagonism. Aiden believed he could read them all.

"I'll leave you in Lon's capable hands as I have business I have to attend to," he said fobbing him off on his butler who had shadowed them as they circumnavigated the room. "Enjoy yourself. You will find everything here to delight the senses."

After Satan's departure Aiden turned to Lon, "Why was I invited?"

"You intrigue him," Lon replied.

"But I've never met him. How does he know me?"

"It's a long story and one best told by Satan himself."

The front door bell rang again and Lon excused himself to attend to it. Aiden wandered the room sometimes pulled into conversation with groups of attractive men who fondled his ass, penetrating his ring with their fingers until he was loose enough to take a cock. A guest with the head of a cat pushed Aiden's head down onto the prick of his friend, commanding him to suck it, while he positioned his cock at the entrance to Aiden's guts and pushed. A small crowd gathered to watch the defilement which Aiden found less painful than he thought it would be. Both men fucking him had prodigious weapons and knew how to prolong his pleasure. Eventually they flooded both his holes with their spunk and Aiden was pleased to receive it although he was still unsatisfied himself.

Another group, watching his obvious dissolute behavior summoned him to join them. It seemed rude to refuse their invitation even though they were dressed as bats, particularly ugly bats with rodent-like heads, small sharp teeth, leathery wings, and black furry bodies that emphasized their cocks. He was forced to his knees as one of the creatures pushed his cock into Aiden's salivating mouth. It was black and pungent but not unpleasant. As he sucked, Aiden marveled at the costuming and masks, and the lengths to which some of the guests had gone for the costume party. His angel costume faded into insignificance beside the realistic bat costumes and the half-man/half Minotaur he saw scratching his hoofs at the marble floor as he watched Aiden's prowess sucking the bat man, his own cock stiffening frighteningly.

Aiden's feathers were spattered with bat man spooge as they encircled him, thrusting their black swollen weapons at his mouth until they came down his throat, over his face or else on his wings.

Before he could stand, a partygoer with the head of an eagle grabbed him, thrusting his head into a decorative urn in order to have free access to his ass. Using his beak as he fucked Aiden mercilessly, he plucked feathers painfully from his wings, spitting them on the floor.

The eagle man whispered in Aiden's ear as he rammed into him. "Don't think you're anything special. You're just a whore like all the rest of us." To demonstrate his superior strength, he pecked at Aiden's shoulders, drawing blood which trickled down Aiden's back dyeing his feathers.

He was passed from group to group to do with as they wanted. It was neither pleasurable nor yet unpleasurable: it just was. By the time they had finished with him, Aiden's muscles were sore, his wings unpleasantly stained and torn. He was in need of a bath. However, he had reckoned without the Minotaur.

The man with the giant bull's head and the huge muscular man's body had a magnificent cock to match.

It was so large it was unlikely many people could take it without splitting. He lifted Aiden into his arms, carrying him to the center of the ballroom where he spread him on his back, his ass splayed in order that he might have greater access.

Aiden gritted his teeth as the huge bull cock entered his bowels, expanding the ring of his ass until it felt as if all the elasticity would be useless against the battering ram that was being forced inside him. Aiden took deep breaths while the audience marveled that he hadn't already begged for the giant bull cock to be taken out. It wasn't likely the Minotaur would take any notice even if Aiden was prepared to beg. No, he would take the cock and line up for more if necessary.

The bull snorted as his cock impaled Aiden, nailing him to the floor. The crowd murmured in awe as the angel begged for it harder and rougher. The Minotaur obliged until he could not hold back any longer, filling Aiden's gaping hole with his spunk. When he pulled out, Aiden's sphincter was so dilated, the spooge inside him ran down his leg. Some partygoers applauded, others spoke in hushed tones of a performance they had never expected to see.

Lon appeared at Aiden's side, helping the angel to a luxurious bathroom where he was bathed and pampered until he felt like new, his ass cooled by a gel liberally applied to his stretched sphincter. Shown to a private bedchamber, Aiden lay down and soon fell asleep.

He awoke to the feel of fiery lips against his own, opening his mouth to allow the tongue entrance, surprised to feel it bifurcated. It was strangely erotic and Aiden wondered what it would feel like poking into his ass.

"You will find out soon enough," Satan smiled. "First, I think it's time for a blow job."

Satan kneeled over Aiden's chest, pushing his scaly red cock toward his mouth. Aiden licked the head, tasting the bitter cum drooling from the slit. He swallowed and it burned his throat like a superior Scotch or brandy, warming his stomach like a small fire. Aiden closed his lips over the scales hoping they would not rip his mouth apart. They were soft and slimy, changing direction with every movement of his tongue. Aiden wondered whether they would affect his gag reflex. Realizing there was only one way to find out, he pushed his throat against the pulsing red prick until it burst through into his throat. The scales tickled but Aiden felt he could control it; he wanted to give Satan the best blow job of his life.

If Aiden really believed he was blowing the 'real' Satan he would have known it was a losing battle as Satan would have had the best ever born, Aiden just another in a long line. But Aiden didn't know. Spluttering from time to time when he didn't judge his breath right or his gag reflex caught on one or two of the scales, he nevertheless put in a valiant effort and Satan was well satisfied as he blew his sulfurous spunk down Aiden's throat.

As they lay side by side, Aiden caressing his lovers pierced red nipples, he asked, "What did you mean about my father?"

Satan hugged him to his body, his powerful muscles protecting Aiden as well as preventing his escape. "You remember the night your dad went after the kids who tormented you?"

"Hard to forget," Aiden replied.

"That's the night I met your father in person. I helped him beat up those thugs."

"I thought…" Aiden stopped himself before he could finish the sentence. He'd been about to treat this man, painted all in red, as the bona fide Devil.

"Not my sort at all," Satan said. "I like my thugs with a bit of finesse. Like your dad. After we took care of the bullies, your dad and I went for a beer. We became good mates. When it was time to go our separate ways, I told him if he never needed anything to just holler. A few years later he did just that."

"When he had his heart attack."

"Yep. Called on me to help him. He didn't want to die. You were still young. Your mum would have been left in dire straits. Plus he wanted to see his grandchildren grow up. Not much chance of that with his ticker."

"Unless he signed over his soul to you."

"Aiden, that's so old fashioned. What the fuck would I do with a soul? No, I asked for something much more to my liking."

"What?"

"I asked for you."

"Me?"

"Yes."

"My dad sold you my soul in exchange for his life?"

"Not quite. Your dad sold me you, body and soul, in exchange for his life. It was deal or no deal. Your dad took it."

"Bastard."

"Look at it from his point of view. He knew you were gay. He knew I have a thing for men with hot asses. He knew I have power and influence. Plus, I'm hot as fuck."

"You think I have a hot ass?"

"Let me show you."

Satan rolled Aiden onto his stomach, parting his legs to get his snake-like tongue between his ass cheeks, burrowing into his snug moist hole.

"Why did you turn me into an angel?"

Satan withdrew his tongue. "It was the only way to get you here. Mortals cannot enter the kingdom unless powered by immortal means. It took a little subterfuge but Lon planned it all perfectly. It tickles my fancy to corrupt a creature as pure as an angel."

"Is Lon your…"

"No," he laughed. "He's my left-hand man. My personal assistant, if you like."

"I'm your fuck toy for eternity?"

"No. Just for a year. Your father wouldn't sign without an escape clause."

"Won't people miss me?"

"Not at all. While it will be a year in my world, it will be tomorrow morning in your world."

Aiden cursed his dad for signing such a short-term contract.

As Satan slipped his cock into Aiden's receptive ass, the angel was well on the way to falling for the powerful red man whose cock stretched his ass so expertly. "That was you, wasn't it?" Aiden enquired.

"The Minotaur? Yeah, that was me."

"You can change into anything at all?"

"You just have to name it."

As their bodies moved as one, Aiden's brain almost exploded under the sheer weight of the fantasies he was brewing. He wondered if a year was long enough. He'd have to see if there was an option to extend.

OMG! MY DAD'S GOT TITS!

*What do you do when the town
MILF is your own dad?*

Jaw dropping. Mouthwatering. Cougar supreme. Definitely a MILF – Mother I'd Love to Fuck. Of course, I had no idea if she was a mother, but she'd certainly turn me into a mother fucker if she were. By now you get the drift that the woman who answered the door was one of those heavenly creatures that powers wet dreams.

She smiled at me as I stared, waiting for me to say something. Like what? "Please remove all your clothing and let me suck the nipples on your magnificent breasts." Her breasts were exquisite. That's not a word that springs into my vocabulary very often. In fact, I think that's the first time in my life I've ever used it. But I have to use it again. Her breasts were so exquisite it was almost blasphemy to think about pushing my dick into the cleavage, squeezing them together so I could fuck the tits off her, finishing off by giving her a pearl necklace. Almost.

I must have stared a little too long – is five minutes too long? – because she said in a demure sexy voice, "You like them?" When I looked up her smile had turned to a smirk.

My words tumbled out in a garbled mess until I stopped the blabber, cleared my throat, and tried the direct approach. "Excuse me for saying so, but those are the most exquisite [third time lucky?] breasts I have ever seen."

Suddenly she went all coy. "How kind of you to say so. I've always liked them." She tweaked the nipples through her clinging T-shirt. My dick did a sort of dance in my briefs in an attempt to attract her attention. If she noticed she was too much the lady to say anything to embarrass me.

The silence dragged on, until she said, "Is there something I can help you with, young man?" The way she said 'young man' made me wonder if she was flirting with me.

Of course, she had no idea who I was. I'd lobbed up at the front door, no warning, and I expected her to welcome me with open arms. Well, no, I didn't expect anyone to welcome me with open arms. Especially not the person I had come to see – my dad. We hadn't seen each other in two years; not since mum died. I blamed him for the accident and I guess I might have been a bit harsh in some of the things I'd said in the heat of the moment after the funeral.

I'd heard the two of them arguing just before they'd gone to a party. Mum never came back while dad survived the result of a truck broadsiding their car at a major intersection. The police found a high level of alcohol in dad's blood stream. In mum's as well but that was beside the point as she hadn't been driving. Dad's level hadn't been high enough to constitute inebriation but it obviously went a long way to explaining what happened.

Or so I thought when I screamed my accusations at my mortified father beside the grave. He didn't fight back which made him all the more guilty in my eyes. If he wasn't, why didn't he answer me? The fact he was up to his eyeballs with morphine and was confined to a hospital wheelchair may have had something to do with it, but I wasn't thinking straight. In fact, the following year is pretty much a blur. I moved out of home before my father was allowed back from hospital. He rang my mobile repeatedly those first few weeks, leaving a raft of messages pleading for me to get in touch. I didn't. I just stopped listening to his messages, deleting them unheard. Eventually, he stopped calling.

It was through my grandparents, mum's parents, Bill and Martha, that I learned the truth. They had been the only relations to support me in my campaign against dad. About eighteen months after my father killed my mum; they rang to inform me they'd been sent a copy of the coroner's report. It seems the brakes had failed on the truck and it had sped through the intersection, horn blaring, right into the path of my parents' car. They felt bad telling me. I felt even worse after the wild accusations I'd flung about.

I hadn't mellowed in the months since the accident, but I had missed my father. He'd always been supportive, encouraging, and I'd behaved like a Grade A asshole. It was time to make amends. I'm not the sort who apologizes easily, plus I wondered whether a simple 'sorry, I screwed up' would hack it after my distressing behavior. I had to presume there was something to save as he'd made so many attempts to keep in touch; at least for the first few months until he tired of my accusatory silence.

It took me almost six months to pluck up the balls to contact Eden, my dad. I suppose I should say, attempt to contact dad. He'd sold up the house, 'too many memories' my gran told me, and moved across the country to start a new life. They'd lost contact with him as he blamed them for our estrangement. I plucked up the courage one drunken night and rang the last number my grandparents had for him but a woman answered the phone. I'd forgotten the time difference and obviously woken her because her voice sounded groggy from sleep. I was about to hang up when it occurred to me he may have a new girlfriend, so I asked for him by name.

"Who is this?" she asked without answering my question.

I hung up quickly, the fact she didn't deny he lived there confirmation in my eyes that he did. I began to plan a visit during the summer break in my uni studies and, because I'm a coward, I was taking my best mate Chet along with me. Our friendship was based on…who knows what? I admit it; I'm a bit uptight, anally retentive, intense. Guilty as charged. Chet, on the other hand, is free-spirited, adventurous, what would have been called a hippie in the sixties. We were a strange pair. Nah, nothing like that. I'm as straight as a dye although I know Chet has experimented. His attitude is, if it's over the age of consent and it's got a hole and it does actually consent while sober then it's fair game. If that sounds a bit callous, let me tell you Chet has a lot healthier love life than I do and his relationships last a lot longer.

Okay, so we organize to drive across country, taking our time because neither of us has visited the east coast before. We could have flown, air fares were cheap enough, but air travel just seemed like a bull at a gate. A leisurely car trip was much more relaxing, plus it gave me time to psych myself up for the meeting.

Chet warned me about expectations. He didn't want to have to scrape me off the emotional freeway like road kill if things didn't work out. There was no reason dad should welcome me with open arms, in fact there was every reason he might slam the door in my face. On the trip over I did sometimes wonder about the wisdom of asking Chet to tag along as I noticed he was constantly looking at my ass and hinted often enough about 'helping each other out' in the confines of our shared cheap motel room.

In the end, we made it without Chet getting anywhere near my end. We were going to find a flea pit hotel in the inner city but I decided to head straight for my target. If dad rejected my friendly overture then Chet and I would head out of town to the fine beaches to the north. If he was amenable to reconciliation, I was hoping he'd provide a bed or two for the duration. You know how expensive accommodation is on a student's income?

That's how I came to be ogling the best tits in the universe while Chet sat in the car waiting.

"Is there something I can help you with, young man?" she repeated.

Taking a deep breath, it was now or never. "I'm Curtis."

When she looked at me blankly my heart sank. Surely I hadn't come all this way on a fool's errand. I added a little more hopefully, "Eden's son."

That got the response I was hoping for. Her face lit up and she stepped back to admire me. "Why didn't you say so earlier, honey? I thought you were one of those Mormons or someone trying to sell me something. Or just some damn pesky pervert the way you were drooling over my titties. A girl can't be too careful these days."

She grabbed my arm and was pulling me into the house when I managed to tell her, "Um, I've got a mate in the car, we've just driven thousands of miles, um…"

"Bring him in, honey. Any friend of yours is more than welcome. Let me put the coffee on." She headed toward what I assumed was the kitchen then turned, adding cheekily, "Or would you young men like something stronger?"

It was the middle of the afternoon, hell, why not. "You got a beer?"

"Two beers coming up," she said. "Now, honey, you go and get your friend and bring him on in."

I guess the relief showed on my face because Chet was out of the car making his way up the path as I walked down the front steps.

"Everything go well then?" he asked, clapping me on the back.

"Wait until you see what's in the house," I smirked.

Once inside, I closed the front door and she...I realized I didn't know her name...called cheerfully. "You boys make yourselves comfortable in the living room while I get you your beers and little snack, you must be starving after that long drive."

"I don't know your name," I called.

"Sorry, honey, where's my manners?" She came into the hallway with oven mitts on her hands, smiling as she looked Chet up and down. "And who is this mighty fine young man?"

She removed one of the mitts, holding out her hand which Chet took gently and kissed lightly on the fingers. "Chet, ma'am."

"And you must call me Edina."

"A lovely name for a lovely lady," Chet oozed, still holding on to her hand.

Edina withdrew it, somewhat reluctantly I thought. "You boys make yourselves right at home. I'll just scare up a little snack. You are hungry, aren't you?"

"Ravenous," Chet replied looking directly at her tits.

"Behave yourself," I whispered as we made our way into the cozy furnished living room where I flopped in an old padded armchair. Chet took the lounge. The room was comfortable but not ostentatious, neither overly masculine nor overly feminine in its tone. I noticed a number of framed photographs on an old cedar sideboard tucked away in a corner and went over for a closer inspection.

I relaxed. "It's the right house. I must admit I was beginning to wonder."

"Who's Edina?" Chet smirked. "Your dad's floozy?"

"I don't know anything about his life. I suppose she's his girlfriend."

"Did you see those fuckin' tits, man?" Chet could be vulgar sometimes.

"You could be talking about my step mum." I frowned now that I had made vocal my suspicions.

"She's everything you'd ever want in a stepmother." Chet grabbed a handful of his crotch and rubbed it.

"Chet!"

He pretended he was chastised, "Just saying."

Then I found what I'd been looking for. Tucked away at the back of the photos was a pic of me and dad in happier times. I must have been about fifteen and dad was spraying me with the hose and I was laughing fit to burst. I put it back, feeling a catch in my throat. It had been a long time since I'd been that happy.

"That's why I didn't recognize you," Edina said from the doorway. "You've grown up into a fine young man."

I cleared my throat of the emotion I knew would be in my voice if I didn't. "That was a long time ago now. A whole lifetime ago."

"How old are you now? Twenty-two?"

I nodded.

"Your father would be so proud of how you've turned out."

"I'm not so sure," I said. "We didn't part on the best of terms."

Edina put the tray of warm chicken with a bowl of coleslaw and a bowl of potato salad, along with our beers, on the coffee table.

"I know your father misses you every single day."

"I wasn't very kind to him," I admitted.

"He told me."

I opened my mouth then shut it because I didn't have the right way to ask the question. It was intrusive and rude.

Edina smiled. "I know what you're dying to ask," she said. "Where did I get such fine titties?"

Chet spat his beer across the room while I almost choked on a chicken wing.

"Just joshing you boys. What you really want to know is where I fit into the picture? Simple, I live here with your father."

I heard Chet mutter, "Damn."

"Where is dad?" I asked.

"That's the bad news, sugar. Of course, he didn't know you were coming and he's out of the country on business. How long you got, honey, before you go back?"

"It'll take us a week to get home, so three weeks or thereabouts."

"That's cutting it a bit fine. You may just miss him by a day or two. Next time I speak to him I'll let him know you're here. I'm sure he'll want to speak to you. He's been keen to see you again. Never stops talking about what a fine boy you are."

"I doubt that," I said to myself but obviously loud enough that Edina heard me.

"Don't you go doubting that for a minute, young man. Your daddy loves you. Okay, you might have had your differences over your poor mum but that's in the past. Leave it there, honey. Say, where are you boys staying?"

"We're going to find ourselves a cheap hotel in the city..."

Edina was outraged. "You'll do no such thing. What would your father say if he came back and found I'd made you go to a hotel? He'd never forgive me. No, you boys must stay here. There's plenty of room."

Chet and I were too tired to argue especially when we saw the comfortable beds in separate rooms which meant I wouldn't have to lie awake half the night in terror that Chet might try something. I just hoped he wouldn't try something with Edina either and told him so later when she'd gone to watch television in the main bedroom.

"But she's gorgeous," he whined.

"She's my dad's girlfriend," I said. "Plus she's old enough to be your mother."

"Oh, right. Like you wouldn't slip her a bit if she wasn't your dad's."

"That's beside the point. Now that dad seems to have forgiven me for the shitty way I treated him two years ago I don't need him to come home to find my best mate shagging his girlfriend."

"Maybe your dad would like a bit of boy pussy while I work over his girlfriend."

"Eww."

The problem was I think Chet was serious.

It was the best night's sleep I'd had for almost a week and I was grateful for the chance of a comfortable bed instead of the lumpy flattened mattresses we'd endured on the trip over. In the morning Edina made us breakfast and because it was the weekend she said she would play tour guide if we wanted. She was self-deprecating enough to add, "But if you don't want an old girl like me cramping your style I won't be offended."

"Why wouldn't we want to be seen with a gorgeous woman like you?" Chet said gallantly. A little too gallantly for my liking.

I wondered whether it was a good idea but Chet over-ruled me and I guessed there wasn't much he could get up to with me tagging along. That's what it ended up feeling like – me tagging along. We took Edina's car and Chet managed to grab the front passenger's seat hogging it for the entire journey.

Edina was the ideal hostess, driving us around the major city sights, allowing us time to stop if we wished or showing us on the large tourist map we'd bought how to get back to certain places to explore at leisure later on. We stopped frequently at pubs and cafés at which we discovered just how popular Edina was. Women seemed to adore her while men were obviously infatuated with her – or her breasts. Men of all ages from Chet's and my generation up to geriatrics. She held them all in her sway.

She was an immensely entertaining guide, laughing easily, always ready with a kind word or a sharp riposte at outrageous behavior. I could easily see why my dad liked her. Chet was right, I was slightly envious of my father. And very pissed off with Chet. By late in the afternoon he'd taken to sitting very close indeed to Edina when we were in pubs for a drink often draping his arm across her shoulders. When I coughed discreetly to draw his attention to how inappropriate his actions were he just smiled and moved closer to his target.

That night when we were alone, I shoved him in the chest and told him to leave Edina alone. He shoved me right back so that soon we were at each other's throats until we realized how stupid we were being and rolled about laughing. "Okay, Curtis," Chet said. "I get your point. Hands off."

True to his word, he allowed me to sit in the front passenger's seat the next day although I noticed Edina adjusted the rear view mirror all the better to see him with. She proved just as popular among the locals on Sunday, a few young men quite open in their admiration for her, claiming her as the hottest MILF in the city. I hadn't had a chance to compare but I had no reason to doubt their appraisal.

We hit the beach where she was well-known and had any number of volunteers to rub sunscreen into her back. Chet grabbed the squeeze bottle, refusing to relinquish it to anyone else, rubbing the cream into her shoulders in a very intimate manner and getting much, much too close to her more private areas when he creamed her inner thighs and the tops of her breasts. I'm sure he copped a surreptitious feel or two. Especially when I heard Edina's little hiccup of surprise.

Edina dropped us off early citing a prior engagement and showing us the best dance venue to pick up in the city. "Satisfaction guaranteed," she smirked. "And you're welcome to bring your...er...dates home if you wish, be they animal, vegetable or mineral."

"What if we can't find a date?" Chet teased. "Will Edina help us out?"

"You boys won't have any trouble finding someone tonight," Edina replied.

After she left, Chet crowed, "See, she didn't say she wouldn't help us out."

"In your dreams," I scoffed.

Neither of us had the energy and ended up returning to the house early. I wondered if there was such a thing as car lag.

As the week progressed I sensed a subtle change in Chet and Edina's behavior toward each other. It was if they were acting an indifference they didn't feel, the air was positively electric with sexual tension. Bringing Chet along with me was turning out to be the worst idea I'd ever had.

Just how bad I learned that Thursday. Edina had gone to work so I knew it was safe to attend to a few things in the city while Chet stayed at the house, after which I intended catching up with a movie I'd missed back home. Unfortunately, the damn session was too late as I didn't want to leave the two of them alone together after Edina got back from work.

There was nothing else to occupy my time so I went back to the house to work on an email to dad. Edina was allowing us to use her home computer and I was compiling a short history of what I'd been up to over the past two years, wanting dad to be proud of me. It seems he was in some part of Eastern Europe that had very bad phone coverage and was best contacted via email. He'd responded to my first hopeful attempt at communication in which I asked for his forgiveness and he wrote back asking for mine, saying he hoped to get home before I left. Baby steps.

The house was quiet. I guessed Chet had gone out so I went to Edina's computer in my dad's office with my coffee and sat down to type. I was concentrating so hard on composing my email that the various noises in the house failed to register. It wasn't until I heard Chet wail and yell, "Suck it, get your lips around my hard cock," that I realized he must have gone out and picked up.

Wondering if his partner was female or male I decided to throw cold water on his performance by bursting into his room while he was at it. It was pay-back for the hard time he'd been giving me with Edina.

Making my way along the hall to his bedroom, I discovered the sound was coming from the main bedroom. Was I mistaken and my dad had returned from his trip unexpectedly? I'd only surmised I heard Chet's voice because that's who I was expecting. I crept more quietly toward the back of the house even as the dirty talk got louder. My dad sure had a potty mouth. I could identify Edina's voice now. I smiled, dad was certainly nailing her to the bed and she was begging for it harder. Lucky guy. I mentally high-fived him.

Thank God Chet was out or I'd never hear the end of it.

I don't know why I kept moving toward the bedroom. Perversity, I suppose. Yes, the main bedroom door was ajar giving me a perfect view of the bed. Edina lay on her back naked, her gorgeous tits flopping about as my dad rammed his prick into her eager pussy. She was begging him for it, demanding he fuck her harder. She had quite a mouth on her, too. Dad leaned in to suck on her nipples and...

Shit a brick!

Chet was balls deep in her cunt. It wasn't my dad. I stood transfixed as Chet ground his pelvis against Edina's cunt, both of them so caught up in the moment neither of them noticed me watching them. They'd obviously been going at it for a while because they were both drenched in perspiration.

"This is the tightest pussy I've ever fucked. When I fill it full of my spunk I'm gonna flip you over and tap that cute ass of yours, but first I want to blow my load over those great tits."

"Mm," Edina mewled. "Your cock feels so good inside me. I wish we could do this all night."

"We will, baby. We will. Oh fuck, I'm gonna shoot. So help me I'm gonna blow my load all over your tits."

"Go for it, let me see you unload."

Chet rammed in and out of her pussy a few more times before pulling out and shuffling up the bed on his knees until his cock exploded jets of spunk all over Edina's fat tits, some of it hitting her face. She spooned it on to her finger, licking it before swallowing it down.

"Sweet."

"There's more where that came from," Chet boasted. "Give me a few minutes and we can do it again."

"Over my dead body," I screamed as I flew into the bedroom pummeling Chet with my fists. I was in a rage, seeing all my efforts to reconcile with my dad go for nothing, my best mate fucking his girlfriend. I had tears in my eyes as I attacked Chet although it was probably already too late. My blows rained down on my naked friend even though he attempted to defend himself screaming at me to stop. He'd fallen off the bed and I was on top of him wrestling with a naked man actually inflicting damage when a deep masculine voice commanded, "Stop this nonsense at once."

"Dad?"

Shit, that made it worse. My dad had actually walked in on this fracas?

"Your dad's caught us?" Chet whispered as we'd both stopped fighting. "Oh fuck."

I stood up, wiping my face while Chet grabbed for his underpants.

"Dad?" I said again.

All I saw was Edina wrapping herself in a kimono.

"Dad?"

I was in serious danger of becoming repetitive.

"This is not how I wanted you to find out, son. I thought you were at the movies otherwise I wouldn't have ..."

Was I going insane? Dad's voice was coming from Edina.

Chet looked as amazed as I was then he had to go and make matters worse by laughing. "Edina's your dad?"

"Not now, Chet," the deep-voiced Edina snapped. "Both of you get yourselves respectable and out in the living room while I get dressed. And if I catch either of you fighting I'll smack heads together, got it?"

"Yes, ma'am," Chet said, still chuckling.

I pushed him rather hard out of the bedroom, following forlornly behind. I sat like a disappointed schoolboy in the living room while Chet was all mirthful anticipation. At this precise moment I hated both of them.

"Man, you could have told me," Chet said, not trying very hard to suppress his excitement.

"Fuck, Chet, I didn't know. Would it have made any difference if I had told you?"

"None at all."

"You still would have fucked him?"

"Her. I would have fucked her."

"Eww. If I'd known, I wouldn't be here. I wouldn't have come in the first place."

"And that's why I didn't tell you when you first arrived," Edina said from the doorway. "I couldn't afford to let you go again. Curtis, I've spent the past two years regretting our lack of contact every single day. You're my son, I love you."

"You certainly have a funny way of showing it," I snapped.

"What? By becoming the person I always wanted to be?"

"So you're gay? Big fuckin' deal. I could handle that." I was still angry. "But why...this?"

Edina kept her cool. "I'm not gay, Curtis. Never have been. I loved your mother, we were very happy together."

I tried sarcasm. "Oh, so you're not gay? Then what do you call it when Chet has his cock slamming into your..." I stopped suddenly when I realized I was about to say 'cunt' and how stupid it sounded. It knocked the belligerence out of me.

"Yes?" Edina said.

The best I could do was mumble, "You know what I mean. Underneath all that makeup and shit, you're still a man."

"Oh no she's not!" Chet added. "I can vouch for that."

"It's not helping, Chet," she said.

I changed my attack, turning on my friend. "And you! Can't keep your prick in your pants for five minutes. You could have ruined my chances with my dad by fucking his girlfriend." Every time I opened my mouth I sounded like a bigger dickhead.

"I wasn't fucking your dad's girlfriend, I was fucking your dad!" Chet snickered. "Oh, man, this is so cool."

"Can't you take this seriously for one fuckin' moment?" I screamed. "You think it's a big joke while I'm dying here."

Edina was by my side in seconds. "Take a deep breath, Curtis. Come on, deep breath. That's it. Deep, deep breath. In. Out. In. Out." She held my hands as the panic attack slowly receded. "Take it easy. In and out. In and out."

She sat me on the lounge and wrapped a protective arm around me and for a few moments I was that scared little boy who suffered similar attacks who was comforted by his concerned dad. But my dad wasn't dad anymore and it was doing my head in. I needed air.

"I'm going out," I said, heading for the front door.

"I'll come with you," Chet said scrambling to catch up in his undies.

"I don't think so," I said. "I have to work out whether I still want you as a friend."

Chet was exasperated. "Oh, come on, is that your solution to everything? You don't get your own way, so you cut and run?"

I turned on him. "I don't need advice from Mr. One-Track-Mind."

I emphasized the point by slamming the front door so hard it made the windows rattle.

I'm not sure now of everything that went through my mind as I sat on the beach staring out to sea. I watched the waves roll in and withdraw like they had not a care in the world making me wonder why I cared.

You were supposed to care, weren't you? It showed what a compassionate human being you were. Or was that just for tsunamis and famine? Donating a few excess dollars to a worthy cause to make us feel better. Where was the charity I could give money to in order to make the problem with my dad disappear?

Problem? There was a good starting point. Whose problem was it? Certainly not my dad's...um...what do I call Edina?

First there was the flaunting of her tits. No boy wants his mum...er...dad...er – fuck it! I was so confused. It was like having to learn the alphabet all over again. But I was an adult. I was resilient. Eww, she'd slept with Chet. What? Was I jealous? Deep down did I want Chet? I don't think so. Methinks the lady doth protest too much.

Those tits. Why flaunt them like that? She had every kid in the neighborhood drooling over her chest. Including me when I first arrived, if I was honest. Wasn't that the point of the exercise?

But my dad had tits. Nice tits. Magnificent tits. And, if I let my mind wander to what I'd seen in the bedroom, my dad had a cunt. A cunt that was wrapped around my best mate's dick.

"Get out of my head!" I screamed at the sky, startling a few lazy seagulls that had been picking among the seaweed scattered along the shore.

It was almost dark by the time I returned to the house which, apart from the look of concern on Edina's face, was as I left it after the great revelation. The atmosphere was subdued as if we were all walking on eggshells, none of us knowing how to broach the subject without restarting the emotional conflagration.

Edina had prepared an amazing, but simple, meal on the off-chance, I supposed, that I would return. We ate in silence until I began thinking about the situation and even though I still had a very queasy feeling in the pit of my stomach, I began to find the whole thing ridiculous and I began to giggle. Then I found I couldn't stop. I knew I was blowing my chances but I simply could not match my face to the gravitas of the situation. Or maybe I was.

I noticed Chet peer from under his brow at my attack of the funnies and it must have set him off as well because soon we were taking turns in exploding with laughter, attempting to rein it in but failing miserably. Edina looked at us with consternation although I heard her hiccup in an attempt to swallow her guffaw. In a matter of moments the three of us were hysterical with laughter, tears running down our cheeks as we attempted unsuccessfully to finish our meal.

There was no point trying to talk as it just brought on another burst of uncontrollable hilarity. I put my knife and fork down and held my sides. I'd laughed so much I'd given myself a stitch and doubled over in painful humor.

It took almost ten minutes to get ourselves settled as one of us laughing set off a chain reaction and we'd all end up cackling like hens about to lay an egg. When we finally returned to our meal I asked seriously, "So, you're not gay then?"

I could see Edina was choosing her words carefully. "Not in the way you mean. As a man, I was never attracted to men sexually, but all my life I've felt like I was a woman in a man's body. It's a difficult concept for most people to accept. I tried fighting it for years, including marrying your mother. We were genuinely in love but over the years I became increasingly uncomfortable in my shell. That's how I thought of my body – a shell. It was actually your mother who encouraged me to seek treatment."

She put her hand up to stop my question.

"By treatment I don't mean because either of us saw it as a mental condition. Your mother, bless her, wanted me to have a gender reassignment. I didn't want to take that step until you were older and could handle the situation more maturely. Oh, she had no intention of divorcing me. When she died and you...turned your back on me, I saw no reason whatsoever not to go ahead. This is the result."

To lighten the mood, Edina put her hands under her breasts and jiggled them. "What is it with you straight boys and boobs?"

"Don't you remember?" I asked. "You were one once."

"A long, long time ago," Edina replied. "That's why I moved here where nobody knows the old me. To forget."

Chet cleared the plates away.

"You know, Curtis, I really would like to have you back in my life. You're very important to me, son. I do understand if this is too difficult for you but I have to be true to myself first and foremost."

"Look, dad." I winced at my faux pas.

"It will take some getting used to so don't sweat it. I'll give you time to adjust. You don't have to tiptoe around the subject scared you'll say something that offends me. Ask what you want, I'll answer to the best of my ability."

"I don't want to lie, dad. This is going to take some getting used to. It's a lot to be confronted with. I don't know whether I'll be able to accept it in the long run, but I'd like to try."

"That's all I can ask."

"I think it will help that after this holiday I'll be going back to uni and we won't be in each other's pockets. Give me a chance to get my head around it and maybe get the answers to a few questions. Come back and see you in the holidays."

"Sounds promising."

I could see Chet was getting restless at the earnestness of our conversation. He must have decided to break the mood.

"So," he smirked. "How do you feel about me fucking your dad mum for the rest of the holiday?"

OMG! SANTA'S GOT A SIX-PACK!

Not all Santas are fat, old bastards.

"I've been watching you. You're really wonderful with children."

Holy Bat toast with Robin jam, Mr. Perfect is talking to me!

I snapped my lips together knowing that if I opened my mouth I would make a total fool of myself. See above reaction. My mouth always engaged before my brain even woke up to what it was saying. 'Juvenile' is the word most of my boyfriends used to describe my childish reaction to everything around me. I say boyfriends but most of them didn't hang around longer than the two-and-a-half minutes it took them to blow up my ass.

Those that did last longer usually ended up braying, "When are you gonna grow up?" before making their exit, inevitably after a break-up fuck.

But it's not me you want to read about, is it? If I'd called the story of my life Santa's got a Skinny Butt, you wouldn't even have put it on your Wish List let alone bought it. So let's get to the selling point: Mr. Perfect. Not his real name. I guess you've already sussed that out for yourself. No one's ever accused me of being the brightest bulb in the chandelier.

He looked very patrician. At least I thought so. I was going to call him Patricia, but that seemed a bit insulting somehow. I settled for Mr. Perfect because he looked like my comic book superhero of the same name. But I'm getting ahead of myself.

You see, me and Thelma have names for all the people who line up with their children. Helps pass the time. Usually it's some tic or habit or facial feature we zone in on and then we give them a moniker like the villains in Dick Tracy. We even had a Pruneface. Not that he looked like a prune in this case, it's just his tone and personality gave us the shits. He was the sort of character who spoke in capital letters.

He attracted our attention by snapping his fingers at us, "You There! My Child Has Been Waiting Absolutely Ages To See Santa. How Long Will It Take?" His attitude got him the animosity of the people in front of him in the line and the sympathy of those behind him, except for Mr. Perfect who gave me a sympathetic smile.

Pruneface's daughter clutched his trousers, trying to hide among the pin-stripes, obviously terrified of meeting the jolly fat man in the red suit, but he'd missed that salient point.

"I Can't Afford To Waste My Time With This Nonsense. I Have Important Meetings To Attend," he added.

Keeping my voice level, although I would have dearly loved to shout at him, I told him, "It's not all about you, sir, it's about the children. If you can't spare the time now, then may I suggest you come back at a time more convenient to yourself when you will be able to wait your turn again."

A few people snickered; a few others gave me what I like to think were grins of appreciation.

See what I mean, though? I can't help myself.

Thelma's the same, but much older. She must be close to a million years old but she says she's closer to fifty-five. I think she's injecting monkey glands because she knows so much stuff, she has to be way older, or else she's somehow transplanted Google into her head instead of a brain.

There I go again. You'd never know I was nineteen and studying to be a graphic artist. Ultimate aim? To rule the universe! I say that but it's not true. I'm not the ruler type. More the set square or compass. *LOL* Maybe not. Real ultimate aim, not fooling around? To draw the best comic book ever. That's the ultimate dream, but I won't be too unhappy if I end up drawing the best comic I can.

It's a bit personal. At the moment, I'm doing it for myself, not for publication. See, I'm just starting out, so it's practice. I showed it to Thel and she said I was 'really talented.' She's just being nice. She did say, though, that Mr. Perfect is not a real good name for a superhero and that if her hubby had been as packed in the underpants department as my cartoon Mr. Perfect she never would've left him. I stopped showing her after that. She knows I'm gay, I'm not ashamed or embarrassed by that, but I was scared she might think I was an unsuitable candidate for this job.

Both Thel and me are elves. Not real elves. All we get to wear is the hat and booties. Green felt rubbish that makes my hair and my feet hot. The real elves get to wear the total green outfit which is even bigger rubbish. But they get more money and have to stay in character all day. They tried me out on that but I was as crap as their costume. They thought my sense of humor was better served looking after the kiddies while they lined up to sit on Santa's knee. Our job is to keep them in line so they don't get too noisy or rambunctious, entertaining them with simple party tricks or jokes while they wait their turn. Parents seem to appreciate it.

So do the Santas. There are a half dozen of them because no one could stand the racket or the unruly behavior for eight hours without a lot of breaks. It's hot and tiring work and sometimes a Santa gets a bit emotional. Or drunk. Then management will dismiss him and find a replacement. A couple of them want me to sit on their laps – when they're naked. I'm polite. It's

Mr. Perfect I want sliding down my chimney. Actually, up my chimney.

That's enough background. You're probably eager to get back to Mr. P. who's still waiting for some sort of response from me whose jaw has dropped to the floor in cartoon surprise at being addressed. Without thinking, I bend down to mime picking it up. He looked at me kinda strange.

"What are you doing?" he asked.

"Picking up my jaw," I said.

At least he laughed. "You're a queer one."

"Queer as in 'oddball' or queer as in 'gay'? Or both. And is it a bad thing?"

Yep, I did say it out loud. I squeezed my eyes shut and screwed up my face at my stupidity, waiting for him to call my supervisor to complain.

Mr. P. did not have a chance right then because a young boy tugged at his coat and in a most severe manner as only a six-year-old can, said, "Mister, bugger off, he was telling us a joke and he hasn't finished."

Apologizing profusely to the young audience, Mr. P. backed off, smiling broadly at the reprimand. Just before I got back to the joke which required all my skills mimicking various woodland animals, Mr. P. whispered, "I liked the way you handled Pruneface. Well done."

I couldn't believe it; he nicknamed him Pruneface as well.

You ever get a buzz so powerful you seem to float through the day? Without drugs, I mean. Everything goes so right it's the moment you want to last forever. Or else, you just want to die then and there because life will never get any better. That moment was mine.

After work, when I got back to my bedsit, it looked like a palace not the cockroach infested dump it really was. The vermin became horses carting me off to the ball where I'd dance with the handsome prince and…

I grabbed my draft paper and my pencils; the work flowing out of me like my body was a conduit to that big library of ideas in the sky. I was so happy, I forgot to eat, almost forgetting to sleep until fatigue overtook me and my head flopped onto my drawing board.

I would have probably remained in that position all night except the knock to my head woke me enough that I staggered to bed. I was so tired I slept in the next morning and was almost late for work. No time for breakfast, I just grabbed my sketches and ran down the stairs. I got through store security and was at my locker with five minutes to spare, enough time to ram the stupid hat on my head so I looked like a stick of asparagus, but not enough to grab a muffin from the canteen.

You might wonder why I'd want a job like this. Well, I actually enjoyed entertaining the kids. They could be little brats, sure, but I identified with their wide-eyed wonder at a world still full of possibilities. Too many of them would grow into the Prunefaces of the future. I hoped I could help just one or two of them avoid that fate. I think the word you're looking for is 'naïve.' Hell, I've been called worse.

The main reason for liking this job is that I don't have to scrub the stink of fried fat off my clothes and my body and out of my hair when I get home at night like I do the other ten months of the year to pay for my tuition and my rent and my paper and ink and pencils. It's great there are fast food outlets that employ young guys like me, dreamers I mean, otherwise I don't know what I'd do.

It's not like my parents would or could help me out financially. I put 'would' first because dad wanted me to work on the roads like him. "Good solid, dependable work, boy," he often told me as I was growing up, there's those words again, floundering about searching for something I wanted to do. "It's not all about you, you know," was his favorite expression. I guess that's why I used it on Pruneface.

Dad would then say something like, "Dreams are all very well in the bedroom late at night, but best to leave them there when you wake up to the real world in the morning. What you need is something dependable. Something that will pay the bills and put the food on the table."

When he said that, I'd think about what was in the fridge: cheap cuts of meat on the turn so they'd inevitably be cut up and disguised in stews, vegetables so flaccid and pock-marked it was a wonder mum could cut enough nutrition from around the spoiled bits to make them worthwhile, and, let's not forget his beer.

Food was a necessary evil to dad. He hated spending money on it. His ill-fitting dentures didn't help the cause of better dietary habits either. Most of his food was mushy because it hurt him to chew. Beer was an entirely different matter. He was praying for the day nutritionists declared it a 'food.' Until then, he had to have the best. Well, why not? You don't have to chew beer.

It wasn't until I left home that I realized what a bang-up job mum did with the little she had. Still, it came as a bit of a shock to discover that food actually had taste, individual tastes, not just some glutinous generic taste of mush.

Oh, hell. I'm rabbiting on about me again, aren't I? Where was I? That's it, almost late for work because… never mind, you've read that bit already. I raced into Santa's Cave to stand beside Thel as security counted down to opening time. There was always an initial rush of parents and offspring, mums and dads not averse to using a bit of elbow power to get to the front of the queue.

Our attempts at crowd control were always short lived. The best we could do was attempt to funnel the enthusiasm, I would have called it the melee if I'd been honest, away from the adult shoppers who were buying exorbitantly expensive decorations, wrapping paper, and the other bib bobs that go with the holiday season, at the counters adjacent to Santa's Cave.

I wasn't going home for Christmas this year. Mum and dad didn't need me freeloading and it's not like we were all that close anyway. Not since they'd found certain drawings of mine which revealed it was as unlikely I'd ever settle down and marry that nice Kylie girl from down the road as it was I'd end up with a job on the roads. As a result there was a minimum of fuss when I declared my intention of moving to the city to study graphic arts for a career in advertising, apart from dad declaring that "No good will come of it, you mark my words," and a slight moistening of the eyes when mum came to see me off at the station.

I sent gifts and received a card from mum with a ten dollar note inside plus instructions to 'buy yourself something nice.' I loved my parents; I just didn't want to be them. So, even though my stomach rumbled its rebellion as I marshaled kids like sheep to the Santa, I was happy. Okay, my bed-sit was crap, I had a lousy paid job, but I still, with pretty strict economizing, had time and a little cash to do what I loved – drawing. And the absolute blue icing on a green cake: I'd met my model for Mr. Perfect which is why I was so bloody tired and hungry right at this moment.

My head rang with the shrieks and screams of young children demanding rewards from Santa for being good for the whole year. It really was the wrong way to go about it. I never believed you should bribe children into good behavior. What did I know? I would never have any of my own.

My stomach gave a volcanic rumble, enough to startle the kids standing near me, bringing to mind the old adage that breakfast is the most important meal of the day, and therefore I should not have been surprised when I could scarcely concentrate on what I was doing. One minute I was turning my hunger grumblings into a creature attempting to claw its way out of my belly to the delight of my young audience as well as the stunned disbelief of some of the more staid parents, the next I was lying on my ass among the plastic bunting that surrounded Santa's Castle, a young worried face hovering over me, asking, "Mister, are you all right?"

Holy Batcrap, I must have fainted.

Parents pulled their children away lest I have some contagious disease before Thel was kneeling beside me, her face a mask of concern. "Are you all right, love?"

I didn't have time to answer before an authoritative voice broke through the confusion. "Stand aside please, I'm a doctor."

"I don't need a doctor," I whined, until I saw who the voice belonged to. Mr. Perfect kneeled beside me, placing the palm of his hand on my forehead. Mmm, maybe I did just need to lie here like Sleeping Beauty waiting for my prince to kiss me better.

"I just didn't have any breakfast," I hissed at him. "I'm fine."

I didn't want to attract an audience as it might mean my job.

"If you're a doctor, where's your scalpel?" one smart little girl asked.

"I can see you're going to be a detective when you grow up," Mr. Perfect smiled at her. "You don't miss anything, do you?"

She beamed at the praise. He leaned into the crowd of children and said in a stage whisper, "I didn't want to scare the patient, but his condition is serious. If I don't operate soon, the monster in his stomach will eat its way out and then we're all doomed."

His audience giggled nervously as Mr. P. swept me up in his arms and carried me toward the staff canteen like a prince carrying off his princess. I knew I would never feel like this again as long as I lived so I breathed in, storing his masculine aroma mixed with soap and a citrus after shave for later fantasies. Surreptitiously, I snuggled against his chest, wondering what mountain they'd carved him from.

Kicking open the canteen door marked STAFF ONLY, he carried me to an empty table and poured me into one of the chairs. He seemed as reluctant to let me go as I was to leave the safety of his brawny arms.

"Sit!" he commanded as the few late morning shift personnel sipping their heart starting beverages of choice stared open mouthed at my superhero striding to the counter to order my breakfast. None of the soggy Bain Marie slush for him. He demanded freshly made eggs and sausage and when the cook went to refuse, he kept his tone quiet which was infinitely more authoritative than if he'd shouted.

Brad Levard, the floor manager, strode in, making a beeline in my direction, his face so thunderous I imagined lightning strikes emanating from his head. "What sort of shit are you pulling?" He'd never liked me since I'd ignored his very obvious attempt to hit on me the day I began work on his floor. Mistakenly, I'd believed his feelings would be less hurt if I'd ignored him instead of giving him the brush off or a polite refusal. My belief was wrong.

I jumped up as he approached my table, earning a stern rebuke from the canteen counter. I was commanded, "Sit!" Mr. P. intercepted Levard before he even reached me, holding out his hand in a warm greeting. Peering at his name tag, he said, "Mr. Levard…Brad. I'm Dr. Crichton. Fortunately, I was in the store shopping when this young man collapsed. I know an organization such as yours would not want any fuss so I brought him in here." Placing his arm across Levard's shoulder in a comradely gesture, Mr. P. steered him away from me as Curried Pearl delivered my breakfast with a flourish. We called her that because she always smelled of whatever was on the lunch menu.

Usually curry. She gave me a wink and a nudge, adding "He's a real keeper that one, eh?"

I must have blushed because she went back to the till cackling like a hen about to lay the golden egg.

Mr. P. spoke confidentially to Levard, but loudly enough that I could make out what he was saying. "You know how litigious people are these days and I thought it prudent to short circuit that possibility, that's why I brought him in here out of the public gaze. You don't want Health and Safety throwing their weight around."

"Quite right, Dr. Crichton. The management appreciates your diligence."

"If I may make a suggestion…"

I wanted to make a suggestion myself. Get your arm away from Levard, who seemed to be enjoying the intimacy far too much for my liking, and put it around me.

Please.

"Suggest away," Levard replied with just a hint of flirtation, obviously hoping the suggestion might include the chance of getting to know the doctor a little better.

"The young chap's blood sugar seems to be abnormally low which is why I took the liberty of ordering him a few carbs to get it back up to within normal range…"

"Very good idea," Levard clucked as if he knew fuck all about medicine.

"I think if he may be permitted to stay off the floor for about half an hour to recoup his strength—"

Levard drew breath to reply, but Mr. P. added quickly, "I know, I know what you are about to say. It's a very busy period for you and the young lad is one of your very best workers…"

I almost choked. My superpowers don't include the ability to read thoughts but I can absolutely guarantee that my being a good worker didn't feature anywhere in Levard's mind.

The floor manager was vacillating in his concern.

Mr. P. easily persuaded him back on side. "I'll tell you what. I'll stay here with the lad until he's fit to return to work and then I'll come to your office, with your permission of course, and give you a full debrief. If you like, I could pop in each day and, if you have time from your very busy schedule, we could perhaps have a coffee and discuss his progress."

Oh, Happy Homos, Robin. I'll get to see him every day. I wonder does that include weekends.

He was laying it on a bit thick. I wasn't sure Levard would fall for it, but a manly squeeze of his shoulders and the floor manager capitulated.

"That sounds like an excellent solution to me. I'll be in my office when you're through here."

Said the spider to the fly.

Levard gave me a cheery wave as he left the canteen, while Mr. P. slid into a chair opposite me. I held out my hand. He looked at me, his handsome features screwed up with confusion.

"Well, Dr. Crichton, aren't you going to take my pulse?"

Discover for yourself, it's racing.

He laughed. "I'm not a doctor."

There goes my chance to impress the parents by marrying a medico.

"No shit, Sherlock," I said. It came out a bit snarkier than I intended. "Look, I'd better get back to work; Thel can't handle all those kids on her own."

"You stay right where you are."

He was so authoritative, I got hard.

"If I have to put up with half an hour of that slimy Levard then the least you can do is make it up to me by having breakfast with me first."

"And that would make it all worthwhile?"

"Oh, yes. Very worthwhile."

Shiver me timbers and call me Shirley, I do believe the man is flirting with me.

"What are you doing this weekend?" The smile that accompanied his question made me lose my sense of decorum.

"Why? Are you asking me out on a date?"

"I've never asked a man out on a date before."

Don't say it, Kaz.

But I did. "Why not?"

"You want me to ask you out on a date?"

Is the sky blue? Does bacon on a string pass straight through a goose?

"It would sure do wonders for my image."

"Not sure what it would do for mine."

Ouch.

At least he was still smiling.

"But seriously, what are you doing on the weekend?"

"I was serious," I muttered to myself, but the look of surprise on his face suggested he just might have heard me. If he did, he let it pass.

"I'd like to make you a proposition. I'll make it worth your while."

I was taken aback. "When people proposition me, money is usually not involved, unless it's taxi fare home."

He seemed genuinely perplexed, and then blushed to the roots of his hair. "What? Oh god, no. Sorry, don't misunderstand me. I am an awkward klutz sometimes. Not that sort of proposition. I mean a real job." He looked at the expression on my face. "I've just made it worse, haven't I?"

I nodded my head, my feelings fighting for space among my toes in my elf boots.

He took a deep breath. "Hi, my name is Patric Charles Crichton, no k on the Patric. What can I say? My parents were pretentious. I'm thirty-three years old and I'm offering you employment at a children's Christmas/birthday party this coming weekend because I admire the way you handle the little bastards in large numbers."

Effective way to get me onside then offside in the same breath.

"No thanks," I said, turning my back on his attitude. "I'd better get back to work."

I'd only taken a few steps when he stopped me in my tracks with, "The job pays…" then mentioned a figure so high it took my breath away.

"Exactly who do I have to kill?" I asked.

His laugh echoed around the canteen, causing Curried Pearl to drop a metal tray which clanged to the tiled floor. Laughter was not exactly an everyday occurrence among the nondescript plates and cutlery and the warmed up remnants of what once passed as edible sustenance.

"You obviously don't know your own worth," he said. "That's the going rate for what I'm asking you to do."

I swallowed, both the lump in my throat and my pride. "Upper or lower end of the going rate?"

"It's about the middle."

"What do I have to do?"

"A car will call for you on Saturday morning, bring you to the party where you'll entertain about two dozen kids from mid-afternoon until the early evening, that's when Santa will arrive. You just have to help him cope with the crowds. Then you can join us for dinner and stay the night, take advantage of the facilities, and a car will take you back home the next day. Or, if you wish, the car can take you back after your job is finished on Saturday night."

"And there's no surrendering of body parts to keep alive an ageing patriarch or the slow extraction of all my blood?"

"Now there's a thought," he said.

I didn't want this job under false pretenses. "You must know it would take me six weeks to earn that sort of money here."

"That's because your skills are under-valued."

"Or other people are taking advantage of your gullible nature," I suggested. "I'll tell you what, I'll do it for half what you're offering, and we'll call it a deal. That's how much it's really worth."

"I can afford to pay you," he said, puzzled by my attitude.

"No, we'll do it my way or not at all."

"All right, we'll do it your way."

He got me to jot down my address, suggesting a time that I should be ready, although I immediately wished I had suggested making my own way or having the car pick me up on the corner somewhere far away from my depressed neighborhood.

I felt that even more keenly when the following Saturday a limo arrived. I heard a vehicle pull up in a neighborhood that usually rang to the sound of clapped-out bombs that wheezed down the road at snail's pace held together with hope and the leftovers of last year's pay packet, or else rocked to the beat of loud techno music as they boasted their alpha superiority by performing wheelies, leaving a wake of smoke and particulate rubber on the asphalt. I thought Patric, Mr. P., might call personally but he obviously had a party to organize.

Calling to the driver from my window, I told him to wait, I would be right down. That was no lie as I'd been up and ready since daybreak, nervous as the Bride of Frankenstein before she met her mate. I feared, too, that if the driver strayed too far from his vehicle we might turn up at the party in a limo minus its hub caps. They were an official currency in these parts.

The trip itself was uneventful, taking a little over an hour to the outskirts of the city where a large Victorian mansion awaited my presence. It was just dilapidated enough that I found it fascinating, full of character, and an ideal model for the villa I was having problems with in my Mr. Perfect comic. I was pleased with my prescience in bringing paper and art materials. Perhaps Patric would let me sketch him, provided his wife didn't mind. I was under no illusions in that department. I knew I was here to entertain his son, Damien, and his friends and that there were no sexual overtones connected with my visit.

I could live with that. I'd take the cash and run, after doing my darnedest to make the Christmas party the best I could. Mr. P. came out to meet the car when it pulled up on the gravel driveway outside the main weathered wooden door that had all the cracked and flaky majesty of an ageing diva.

He was all smiles. "Welcome, glad you could make it."

His greeting puzzled me. "You sent a car. Were you expecting it to break down on the way?"

"No, sorry. You'll have to forgive me if I'm a little distracted. Here, let me carry your bags up to your room." He picked up my canvas bags, straining to lift the larger of the two. "What have you got in here? An elephant?"

"I never travel anywhere without all the necessaries. Sorry, it's heavy."

Once he'd shown me into the vast tiled foyer and closed the front door, plunging us into the gloom of dark wood paneling and heavy velvet curtains so redolent of Victorian fussiness I expected to see maids and manservants bustling about to keep the mansion functioning, he put the bag down.

"Listen, there's something I must tell you about this afternoon. But not here. Come with me."

I wanted nothing better than to open the curtains and windows to let in light and air, but I knew my place, so I followed him down the corridor like the governess in Henry James's ghost story, *The Turn of the Screw*. Melodramatic? Certainly, but with an ounce of truth as Mr. P. explained once we were in the book-lined library.

I refrained from that old cliché, "Have you read all these?", because the leather bindings revealed they were inherited rather than purchased recently. I was pleased to see a few books on an antique side table alongside a comfortable old grandfather of an armchair situated beneath a reading lamp.

He hesitated between the armchair and the more modern chrome and leather seat behind his desk. Professionalism won over friendliness and he sat behind the large wooden desk, reinforcing the gap between us. I took a seat situated conveniently to give Mr. P. dominance. As it was on wheels, I moved it so that he had to turn to address me. He was irritated at my impertinence but, what the hell, I wasn't here to play games. Well, not with him anyway.

Whether he was wrestling with what he wanted to say or whether he was attempting to control his temper at my temerity I could not tell, but the silence became uncomfortable. I had examined the bookshelves a number of times from my seat and was about to start on the ceiling when he finally spoke.

"I may have lured you here under false pretenses," he said at last.

I certainly hope so. And, yes, I will marry you.

He obviously didn't hear my thoughts because he continued in a totally irrelevant vein.

"To put it frankly, Damien is not exactly the most popular pea in the pod."

He seemed relieved to have unburdened himself of that piece of news. I did wonder, though, how the kid could possibly have inherited a charisma bypass with Mr. P. as his dad.

"The other children tolerate him because their parents tell them to. He's even more morose this year because his mother is away on assignment and won't be coming home for the usual Christmas celebrations although she's managed to organize a hook-up from wherever it is in the world she is."

My look of surprise must have galvanized him into explaining further.

"Sorry. There's no reason you would know his mother is Endive Veroche."

My mouth dropped open in surprise. And admiration. Mr. P. was married to the most important war photographer of the modern age? I was stunned. Everyone knew her work. I understood now, too, why Mr. P. and Damien may not know the exact location of their nearest and dearest. She worked undercover, never embedded with allied troops because, she maintained, they just fed her bullshit. She preferred to branch out on her own recording the day-to-day atrocities of a war zone. She was probably on the hit list of both sides.

"I'm impressed," I managed to say.

"Well, Damien's not. Of course, he's too young to understand and he's becoming more and more withdrawn as the days go by, therefore alienating further those few acquaintances that he does have. So today's party is of the utmost importance if not to him, then to me. It has to turn around the other children's perceptions of him."

"Oh, good, make it easy for me," I said sarcastically. "Don't pile on the pressure."

"I don't expect miracles," he said.

"Not like raising someone from the dead, just a minor loaves-and-fishes style of rabbit-out-of-hat miracle."

"No, the party's catered."

I laughed at his little joke but failed to find anything about this situation amusing.

"I'll show you to your room. It's yours for as long as you stay. It may look as if the house should have a lot of servants but those days are long gone. There's a cook comes in to make breakfast and she's a stickler for punctuality. If you want a hot breakfast, you must be at table before 8am or it's leftovers for you. For today, there will be ample food catered, so just help yourself. By all means, set a plate aside in the refrigerator if you wish. Ah, here's your room."

He showed me into a magnificently furnished boudoir, the bathroom of which would have contained my entire bedsit. "Oh, my," I sighed. "It's magnificent. I feel like Norma Shearer in *Marie Antoinette*. I love it."

He seemed surprised by my enthusiasm.

Hustling me out, he pointed to his room at the end of the hallway, before climbing up a flight of stairs to what looked as if it had once been servants' quarters although now converted into a nursery-cum-play area. "Of course, you have the run of the house and the grounds," he explained, "but as best you can keep the children away from the kitchen. Oh, and the library. If you need anything, that's where you'll find me. Any questions?"

"What time is Santa arriving?"

"About 4 o'clock. See if you can get them to have a nap before he arrives. Their parents will pick them up around six."

I accompanied him downstairs to grab my bag and haul it to my room where I spilled the contents all over the bed in a flurry of activity. I had requested that Mr. P. buy a few items to which he readily agreed and I took them up to the Secret Room as I renamed it and set about my preparations, occasionally popping back to my bedroom when I needed further inspiration.

I was in the middle of transforming the upstairs room when I heard a little voice behind me. "What are you doing?"

I turned to study the forlorn little figure. "I'm getting everything ready for your party."

"They don't like me, you know." Such a sad little boy, and only six years old. Time enough to be disappointed when you reach adulthood. Still, I wouldn't lie to him and hope that would make everything better.

"Then we'll just have to get them to change their minds, won't we?"

"How?"

He was inquisitive, so there was still hope.

"See that packet over there?" He nodded. "Can you write your name?"

"Of course." He was indignant that I would even doubt it for a moment.

"In that case, I want you to pick out one of the T-shirts in the packet, they're all the same, and then I want you to write your name in really big letters on the front and the back. Think you can do that?"

I handed him a black marker pen, watching as he chose his shirt carefully then sat on the floor, his tongue poking out of the corner of his mouth in concentration as he laboriously wrote his name. When he completed the task, he held it up proudly.

"Good boy. Now hand me the shirt and you take a seat just over there and try not to move for a few minutes. Got that?"

"I'm not stupid," he admonished me.

"Sorry," I said.

He took a seat looking very stern. I searched his face for traces of Mr. P., but could see none. He must take after his mother. With a few quick strokes of the pen, I had drawn his likeness, holding it up for his approval.

"Is that me?" he asked.

"Uh huh. Try it on and go and have a look at yourself in the mirror over there."

I helped him pull the T-shirt over his head; it was adult sized so it fitted him like a smock, which was my intention. He stood admiring himself and his drawn likeness for an age, and then he said, "Cool. Can I keep it?"

"It's all yours. But take it off now because you'll need it for the party."

I helped him when he struggled to remove it by himself. He folded it, placing it over a chair.

"Can I help?" he asked, coming back to my side, definitely more involved now.

"Of course, I'd like that."

The preparation time rushed by so that I was still putting the finishing touches to everything when I heard the first cars arrive. The playroom overlooked the front of the house and we could hear none-too-excited voices complaining they didn't want to be here, begging to be taken home. I marveled at Damien's equanimity under such a barrage of negativity and attempted to save what little of his dignity remained by talking loudly enough to drown out their voices.

"It's all right," he said. "I know they didn't want to come to my party."

"Time to put your special shirt on. I'll put mine on as well." Mine had a caricature of me, my features much more exaggerated than Damien's; his was as lifelike a portrait as I could make it.

I took his hand as we went downstairs to greet the guests, feeling the tension in his grip. The parents put on a brave face as they deposited their unwilling offspring. Mr. P. must have heard the hubbub because he made a special guest appearance greeting the mainly mothers by first name, some of them flirting openly with him. A few asked after Endive, they and their children scrupulously avoiding Damien until one little girl pointed at his T-shirt of which he'd become inordinately proud and said sarcastically, "What is that you're wearing?"

The other boys and girls, busy until then playing games or texting on their mobile phones, looked up.

The parents all turned to stare at Damien. Mr. P. looked to me for an answer.

"That's part of this afternoon's activities," I said. "Part of the games."

Some of the parents gave me a sympathetic smirk, while others smoothed out party dresses that cost more than a week's wages for me, or attempted to pat down unruly hair on the boys. The children were all between five and seven but it was the males who looked most unhappy to be there. This group was going to take some winning over, something Mr. P. must have realized as he bid goodbye to the parents and fled back to the safety of the library.

When I was finally alone with the kids, I corralled them upstairs to wait outside the door to the playroom upon which I'd taped a very large sign dominated by a rough illustration of children having old-fashioned fun. No sooner had we reached the door than some of the guests recommended playing with their mobiles.

"Right," I said to gain everyone's attention. "From this point on, all phones off!"

"What if we don't want to?" one little boy piped up.

"Let me see," I said in my most cordial manner. "You're all grown-ups here, so I'll treat you like grown-ups." A few chests thrust out in pride. "You make your own decision about your phones. If you want to come inside and play, then turn your phone off and then seal it in one of those envelopes after you write your name on it. Otherwise, you can sit out here or down in the foyer and wait for your parents to come and pick you up. Right?"

"What's inside?" one of the girls asked.

"Games," I said.

"Computer games?"

"No, old-fashioned games. Come on, who's coming in?"

Three of the boys shrugged, switched off, then sealed the phones in one of the envelopes each. As instructed, Damien led them into the room, instructing them to write their names on a T-shirt. He closed the door behind him.

"Anyone else?"

One of the girls stepped forward but her best friend stamped her foot impatiently and squealed, "Debbie!"

But Debbie was not for turning and I soon let her into the room to join the very small party indeed. There were twenty in all, including Damien, and so far, only five were inside. I had taken a calculated risk but I knew I had to separate the guests from their electronic distractions. Don't get me wrong, I have no beef with modern technology when it's used for good but when it becomes an anti-social device, then look-out kids!

It took a further twenty minutes after I closed the door on the hold-outs before they all ventured inside lured no doubt by the gales of genuine laughter from those favored few inside. They came in dribs and drabs, the final hold-out, not unexpectedly, being the rude little girl from the initial meeting at the front door. She sulked into the room and rather than make a big fuss I spirited her straight over to the T-shirts and got her to write her name then sketched the most flattering portrait I could. She baulked at wearing it as her mother had obviously gone to a lot of expense to doll her up, but when I insisted she would have to go back outside, she relented begrudgingly. She soon overcame her snit, fortunately, and joined right in.

The T-shirts served a two-fold purpose: to keep the children's good clothes from getting soiled and to give me a reminder of their name.

The games we played were fairly conventional but their newness to these children was such that they enjoyed them out of all proportion to their origins. Once they were exhausted from all their screaming and running about inside, I took them outdoors, still without their phones, in order to explore the lawns and gardens for insects and bugs from which I wove a fantasy story about fairies who lived among the flowers and elf princes who rode snails like wild water buffalo and which I illustrated on my giant draft-paper pad.

It was an absolute joy to see the kids getting their hands dirty. I marched them off to the bathroom to wash up when catering arrived. We set up trestle tables on the lawn and gave the children blankets to lay about on in the shade because the sun was scorching hot that summer. Mr. P. joined us for the food which I'd insisted be healthy with a minimum of sweet, sugary biscuits and lollies. To deflect any young complaints, I'd had each of the children pick a flower or leaf from the garden, telling them that the caterers would cook it up in the big kitchen inside and bring it out for all to share.

Admittedly, there was a degree of skepticism when a rose petal re-emerged as tomato flans, and a cicada shell transformed into vol au vents, dandelions into small quiches, but they ate them anyway. The caterers boxed up each child's garden choice with a couple of examples of what it had transformed into to take home with them along with a piece of the delicious tiramisu birthday cake.

Mr. P. sang louder than all of us when the cake appeared with its six bright sparklers instead of candles, the partygoers oohing their wonder. I told Damien to blow them out when I judged they'd just about sparkled themselves to death, and he made his wish, screwing his eyes up tightly. Then he ran back to join a group who welcomed him with a warmth that had been sadly lacking earlier in the day. Some of the girls sought him out to talk to him which was such a turn around that Mr. P. looked at me as if I had some sort of magical powers.

"I knew I made the right choice," he said before heading back inside the house.

I regretted he didn't have more time for his son but many adults lack the patience for hours of exhausting game playing. After they had finished their snacks and their fruit juices it was time to head back inside for a nap. It would also give me a chance to recharge my batteries which were seriously in danger of running out of energy.

When the youngsters were all asleep, I crept out to make my way downstairs to the library where Mr. P. was engrossed in paperwork when I tapped on the door and entered.

"Ah, Kaz," he said, pausing in the midst of an important pile of documents.

"They're all napping," I said by way of explanation.

"Any problems?" he asked.

"In the beginning. Nothing I couldn't handle though."

"Damien?"

"He seems to be having a ball. He's made a few friends. I think they might stick."

"That is a miracle in itself." He sat back in his chair. "I hope you'll do me the honor of joining me for dinner."

"Yes, I'd like that," I said.

"Good," he replied then went back to his paperwork signaling our little chat was over.

I went back to the play room and was soon as fast asleep as my charges only snapping out of it when I felt a small body jump on my chest. They would definitely be friskier after their sleep and I had to channel that energy or it would be the end of me. Seating them in a semi-circle, I had them call out their favorite animal, real or mythological, and then directed them to the large sheets of paper and paints, the other items I had asked Mr. P. to buy, to draw the animal they'd named, explaining it should be a large picture so they could see it from the air. I thought they may have guessed they were drawing a design on what would become home-made kites, but they painted on blissfully unaware. When they finally twigged, there was a hush of disbelief that they could actually make their own playthings. They had only ever heard of store-bought toys.

With perseverance, and a lot of help from me, each child eventually created something approximating a kite, weird and wonderful though they were. It didn't matter whether they flew or not, it was the excitement of having created something themselves. In the event, they all flew even if only for a matter of seconds but no one minded as they were having too much fun running around the lawns dragging their kites behind them, making enough noise to be heard on the moon.

They were still at it when the limo came back with Santa seated regally in the back. Kites forgotten they ran after him until I managed to calm down their unruly behavior. Santa was a consummate professional, listening to each and every child's request, gently steering them away from impossible gift ideas, like the boy who wanted a real sabre sword to chop up his teachers at school. He gave out a small gift to each of them after they'd solemnly sworn to him that they'd been good all year.

When he'd finished I took him down to the library where Mr. P. had drinks and a little food waiting for him. I went out to the lawn to gather up the kites just as the cars started arriving to pick up the partygoers. I gave each child his or her kite plus their mobile as their parents arrived.

Damien stood proudly in the driveway saying his farewells to everyone while some of the guests bombarded their confused parents with requests that they invite Damien to their Christmas party because they'd had so much fun at his. A few of them looked at me suspiciously as if wondering what strange power I'd used on their child.

Not all of them would reciprocate, just enough that Damien would no longer be a pariah. One little girl even ran over to peck him on the cheek and although Damien made a big deal of wiping the kiss off with his sleeve there was no disguising his secret delight. I scooted him off to his bedroom after everyone had left in order that I could debrief with Mr. P. but when I opened the library door, he was nowhere to be seen. Santa, still in costume, savoring an amber liquid topped with ice, waved me in.

"Sorry," I muttered. "I was looking for—"

"Come in, lad," he said. "Close the door. Mr. Crichton said for you to wait for him in here. Care for a drink?"

"Uh, no thanks."

"I hear very good things about the way you handled the children before I arrived. They were very docile in comparison to some of the other groups I've had."

"Thanks," I said, warming to him.

"So what can old Santa bring you for Christmas? Is there something you want above all else?"

I snickered. If only Santa knew.

"That was a very dirty laugh, lad. Come on, spit it out!"

"As long as Santa won't be shocked," I said.

"Ha. Nothing shocks this old Santa. I've heard just about everything. If it's that shocking come and whisper it in my ear."

I found myself walking over to him. What the hell was I thinking?

"Park your butt here, young man," he said patting his knee.

I did it automatically as if I were a young child again.

"So tell me what it is you most desire in the world."

He looked so comforting I couldn't help myself.

"More than anything in the world, right now I want Mr. P."

"Who's Mr. P.?" he asked.

"Patric."

"Mr. Crichton? Your boss?"

"Mmm."

"Why do you call him Mr. P.?"

I explained about my comic hero, Mr. Perfect, and how much I'd modeled him on Patric. I rambled on and on, hoping I wasn't embarrassing myself, but the old guy chuckled conspiratorially.

"Why don't you tell him?"

"He wouldn't be interested in me. A hot guy like that. I'm just a scrawny stick. He's smart…" I was going to go on and on about Patric's good points but I thought that was probably unwise.

"Is it his money you're after?"

"Has he got money? It can't be much; this old place is falling down round his ears. It's a lovely old house though."

"If it's not his money, you after an overnighter or for keeps?"

"For keeps would be nice."

"What if he doesn't do for keeps?"

"Then I'd settle for once. I can't stop thinking about what it would be like."

"Here, son, close your eyes, make a wish and put your hand in here."

I should have known. This guy was just another filthy old Santa turned on by having a young guy perched on his knee. Before I could stand up, Santa grabbed my hand and pulled it toward him, thrusting between the buttons on his jacket, through the rent in his fat suit. Okay so the guy wasn't as fat as he looked, big deal, he was still a sleaze.

I was surprised when my hand reached bare skin: hard, muscular flesh. I stopped struggling, running my fingers from the guy's muscular chest down over his hardening nipples to his abs. Oh my God! Santa's got a six-pack! But he hadn't finished with me yet, guiding my hand a little lower until it reached a very hard cock poking up toward his navel.

I withdrew my hand as if I'd been burned.

"What's the matter, you don't like?"

Santa was an old fraud. I pulled his beard off to reveal Mr. P.'s laughing face.

"You bastard," I cursed. "That was a mean trick."

"It's only mean if Santa doesn't grant your wish."

I was still on his knee. He had an erection. I had an erection. What more did I need to think about? I grabbed Santa's face and planted the sloppiest, tonguiest kiss on his mouth that I could manage, while I unbuttoned his jacket to get my hands on those fabulous abs again.

It was fun playing with his muscles but I was after that jutting monster between his legs. I pulled down Santa's baggy trousers and palmed his cock which was already straining for release. He attempted to stand up to remove his pants totally but I pushed him back in his seat. I had enough leeway to suck his brains right out of his skull via his prick. That's how determined I was at that moment. I nuzzled his balls with my nose and lips, before working my way slowly up his shaft, thumbing his slit, admiring his large cut cock, happy to spend the night worshipping it.

Eager to taste him, I slid my lips over the crown, suctioning down as far I could without opening my throat just yet. That was a gift for later, once I brought him to a peak. He seemed content to sit back and watch me while I paid homage to his beauty. He wasn't arrogant, just superior as if the world owed him their sexual obedience. Who was I to argue when the object of my lascivious thoughts was within blowing distance?

"It's been so long," he groaned, as he ran his fingers through my hair.

In that case, it was time to reveal my true talent. I took a deep but silent breath before I plunged downward not stopping until his prick was pushing into my throat.

Controlling my gag reflex, I bobbed in short arcs to keep him wedged tight until I needed to breathe. He grasped the arms of the chair as if an electric shock had surged through his body.

"That is truly spectacular," he sighed.

If that wasn't a signal to do it again, I don't know what would be. I went back to ministering to his needs, his cock constricting my throat until I thought I would burst. I didn't know how long I could keep this up but I reasoned that as he'd asked me to stay the night that this was but a preliminary round.

Giving it my all, I bobbed until his cock was buried as deep as it could go, using my tongue, my teeth, every oral trick in my armory, until he called out as if in pain and I felt his spunk squirt down my willing throat. I regretted that I didn't get to taste him but his obvious relish of my skills offset that disappointment. Plus the fact I would get to taste him later.

"That was absolutely amazing," he said.

"Would you like a repeat?"

"Later," he puffed. "Let me get my breath."

Then I was hoping he might take care of the throbbing I had between my legs.

"If you were interested, why didn't you say something before?" I asked.

"I didn't want to jeopardize Damien's party," he said. "That was the most important thing. But now that's out of the way—"

"There's nothing stopping us."

"Plus I had to be sure you were really interested—"

"Could I have made it any more obvious?"

"I thought you may have been after me for my money?"

"Why, have you got tons of the stuff?"

He stilled my wandering hands, holding my wrists together, making me look him in the eyes. "You really don't know who I am, do you?"

"Holy Batcrap, you're a serial killer or a vampire or some shit like that, aren't you? And I'm in deep trouble?"

"Nothing like that. I'm Patric Charles Crichton. Head of PCC Industries."

"OMG!" I screamed. "Not the Patric Charles Crichton of PCC Industries?"

I had no idea what the fuck his name meant, so I laid it on thick. His smile of satisfaction showed I'd done the right thing.

"So you can see why I'm a bit wary of getting involved with just anyone."

I let go of his cock which I'd been pumping slowly while we got the talk out of the way. His idea, not mine. The talk part of it. "Why don't you open your mouth a bit wider and insert the other foot?"

That took his breath away. I stood up, gathering my clothes.

"Just for the record, your name and the name of the company mean nothing to me so, big shot, save the self-importance for the people who are impressed by that sort of pompous priggery, like those puffed-up harridans who brought their poor kids here today. I wanted you because I liked you. Get it? I don't suppose you do. Oh, and by the way, yes, I got those none-too-subtle hints you dropped as Santa Claus that just maybe Mr. Perfect was not into relationships. Still I was willing to settle for an overnighter if that's all I could get. Because I like you. Make that liked. You're so far up your own fundament, you can't see what's in front of you. No wonder Damien's so screwed up."

That was below the belt but I was angry as hell.

"And how patronizing can you be?" I was like a dog with a bone and not about to give up. "You don't want to get involved with 'just anyone'? How about I just duck home to get my vaccination certificates, my passport, my driver's license, my employment record, my college exam results, and my criminal record so you can make an informed decision? Then, how about you do the same for me so I know I'm not sucking 'just anyone'!"

He seemed shocked. "You've got a criminal record?"

"See? No, I don't have a criminal record; I was trying to make a point. I thought you were a free spirit but you're even more timid and uptight than all the others." I was dressed by this time. "If you don't mind, I won't be staying the night. I'd like to leave."

I didn't exit grandly like Norma Desmond; I shuffled out in case I burst into tears. How could my Mr. P. go from Perfect to Puerile in such a short period of time? Upstairs, I packed quickly, sitting in my room hoping he had called the limo back because there was no way I was staying under the same roof that night.

About twenty minutes later, there was a knock at the bedroom door. I dreaded facing Mr. P. again but I took a deep breath, wiped my eyes, and answered. It was the limo driver.

"Seems I have another passenger going back? You about ready?"

Of course, Santa was still here. I grabbed my bags, the limo driver helping me with the heavier one, and we manhandled it down the stairs. As we passed the library, I couldn't help but call out loudly enough that he'd hear me. "Do you want to come out and search my bag, just in case I'm stealing any of the cutlery?"

I heard a crash of something breaking from inside the closed room.

"Ouch," the limo driver commented.

Santa was waiting for me in the limo, already helping himself to the alcohol for the long ride back. His name was Colin and by the time we reached the city proper, and my place in particular, we were the best of drunken mates, so much so the limo driver had to help me up to my bedsit, leaving Santa as hubcap guard. Patting my ass, the driver lay me down on the bed fully dressed.

"Don't think I'm not tempted, mate, but I don't take advantage of the inebriated. Maybe if we run into each other under different circumstances…"

He let himself out leaving me to sweet oblivion until I woke up the next day with a Holy Batcrap of a head.

I was sick, so sick, physically and psychically. The physical demanded immediate attention, my head poised over the toilet bowl and then a long draft of seltzer to settle my stomach and a handful of aspirin for my head, the psyche having to be stored away for later. The remainder of the day was spent feeling sorry for me and wondering if I was going to die.

Here lies the body of our dear departed son, Kaz, who remained undiscovered because no one even missed him.

I couldn't believe my head was still pounding. I just wanted it to stop. Not only was my head jabbering like a jackhammer, I was now hearing voices. "Kaz, open up. If you don't open up soon I'll break the bloody door down. Come on, it's Thel."

What? The voice inside my head was a trannie named Thel?

I sat bolt upright in bed, regretting it immediately. I groaned, stumbled out of bed, and unlatched the door, letting Thel push her own way in while I collapsed again.

"What are you doing here?" I groaned.

"When you didn't turn up for work, and didn't ring in, I was worried."

"What do you mean work, it's Sunday?"

"It's late Monday afternoon and Levard is spitting chips. You'll be lucky to have a job come tomorrow." Thel went to the bathroom and turned on the shower. "Right, now you can get yourself into the bathroom and scrub up or you can give Thel a cheap thrill and make me undress you and shove you in the shower. Your choice."

I was unsteady on my feet, but determined. "Loath as I am to deprive you of an opportunity to feast your eyes on my privates…"

"Good boy. You must be getting better if you can string a sentence together that long without stuttering. Now scoot."

The shower was the first step in my recovery, the second was going out for a cheap meal with Thel. I explained what had happened over the last few days, not sparing my own stupidity from her derision, but instead I got sympathy.

"He seemed like such a nice man, too. Not at all like I expected."

"What do you mean?"

"You really don't know who he is? That wasn't all an act?"

"Have you ever known me to act that well?"

"No, love, your feelings are always plastered all over your face."

"So, who is he?"

"Worth a fortune if the papers are to be believed. Gives a lot of it away to good causes."

"So he's a philanthropist?"

"Wouldn't know about his religion, they never mention that. He's a bit of a recluse."

"No wonder he doesn't date."

"Must be scary to have that much money," Thel sighed, probably wishing just for once in her life she could be that frightened.

The remainder of the meal was taken up with small talk while at the back of my brain, my conscience was attempting to work out whether I had wronged the man. It was a moot point as I'd never see him again to apologize whatever the outcome of the moral dilemma.

When it came time for Thel to return to her long-suffering boyfriend I went to pay the bill over her objections only to discover an envelope in my coat pocket, an envelope stuffed with cash. I saw her to the train then raced back to my bedsit not daring to count the money in public.

The limo driver must have put the envelope in my coat when he walked me up to my apartment. I couldn't believe my sudden wealth. It was the full amount that Mr. P. had suggested, not my lower acceptance. I wrestled with my conscience for a few seconds until I overpowered it for the mandatory count of ten then put the money aside for a rainy day. Beneath that hot, muscular, cheating exterior, there was a heartless of gold. Besides, I had no way of returning the extra cash.

I looked vainly for a note, so I slept only fitfully that night, my dreams full of my tarnished hero and the wrong I had done him.

Levard was surprisingly sanguine about my no-show the previous day, dismissing my apology airily with the rejoinder, "It's of no importance, Kaz. Dr. Crichton rang in on your behalf saying that he had seen you on the weekend and in his opinion, you were unfit for work yesterday."

My look of surprise didn't seem to register with the floor manager, but at least my job was safe. Thinking it over, that bastard limo driver must have reported back to Mr. P. on my condition. Well, he could make of it whatever he wanted.

Thel welcomed me back like I'd been gone for months instead of just a day and by morning tea she'd cajoled me into my normal childish, good-natured, optimistic self. Optimistic in most respects but not about Mr. P. I didn't want to invest energy and emotions in a relationship with a married man, even if his wife was away most of the year. I wanted a superhero all my own. Was that selfish?

"No, love," Thel said. "That's what we all want, but there should be a rule we can trade 'em in every ten years or so for a better model."

"Ain't that the truth," Curried Pearl added. She had joined our table for her allotted ten-minute break, slurping her coffee like she was drinking it through a straw and smoking like the proverbial chimney even though there were No Smoking signs dotted on all the available wall space between notices for the staff badminton championships and the social club outing to see Mamma Mia.

So the days passed as I marshaled faceless children toward Santa for their three-minutes of annual greed (photograph $10 extra) until a week later a tiny hand tugged at my sleeve. "Damien?" I squatted so I was on the same level.

He was pouting. "You didn't stay for dinner."

"Oh, I'm sorry about that. I had urgent business in town. You were taking a nap when I left and I didn't want to wake you."

It was the truth. I didn't want him to think I'd just walked out on him. I'd done a quick sketch of him sleeping, leaving it on his bedside table so he knew that I cared just a little.

"I know. Patric framed your picture and it's hanging in my room. It's cool."

I didn't want to ask, I really didn't.

"Where is Patric?"

He pointed. There was no use in not turning as the object of our conversation would have noticed we were talking about him. Fortunately for me, Levard was oozing all over him, keeping him distracted.

"Don't you like Patric?" Damien asked.

I was taken aback by the forthright question. Well, yes, I did, do like Patric, k or no k.

Before I had a chance to answer, Damien added. "He misses you."

"And I miss him, too. But don't tell him."

He crossed his heart, although I noticed he had his fingers crossed.

"Did you want to see Santa again today? Did you forget to ask for something?"

"Yes," he said earnestly.

I placed him in the line before returning to my regular duties, making sure to keep an eye open for his welfare as he moved patiently forward. When at last he hopped on Santa's knee, whispering in his ear, I saw him point in my direction. I hoped he wasn't vindictive enough that he was asking Santa for a hit man to take me out.

When he'd finished, I fetched him, offering my hand which he took as I made my way over to Mr. P., my heart beating until I thought I would be unable to go through with the meeting. Both he and Levard turned their beaming smiles in our direction as we approached. Damien pulled at my hand for the last few meters as my feet seemed remarkably reluctant to take the necessary steps.

Mr. P.'s face was a study in neutrality as I nodded my greeting. "Thank you for ringing Mr. Levard to let him know I was feeling unwell last week."

I saw a slight curling of the corner of his mouth on my use of the word 'unwell.'

"That's what…doctors are for," he replied. My heart stopped when he paused, hoping he might say 'friend' but I guess he couldn't. That would be unprofessional. Anyway, I didn't need a common or garden variety friend, I needed a boyfriend. Preferably one who was available.

We stood around awkwardly until I let Damien's hand go to return to my job. I saw the look of distress on Damien's face.

"Ask him Patric, go on." A little voice pleaded.

Mr. P. looked mortified, speaking harshly to his son. "Not now, Damien."

That was my cue to leave and after wishing Damien an effusive goodbye which just seemed to embarrass Mr. P. further, I made a hasty exit. I had no idea what was going on there but I knew it was not a good place to be. Maybe Mr. P. had transferred his affections to the odious Levard. The guy wasn't bad looking but his personality, let's just say, if it came down to a choice between Levard and a cobra, the snake would win every time.

As I went about my shepherding task, I watched as P. shook hands with Levard, leaving the floor without so much as a backward glance although Damien gave a little wave. I waved back. It wasn't his fault his dad was such a bastard. A sweetheart of a bastard.

The afternoon was so busy I had no time to think any further on the matter until my tea break when Thel and I slumped exhausted in the canteen chairs, so over the Christmas bustle we failed to notice how putrid the coffee was.

"There you are, Kaz," one of the friendlier Santas said, plonking himself alongside. "None of my business, but I just thought you'd like to know, that little boy you were so friendly with—"

"Damien. He's a friend's son," I said to clarify my relationship.

"Well, it's just he had a mighty funny Christmas wish. You get all sorts, of course, some would just tear your heart out, but he was very specific. He even offered to give up his other Christmas presents. Most unusual for a little boy to give up presents. But, what I'm trying to say is, when I asked what he wanted for Christmas, he pointed at you and said 'I want him as my daddy.' There you go, for what it's worth."

Oh shit, I had a sudden need to run to the men's room so I could bawl my eyes out in private.

My eyes were still red when I got home in the early evening. I wasn't depressed exactly, just a little heartbroken for Damien, and feeling sorry for myself. I tried working at my drawings, wallowing sufficiently that I didn't hear the tap on the door until it became more insistent. I really was not in the mood for one of the other occupants of the building coming to me to borrow money or ask if I was selling drugs. I ignored it for as long as I could then reluctantly put down my pencil because I was in danger of scribbling all over my portrait of Mr. P. in annoyance and flung open the door.

My first reaction was astonishment, which gave way to embarrassment, in turn becoming irritation, then finally lust. Mr. P. stood at the door to my scummy bedsit. Although all those emotions ran through me in record time, I was still gaping.

"Are you going to invite me in?"

I so much didn't want him to see how I lived, but to have him in the same room as me over-rode my good sense. As I stood aside I was curious. "What are you doing here?"

"To see you, of course. Do you need to ask?"

"Yes, I do. I thought we'd already established I'm not suitable. Oh wait, you would have needed time to check me out first to see that I wasn't 'just anybody'." *I really must to learn to keep my mouth shut.*

I wouldn't have blamed him had he walked out after that welcome but he said simply, "I deserve that. Now it's out of your system, let's move on." Taking in my room, he retaliated with, "I see accommodation for students hasn't improved much since my day." Somehow, though, I just couldn't picture Mr. P. living in such squalor.

"What do you want?"

"I came to invite you out to dinner. At a restaurant."

"You think I need fattening up? Don't let these surroundings fool you."

"No, dammit! A date."

Holy penguins in a burnt butter sauce! Me. On a date. Call the Daily Planet. Hold the presses! Scoop of a lifetime. Kaz asked out on an actual date by the hottest man in the universe…

Unfortunately, Mr. P. chose that exact moment to find the comic book Mr. Perfect, the Hottest Man in the Universe ® ™ (patent pending) who bore a remarkable likeness to his inquisitive self.

"Is this me?"

I didn't dare speak, so I nodded my head.

"What am I supposed to be?"

Clearing my throat, to give myself time to censor my thoughts and give him the family rated version about him and my libidinous superhero, all my reservations went out the door and I babbled away like some stupid kid seeking approval from grownups. In his favor, Mr. P. listened patiently, didn't interrupt the more ludicrous aspects of what I was telling him, until he couldn't stand it any more and he placed his index finger on my lips.

All he had to say was, "I missed you," and I was in his arms.

I was hoping the way I ravaged his tongue was answer enough. I still couldn't believe that he was in my bedsit, that he missed me, and that I was succumbing to a married man.

Ain't love grand?

He backed me onto the bed and began divesting me of my clothes while he shucked off his own shirt and I struggled to undo his belt. "I want you," he muttered, blotting out the few remaining reservations I had. No one had ever wanted me like this before.

He lay on top of me, both of us totally naked after the undignified wriggling to divest ourselves of our clothing, pinning my arms above my head.

He gently bathed my lips with his tongue before gently pushing his way inside, my tongue eager to greet him. There was none of the hurried exploration like the last time we'd found ourselves in this situation.

"Mmm, sweet," he murmured when he came up for air, "I should kiss you more often."

"Make a booking. My dance card is pretty empty at present."

I snacked on his tongue, sliding my lips around it as if it were a cock, rocking back and forth in a facsimile of a blow job. I've had kisses rough and kisses gentle and his was by far the most arousing I'd ever experienced. He took it to a whole new level. I couldn't get enough as he ground his hips against my body in rhythm with his tongue in my mouth. It wasn't all selfish domination because he withdrew to allow me access to his warm wet mouth when I tried so hard to imitate his technique. He was obviously more experienced than me, so I added a small playful flourish. I tickled his gums with my tongue, making him squirm.

He pulled away, disappointing me because I was in no great hurry now that I had him in my bed, but he made me gasp when he ran his lips down my throat and across to my nipple, nibbling at it until it was hard as the tip on a frozen ice cream. He repeated the exercise on the neglected one before burrowing his nose between my feeble pecs then, snorting his breath on my skin, he licked his way down to my navel where he stopped for a brief inspection before continuing farther south, past the pubic jungle, to the leaning tower that was my busting-for-action cock.

Expecting a few tugs with his hand, I was totally unprepared when he opened his mouth and swallowed my prick whole. I called out in surprise, my body bucking on the bed, as his tongue made merry with the underside of my shaft and he bobbed his head up and down to take me to the root. I watched as my dick disappeared between his lips which only made my orgasm even more perilously close. I tried to pull his head away without success so I warned him, "If you keep doing that, I'm gonna come."

He took his mouth off, which gave me a chance to recover, and said, "Can you come more than once a night?"

Does Superman need a new costume designer? Does the Green Lantern need a new color chart? For Mr. P. I could come as many times as he wants.

That ran through my mind. What I said was, "Uh huh."

"Good," Mr. P. replied and went back to his expert blow job, bringing me off in record time and…

Jiminy Grasshopper, he swallows!

I moved on the bed in an attempt to grab his cock, memories of it plowing my throat surfacing in my mind. I was keen to repeat the experience. Unless—

"Lie still," he commanded. "This is all about you tonight."

Even my mind went blank at the thought of that.

"What would you like me to do next?" he asked softly.

You mean apart from move into my bedsit and spend the rest of your life loving me, being my superhero?

"I want you to fuck me," I whimpered.

"You got…?"

I'd already leaned my arm over to the bedside table and fished the makings out of the drawer. He ripped the condom wrapper with his teeth, and then rolled it down his shaft as he asked, "How do you want it?"

This was no time for the obvious smartass answer.

"I want to watch you as you fuck me."

He smiled. "Just the way I like it."

Hoisting my legs onto his shoulders, he slicked my ass with lube, pushing his finger inside so gently I barely felt it. Then a second and a third until I was ready for him.

I was so ready, in fact, that when he aimed his cock at my entrance and pushed, there was hardly any sting at all, and I welcomed his intrusion. As he sank slowly inside me, filling me, I had never felt so at peace. He watched me intently for any signs of discomfort and when he found none he began to thrust, withdrawing until the head of his cock was just inside my sphincter, then sliding back down until he was buried up to his balls.

He was fucking me like a well-oiled machine, deliberately hitting my sensitive spot every third or fourth thrust so I didn't climax too quickly for my cock was hard again. I sighed contentedly because this was so unlike most of the men I picked up who treated screwing as an event on the Spring racing calendar. I squeezed my ass muscles in appreciation and he gasped.

"Do that again and I won't be able to hold off. I want this to last."

I did it a few more times in rapid succession, holding off my natural inclination to pleasure him more. After all, I wanted him inside me forever, maybe with time off for public holidays.

Suddenly, I realized not only was sex the greatest thing ever invented, but it was actually fun. I wasn't gritting my teeth, I wasn't wondering when he would blow and go, I wasn't looking at the clock, and I wasn't even working out in my head what I was going to eat for dinner tonight. I was giving Mr. P. my full attention.

He kissed me as he pumped my ass, the speed increasing, his breath coming in short, sharp bursts. I clung to his body, trying to thrust my ass back to meet his penetration, wanting him farther inside me than was humanly possible. Whimpering, I clung to him never wanting to let go as he bellowed, shuddered, and thrust his load inside me, quivering with each spurt.

I squeezed my ass as hard as I could to milk every drop out of him, until he collapsed on top of me. I caressed his hair and down his back, tracing my fingers lightly over his ass cheeks. It must have tickled because he swatted my hand away.

"I'm crushing you," he said, moving off me and onto his side. He removed the rubber, tossing it in the bin beside the bed. I missed the feel of his strength, expecting him to beat a hasty retreat now that he'd had his fun, but he scooted me over so we could spoon, my ass cheeks rubbing against his slick cock.

"I..."

"Don't talk," he said. "Let's just lie here for a spell. Then you can say whatever is on your mind. Okay?"

"Mmm," I agreed.

We fell asleep in that position, waking up cramped and uncomfortable about an hour later. Still, for all my discomfort, I didn't want to move.

"Shit, I was going to take you to dinner," he said glancing at the clock. "There's still time."

I decided to be selfish. "I'd rather stay in bed with you."

Even though his tummy rumbled, he said, "That would be my choice, too."

My cock strained at the thought of another session with Mr. P. He must have read my mind because, this time, he leaned over to grab another condom from the little pile I'd left on the bedside table.

"Expecting a crowd, were you?" he asked, but he was smiling.

He ripped open the packet, I wriggled in anticipation of another good screwing, but instead of sheathing his dick, he rolled the condom down over my cock.

"What?"

"Keep still, it's your turn."

"But…"

"Don't you want a turn?"

"No one's ever asked before," I said sheepishly.

"I'm asking," he said.

"Yes please," I said, sounding a little bit too much like a kid who's just been asked if he wants an ice cream.

"Let me do it my way first, until I get used to it. Then you can do me any way you like."

I nodded, afraid if I spoke this would all prove to be a dream.

He greased his ass before squatting over my cock, guiding it toward his hole. I lay still, allowing him to do all the work, feeling the tingle as he rubbed it around the entrance to his guts. Working it in slowly, he flinched when it breached the muscle. The last thing I wanted was to hurt him, not that I'm suggesting I'm horse hung or anything, but I couldn't bear to see my Mr. P. in any sort of pain.

Eventually, like all tough guys, he gritted his teeth and got on with it. He plunged down until I was as far inside his ass as I could go. My eyes opened in wonder. So this was why guys were lining up to fuck other guys' asses. Oh, I could totally get used to this feeling.

"Nice, eh?" he grinned. "And I'm not even very good at it. Imagine what an expert, someone like you, could do."

I couldn't have been happier. "You're good enough for me."

"Start slowly," he pleaded.

I moved my hips, pushing in and out of his ass slowly, letting him get used to the feeling. Been there, done that, so I knew what he needed. I tried to keep my rhythm as fluid as possible because the worst kind of screw is from someone who pokes like his cock is stoking a fire in a grate.

Concentrating on finding his little knob of a prostate, I changed the angle of entry ever so slightly until he rewarded me with an expletive so loud they must have heard him downstairs.

"I want you on your back, the same way you did me."

With a minimum of disruption, he leaned back in the bed and held his legs apart. If you've never seen a wall of muscle with his cheeks spread open to take your prick, then you are missing one of the wonders of the world. Mr. P. was offering himself to me and I was gonna take him up on his offer. I was a little less considerate this time, allowing for the fact he'd had time to get accustomed to my dick in his butt. From now on, any man who wanted my ass would have to surrender his in turn.

He grimaced a few times until I heard him expel a deep breath, signaling he had relaxed and was now enjoying the right royal buggering I was giving him.

Does anyone last long their first time? I doubt it, and I wasn't going to be the exception to the rule. Mr. P. stared into my eyes as I rode his ass, more side-saddle than full on home on the range, but I was enjoying myself and I think he was too if the way he was bucking under my inexpert fucking was any indication.

I blurted out, "Sorry," as I increased my thrust, a matter of seconds later spewing my sperm inside him, muttering 'Oh, my god,' over and over until I couldn't squirt any more.

I pulled out slowly, proud of my first effort, grinning sheepishly as I disposed of the rubber. Mr. P. lowered his legs, pulled me to him, sheltering me in his powerful arms. Neither of us needed to say anything and I fell into a contended sleep listening to his heart race in his chest.

I would have been more content if I hadn't awoken the next morning, the right side up in my bed, the sheet and blanket covering my naked body, my hero disappeared.

Too late, I remembered that he didn't do relationships.

It was exquisite agony to get myself ready for work: agony that my body felt like it had been slept in, and exquisite because for a few hours Mr. P. had been mine. He'd shown me more respect than all my other lovers put together, but it galled me that he ran out rather than tell the truth: that our liaison was a one-night fling while his wife was away.

All that was before I discovered he'd stolen the portrait I'd done of him as my superhero. I'd put everything into that. Sure, I could do it again, but I wasn't sure I wanted to any more; it would just serve to open up the wound. I'd try my hand at something else, something more down to earth, more practical.

Fortunately, by the time I got to Santa's Cave my sprits had lifted and the idea of capitulating to the mundane had so horrified me on the bus that I swore to myself I would never travel down that route no matter how appealing it seemed.

I plugged into my memories of Mr. P. whenever I needed a boost to my flagging energy in the lead-up to Christmas during which the kids seemed to become more unruly and the parents more snarling and unreasonable. Stress compounded, screaming headaches were common place, tempers flared, and I worked with the persistent nagging emptiness where my emotions should be.

Fuck it, I missed him.

Then, all too soon, Christmas Eve rolled around and the thought of the holiday period alone in my bedsit suddenly made me look like a major loser, even to myself. Thel invited me over to her place but she had a large family among whom I'd feel totally out of place. No, I'd sleep in and go to the movies at midday to watch the latest blockbuster, maybe treat myself later to a slap-up burger and fries on the way home.

After we finally saw the last children off for the year, we could have our own little celebration, just a few drinks and canapés before heading home to family. I wouldn't make the mistake this time of imbibing too much although sleeping through the entire day was not without its good points. Even Levard joined our little group complimenting us on what was likely to be the store's best Christmas ever.

"Sorry if I was a little hard on you this year," Levard slurred as he maneuvered me into a corner, placing his arm against the wall so I couldn't escape.

Don't let him proposition me. I want to work here again next year.

I tried to attract someone's attention so they could come to my aid as Levard rabbited on and on about how impressed he was with my commitment which became what a good worker I was and then not-so-subtly morphed into what an attractive young man I was.

Help me!

I noticed everyone had their eyes toward the lift which was behind me, the only sound Levard's inept attempt at a pick-up, until eventually he stopped speaking, his mouth dropping open in surprise. It was Thel's squeal of delight that made me turn.

I'm afraid I gaped, too. Striding toward us was Mr. Perfect. Not Mr. P. but rather my superhero in full costume as I'd drawn it on the sheet that had disappeared along with Patric Charles Crichton from my apartment and my life. My mind noted a few minor adjustments I'd need to make to the costume color scheme and an important one to the cut of the fabric covering his crotch as currently it was much too revealing, especially as Mr. Perfect seemed to be sporting a mammoth erection. I knew from experience it wasn't padding.

I could see determination in his eyes as he pulled me to his body and planted the most sizzling kiss to my lips, raising me off the ground in the process, with scant regard for anyone who was watching. I thought I heard Thel clap but it could just have been the bells that were pealing in my head.

"Damien wants me to bring you home for Christmas," he said simply.

I couldn't help it. "I don't look good in stockings," I replied.

"But you'll look mighty tasty in my bed."

"Once is all right, but twice makes it look like some sort of relationship is developing."

"I missed you."

"Me, too."

He scooped me up in his arms just like a superhero. He spoiled the effect somewhat by walking to the lift rather than flying from the window. I could live with that. I could live with whatever he decided. I would even be the other woman for him.

"What other woman? What are you talking about, Kaz?" He looked genuinely puzzled as the lift ascended to street level.

"Your wife. Damien's mother."

He guffawed fit to piss himself.

"I'm not married, you dickhead. Endive is my sister. Damien is my nephew. I look after him whenever sis is away on assignment."

I tweaked his nipple really hard until it hurt.

"Ow. What was that for?"

"For leading me on. Making me worry."

Deep down I knew he could lead anywhere and I'd follow.

Once we reached the street, passers-by gawped at the strange sight, until a limo pulled up and Mr. P. deposited me in the back seat before wrapping me in his massive arms, planting another of those lip searing kisses on my mouth. As the car pulled out into the late Christmas Eve party-going traffic, I spied a small box stuffed in the belt of Mr. P.'s costume. I could just make out the words 'Extra Sensitive,' and the number 36.

Holy Batcrap, Robin. A happy ending.

ABOUT THE AUTHOR

Barry Lowe writes about love and sex so he won't forget how to do it. When he's not scribbling his adventures for the Sydney gay weekly *SX*, or out doing field research, he's writing about love's wonderful variations for a series of smut eBooks, novels and anthologies for Lydian Press.

Go to www.barrylowe.info

ANTHOLOGIES By Barry Lowe

BUSTING BILLY'S BUTT - eBook & Print

Four On The Floor
Jolly Rogering
The Devil His Due
Never Take Candy from Strangers
Done Like A Dinner
In The Family Way
Right Up His Alley
Group Therapy

THE MAJOR AND THE MINERS - eBook & Print

A Serpent in Paradise
Desperate Remedies
Joshua's Story
Emerald City
Danny's Revenge
Future Tense

ROMANCING THE BONE - eBook and Print

Carbon Dating
Let the Games Begin
Taking the Bait
Party Whip
Team Player
Davy Jones' Locker
Here's to You, Mr Robinson
Gay Dungeon for the Straight Boy
OMG! Santa's Got a Six-Pack
Vlad the Impaler
Meta-Analysis of the Effects of Love on Tofu

LIKE FATHER LIKE SON - eBook and Print

Man of the Hour
Like Father Like Son
Sonny & Shared
Sonny Side Up
Eclipse Of The Son
Son & Games
Where The Sun Don't Shine
The Sun Shines Out Of His Ass
Have Son Will Travel

BEAR SKIN - eBook and Print

Carbon Dating the Bear
Bumming a Fag
Four on the Bear Floor
Beauty, Mate
There's a Bear in There
Busting a Gut
Steam Punk
Piss Elegant
The Bear's Guide to Depilatory Wax

ROUGH & READY - eBook and Print

Stocks & Shared
Scarface
Ceps: Mad about Muscle
The Plumbers' Mate*
Climbing Up the Wall
Little Red Rides da Hood
The Dex Factor
Jailhouse Cock
The Skinhead Upstairs

THE MORE THE MERRIER - eBook and Print

Marine Biology
Flesh for Fantasy
Buck's Night
Four On The Floor
Sluts & Satyrs
Framing the Picture of Dorian Gray
Fuck Buddy
Seven Card Studs
Dude, Where's The Bar?
New Year's Steve

THE BOY IS A BOTTOM - eBook and Print

Marine Biology
Marine Animals
Attack of the Ass Bandits
The Arab Downstairs
Clockwork Derriere
Creaming the Party Dip
Top of the World
Route 666: Signal Driver
The Butler Did Him
Fifty Shades of Fey
Spinning the Bottom

THE GRAVY TRAIN - eBook & Print

In the Soup
Salad Days
Whores d'Oeuvres
Beefed Up and Porked
Torte A Lesson
Café or Lay

BABY, I'M NOT A MONSTER - eBook and Print

The Vampire's Guide to Dental Hygiene
Stupid Cupid
Gadigal
Pride & Joy
Seeing Things
My Dad's a Vampire
Guys & Trolls

COCK-EYED OPTIMISTS - eBook and Print

A Red Rose Before Crying
Too Frocked to Care
The Three Spooges
Love and the Odor of Red Leatherette
It's All Greek to Me
Hard On His Heels
Salted Mixed Sluts
The New Dad's Club

YOUR BOYFRIEND IS HOT - eBook and Print

From Here to Fraternity
Stripping His Assets
Indecent Exposure
Middle Man for Madame Blavatsky
A Cook's Tour
Topping the Pizza Delivery Boy

For all Barry's titles please visit his page at:
lydianpress.com